IMMORTAL HUNT

AN IMMORTAL STORY OF TRUE
LOVE, MAGIC, AND ADVENTURE

The Immortal Stories Series

Book 5

by

Linda Ashton Trott

Tagger Press

Copyright

ISBN-13: 978-1-7782949-3-8

Cover design by: 100COVERS

Second Edition, January 2023

Adult Content, 18+

Dedication

I am dedicating this book to my husband, who without, it would have been impossible to complete this work.

A huge thank you to Lee Burton of Oceanside Editing for being my editor. He continues to help me improve everything I write. He is a very good teacher and editor.

Also, I would like to thank Dawn Hughes for her work on making sure my continuity from book to book is perfect.

Thanks to you, the reader, for purchasing this book. I hope you enjoy it! If you do, don't forget to leave a review.

Contents

What did you miss?

Book 4 - Immortal Victory

- Falon recovered from a tornado
- Falon and Mark confronted the Council
- Lora lived a sexual fantasy
- Falon had public sex with Mark
- Mark and Falon went through the ritual
- Falon explored her new superpowers
- Rick and Justin prepare to a second restaurant in Montreal
- A vampire hunter went after Mark
- They discovered the Fraternal Order was after them
- Falon decided to end homelessness
- Lora explained everything to Rick
- Brandon was hired by Derek to take Falon from Mark
- We learn more about the order that hunts immortals
- Falon put together an epic Gala to fund-raise for the charity
- Andrews & Gwen get together
- Andrews enlisted the Fraternal Order to help get Derek

1—After the Ball

The charity gala was done, and it was a resounding success. It was truly epic!

After working together so closely for the past three months on the gala, Falon's crew had grown very close. The threat to their lives by Derek Staung had them all strung out. Now that he and his organization had been neutralized, there was a collective feeling among the crew of, "Whew, we dodged that bullet."

This feeling of profound relief was expressed in their group hug at the end of the evening. When Justin and Rick could finally leave the kitchen and join them, the party level went up a few notches. The crew had a blast dancing until every last gala guest was gone at 1:30 am.

They were all there: Greggory, Andrews, Grisham, Parsons and his wife, Rick, Justin, Mark and Falon, as well as Gwen and Lora—all on the floor in a circle dancing up a storm. Each of them took turns doing their thing in the middle and showing off.

The venue staff were busy cleaning up and putting everything away. They were finished by 3:30 a.m. By that time, the crew had dispersed some, with a few couples going off in corners to do more intimate kinds of celebrating.

Falon and Mark were feeling drained from the fun and stress of doing the gala, but more from the fact that they had lived with an assassin hunting them for the past few months.

"Hey, everyone," called Falon. "Why don't we blow this pop stand and go back to our place? We have some munchies and a good bar and lots of space for crashing."

Murmurs of consent from Gwen and Andrews, as well as from Rick and Lora. Justin begged off saying he had to be back at the construction site by 10:00, and, interestingly, Greggory took off with him. Andrews' staff also decided to go home. So the six of those who remained got into the limo and went back to Mark and Falon's.

"I'm so glad we all got through this night," said Falon. "It was really scary waiting to see if we would stop Derek."

"I agree," said Mark. "It was tense for a while."

"Andrews, thank you to your team for an excellent job at protecting us all," said Gwen. "I really don't want to lose my head."

There was nervous laughter.

"Yeah, that was a little too close for comfort," said Mark.

"You know that we didn't take out Derek," said Andrews. "It was the Order who did the dirty work. I saw them carrying out a body when I was heading to the head table to protect you."

"Wow, that means reaching out to them worked," said Mark.

"Yes, it seems to have. I just don't know if that put us on their radar, though."

"Mmmm, yes, I see what you mean," said Mark. They were silent for a minute or so, all contemplating what might happen if the Order came after them.

"Everyone, let's take hands," said Lora. "Now repeat after me: We survived! We are here! We will love!"

They grasped each others' hands, and repeated what she said.

"Oh, come on, people, say it with feeling!"

They all put more energy into it this time.

"Not good enough," said Lora.

"We survived! We are here! We will love!" they all screamed together.

"That's better. We will protect each other," said Lora. She got tingles down her back as they all screamed the chant together. There was something about the six of them that drew some sort of power, or created some sort of power. She couldn't place her finger on it. But being a witch, she surely felt it. It lifted the hairs on the back of her neck. "Now kiss the person on your left."

Since they were sitting in a circle in the back of the limo, Falon turned to her left and kissed Mark. Lora turned to her left and kissed Andrews. Gwen reached across and kissed Rick.

"That was nice," said Lora. "You're a good kisser, Andrews."

"So is Rick," said Gwen.

Once the limo stopped, they piled out and went into the townhouse. Rick took Lora's hand and pulled her into a hug.

"Hey, gorgeous, get comfortable with me?" he asked.

"I think so," Lora said. "Let me go to the bathroom and be right back." Lora went into the main floor powder room and took off her jewels and shoes, then took off the bra that was pinching her boobs, and the underwear that was crawling up her crack. Stuffing it all in her bag, she let down her hair and put the pins in the bag too.

"That feels better," Lora said to her reflection. Fluffing her tresses, she went out to find Rick, who had taken up the corner of one of the sofas. He had removed the jacket and vest of his tux, removed the tie and rolled up his sleeves. He'd also opened a few buttons on his shirt.

"Damn, you look good, Rick!" said Lora. "I'll just have to eat you up." Climbing onto his lap, she proceeded to kiss him ardently.

Andrews was watching with amusement. He glanced at Gwen, who was smiling like a cat with a mouse in her mouth.

"I'll be right back too," she told Andrews in a lowered voice. "Find us a sofa."

Andrews, tingling all over, shucked his clothes like Rick, and sat opposite them on another sofa. Gwen came out a few minutes later, also liberated of undergarments, and sat down beside him.

"Let's see what we have here," she teased as she undid his buttons and kissed his body down the opening to his belt.

Falon was sitting in Mark's lap, her legs swung up and over the arm of the chair while he was liberally applying kisses. He was also making good use of the slit in her dress with one of his hands. The small moans escaping her throat were turning him on even more.

"Falon, you are so sexy right now," he whispered into her ear.

"So are you," she said as she undid his tie and threw it on the floor. Next, she started to undo his shirt, reaching inside for a nipple and tweaking it with her finger.

Mark responded by inserting his finger behind her thong and caressing her mound ever so gently.

"The others are suitably engaged, they won't even notice us," he murmured into her ear.

"I don't care if they do," Falon said. "In fact, I hope they do!" She kicked off her shoes and hiked up her dress so she could straddle him. He pulled her forward so he could take a nipple that was escaping and suck on it not so gently.

The scent of pheromones and sex in the room became elevated as the three couples got more involved in what they were doing. So did the energy in the room. With four immortals aroused, the power in the room became palpable. It wasn't long before they were all emitting moans and sighs.

"Hon, there is not enough room in this chair," complained Mark. "Let me move the chair and table out of the way."

He slid the chair back and moved the table clear of the room, then brought the cushions back. They sat down on the cushions where the chair had been. Falon then straddled Mark with her dress basically gathered around her hips. She was working on removing his shirt, as he had already taken off the jacket and vest.

"That's a good idea," said Lora. She got up and pulled Rick to a standing position, then grabbed all the cushions off the sofa and piled them up on the floor. Rick then stretched out on the floor using the cushions to lean on. Lora stretched out with him.

Sensing this infusion of power again, Lora asked into the quiet, "So would anyone be interested in having sex together?" A couple of people shifted. Lora wasn't sure whether it was discomfort or something else. She scanned the group: all the immortals' eyes were glowing with power, arousal, and interest, even Falon's.

"No one is into a little kink?" she asked again. "We could start slow, by swapping partners."

"I don't know if I want anyone else," said Mark.

"Oh, that's because you've already done it," said Gwen. Falon looked at Mark questioningly.

"Yes, I've participated in such things," he said.

"I haven't," said Falon. "But I'm willing to experiment."

"Who would you have gone with?" asked Gwen.

"Mark takes me, you take Rick, and Falon gets Andrews," said Lora.

Everyone thought about that while looking at each other—and in particular their new potential partner.

"We can make it a game," said Lora.

"How so?" Asked Andrews.

"The girl chooses the kink, the boy sets the method," said Gwen. "For example, I choose to be submissive." Her eyes were starting to glow as she imagined the play.

"And I choose to be the dominant," said Rick. His eyes were glowing ever so slightly.

"Okay, I choose multiple penetration," said Lora.

"Then I'll choose the toys," said Mark.

"Well, what would you like?" Andrews asked Falon. "I'm experienced in all kinds of kink."

"Hmm, I'll choose submission too," she said.

"I will choose master then," said Andrews.

"Now what?" asked Falon.

Rick got up and went to Gwen and looked down on her. She rolled her eyes downward and immediately went into a submissive position. "On your knees, Gwen," he said.

She sank to her knees. "What's your safe word, Gwen?"

"Clock."

He took his tie and tied her wrists behind her back. He walked around her and spanked her ass. The sound of skin on skin resonated in the room. Gwen cried out and then moaned as her body enjoyed the spanking. Rick alternated between spanking and caressing.

"Were you naughty?" he asked.

"I was very naughty. Punish me."

Rick slapped the other cheek, then gently brushed his fingers across her skin, giving her gooseflesh and taking the sting out of the slap. Each slap made her moan as he caressed it. Her arousal was building, releasing pheromones that fed the others too, not just Rick. He had a cockstand that needed attention.

Moving in front of her, he pushed his cock into her face. She opened her mouth and searched for it with her tongue. As he pushed himself in her mouth, she scraped her teeth across his skin. When she sealed her lips around his shaft and started sucking, he almost lost it.

He took her head and held it as he gently moved in and out of her mouth. She was biting down and giving him little shocks of venom. He was about to lose control, so he pulled out suddenly. She whimpered at the loss of her toy. Rick untied her hands in the back and retied them in the front. With the extra mobility, she took hold of his cock and pumped him hard, then drew him into her mouth deeply, purring deep in her throat, and bit his penis. He instinctively started pumping deeper, and as his arousal grew she took him deeper so that when he came he was nearly completely buried down her throat. She grabbed his balls as he ejaculated, gently squeezing them, making him gasp, and cry out.

Rick pulled out and knelt on the floor beside Gwen, undoing all the ties. Gwen glanced at the others.

"Falon, come here and sit," demanded Andrews as he walked to another cushion. Andrews handed Falon a blindfold and told her to put it on. Then he told her to lie down on her stomach. He raised her arms above her head and tied them together with his tie.

"We don't proceed without a safe word," he whispered in her ear.

"How about 'cookie?'" said Falon.

"That will work."

Standing behind her, he pushed her dress over her hips, exposing her ass.

Andrews spanked Falon on her ass and her breath caught in surprise. He kissed away the sting and slapped the other side, again making her gasp, and kissing away the hurt.

Falon was getting aroused in spite of herself. When Andrews took two fingers and played with her vagina, her body responded by getting very wet. He used her own plentiful juices to lube two fingers and pushed them into her anus. This time, the surprise and the pain made her cry out again. But that was quickly overtaken by him penetrating her vagina. She groaned deeply as she felt his fingers and his cock push deep inside.

Andrews nodded and thrust even harder into Falon, making her cry out again. Then he pulled out and was hovering at her opening, not going in. Falon squirmed. She started to speak, but Andrews spanked her for talking, then pulled away from her entirely.

"You are not allowed to move," he told her. "No matter what you hear."

Falon whimpered quietly, her body so hungry to be fucked hard it ached. But she held her tongue and stayed like that, face on the floor, ass high in the air.

Lora had sidled up to Mark when Falon left, removed her dress and pressed her body up against Mark's, grinding. Mark's eyes started glowing like the other immortals, and his body responded. She showed him several dildos, and he chose one that was as large as himself. She presented her ass to him and he started to stimulate her, getting her wet.

Lora was wiggling her pussy in front of Mark. He took hold of her hips and buried his nose in her scent, kissing and licking, making her even more excited. He used some fingers in her vagina to bring her close to climax, and stopped before she got too far. He then took one of his fingers, licked it, and inserted it into her anus. Lora squealed with delight and wiggled even more. Moving his finger, he stretched her anus and applied the lube that she handed him. When she was suitably slick, he started inserting the dildo.

Mark was watching Lora's ass as he pushed the dildo in. Her hips were bucking and she was very excited. Getting up on his knees, he rubbed his cock in her opening and pushed inside her vagina. Lora immediately started keening and moaning, her body pushing back on him to get him deeper inside. She handed him another dildo and started pumping her hips against him. For a minute Mark wondered what to do with it. He glanced at Rick for explanation.

Rick was watching Mark. When he saw Lora give him a second dildo, he knew the answer to Mark's question. He went over to them and told Mark she wanted two in one hole. Mark looked surprised.

"Are you secure in your masculinity?" Rick asked Mark.

"I think I am."

"Let's try something, then," he said. "Lora, do you want the two of us?"

"Oh my God, yes!" she cried. "Separate from me, Mark, just a moment."

He pulled away and Lora turned around and straddled Rick, taking him deep into her vagina. Then she bent over flattening herself against his body, exposing her ass.

Mark looked at them, and asked, "Now what?"

Use a dildo in my ass, and join Rick in my vagina," she said matter-of-factly.

Mark lubed the dildo and inserted it in her ass carefully. Rick and she were groaning with the sensations. Then he lubed his own cock and started to push into her vagina. *Oh fuck it was tight!* Rick gasped loudly as he felt Mark join him. The sensations were wild. Lora was humming with pleasure. Mark kept pushing. He could feel Rick next to him, moving, and it stimulated his cock too.

By the time he had most of his cock inside, all three were gasping with the pain and pleasure of it—in particular Lora, because they were well-endowed cocks.

The guys synchronized their rhythms and thrust together to the maximum. Mark pushed in deeper and Rick indicated he was close to climax because the sensation of the two penises rubbing each other was nearly too much to bear. The men stopped what they were doing for a moment.

Lora couldn't take that. She was moaning between them and couldn't stay still. Her hips kept moving in rhythm on them both, delighted in the fullness, her breath taken away.

As Lora moved herself on the two cocks, Mark's vision started to blur from the arousal. The pressure from her very tight vagina and feeling of Rick next to him inside her was making his head swim.

Gwen was watching this, very aroused. She was watching Andrews and Falon and decided to join their duo to make it a trio too. Picking up a double-ended dildo from the toys, she walked over to Andrews where he was bent over Falon. Gwen lubed up one end and plunged it into Andrews' ass and watched as he yelped and then moaned.

"Ah God, it's been a while—keep going," he said, in a voice thick with arousal. Gwen put the other end into herself and smashed them together. As Andrews was fucking Falon, she was fucking him and getting fucked herself. A win-win-win.

Gwen circled her own clit with her fingers. All three of them were linked as their arousal climbed together. Close to their climax, their hearts all synchronized as they crested the wave as one. Gwen reached across Andrews and placed her hand in Falon's mouth, encouraging her to bite down. She then sank her teeth into Andrews' shoulder, and then Falon's. The venom pushed them to euphoria as they finished.

Lora's threesome came to a blinding climax at the same time. Mark bit Lora, then Andrews. Their hearts had synchronized like the other trio, and all three were screaming and moaning until they collapsed in a heap.

The two trios slumped on the floor in one heap of entangled bodies. Eventually, they all came back to consciousness.

Falon was first. She panicked when she couldn't see, but then remembered she was blindfolded. Her hands were still bound and there was a body on top of her. Gwen became conscious next, and pulled away from Andrews, removing the dildo. She untied Falon and removed her blindfold. Andrews had separated from Falon, sprawled with his head on her stomach. He was still slightly hard.

Falon looked at Gwen and smiled. She felt very close to her now. When she realized it was Andrews who had penetrated her, she got a sizzle inside. She had wanted to fuck him. When Andrews opened his eyes, the first thing he saw was Falon's pussy. His cock stood up immediately. He remembered what Gwen had done to him, and that brought back memories of the experimenting he had done in college with his roommate. It had been enjoyable, but nothing like what it was with Gwen.

Rick, Lora, and Mark were entangled in an interesting way. As Andrews looked at them, he realized that Rick had shared Lora with Mark. They both had penetrated her.

Mark was on top, so he straightened up and disengaged his cock from Lora. When he did, Rick also came out, so she had a small river of semen coming out of her. Mark went to find a towel. Lora was lying on top of Rick, and she wasn't awake yet.

Rick woke up when Mark pulled out. The sensation triggered another hard-on, and his now hard cock pushed up against Lora. Mark returned with hot water, towels, and cloths for them all to clean up. Lora woke up just as Rick took the dildo out of her ass.

Mark realized that Falon was with Andrews and Gwen. He felt a jealous surge rise up in his gut and he didn't know why. There was really no reason. He decided he was going to let that go once and for all. They had all survived a life-threatening event and had all just shared in life-affirming sex games with each other. *Let's leave the possessiveness outside.*

By some unheard yet agreed-upon signal, they gathered all the cushions together and then cuddled in one pile, intertwined and in contact, hands on breasts, on cocks, on asses, touching intimately and completely comfortable with it.

A breakthrough seemed to have happened.

As day broke and sunshine filtered in through the curtains, they were yawning and stretching, still in contact with each other. They looked like a puppy pile.

Gwen broke the silence.

"Well, that was fun!" she said.

All of them burst into laughter.

"That was truly remarkable," answered Mark.

"I had fun," said Lora.

"You started it," said Gwen.

"I finished it," said Andrews.

"You certainly did, my wonderful human," said Gwen. "Which is something I want to correct."

"Are you going to ask for permission from the family council?" asked Mark.

"No, because you were put through hell when you did," said Gwen. "I'm not going to."

"Get permission," he said. "It's easier in the long run."

"Fine," said Gwen. "I will."

"Wow, what a ride!" said Rick, waking up. "How's everyone feeling?"

"I'm surprisingly not sore," said Lora.

"Neither am I," said Falon. "We have to make Andrews an immortal."

"Can we make Lora one too?" asked Rick.

"Oh! That would be interesting, an immortal witch," said Lora.

"Well, we could have our own ceremony," said Mark. Gwen grinned and glanced at Falon.

"Can we participate again?" she asked.

"In the ceremony?" asked Gwen.

"Ya, why not?" asked Falon. "It's just another excuse to have heart-stopping sex with my guy." She looked over at Mark and their eyes connected, like they had so many years ago in that bar. The heat coming off them was palpable to the other immortals.

"Okay, you two, enough of that," Gwen chided them.

"I want to be able to bite my lover too," said Lora.

"Gwen, do you realize that we've gone from lonely immortal singles to creating our own close group of immortal friends?" said Mark. "What a small miracle." He was looking at Falon when he said that.

"I feel blessed," said Gwen.

"So do I," said Rick. "I never believed I would find community and love by other beings like myself."

"We are a community," said Falon.

"Indeed," said Andrews and Lora.

"Who's making breakfast? I'm starved!" cried Lora.

2—The Project Begins

—Falon

The gala had been such a success! Now we got busy with the money we'd raised, getting the Tiny House Project off the ground.

Lora was busy organizing designers. Gwen was busy working with contracts. Andrews was busy building a security company. Mark was busy with his businesses. Rick and Justin were getting Escalata II up and running. And I was swamped with the applications for housing.

Greggory, my assistant, was indispensable in going through the applications and helping me make the selections based on need. He came up with a system of criteria that we applied to each applicant. That gave us a number of stars of need, and those with the most stars got spots first.

The contractors Gwen and Andrews lined up were ready to work. All we needed was a plot of land to use.

In discussions with the city of Montreal, the councillors and community representatives expressed concern that too many tiny houses in one place would put a neighborhood at risk. We ran up against NIMBY—or "not in my back yard."

It seemed that putting the tiny house village in or near a residential area was out of the question. So next I looked for an abandoned parking lot or building that wasn't being used.

We found several sites, but none of them would make a good location for people to live. Our conundrum was: do we locate them centrally or do we locate them outside of the city but near transportation?

There were other projects around the U.S., but the houses were horribly designed and were basically garden sheds, or smaller. We wanted our tiny houses to be four-season safe and to give the owner a sense of pride that it wasn't just a box, but a home. Their sense of self was important to us.

One idea we found in the U.S. that was helpful was choosing useless pieces of land as locations for the tiny house villages. The first such village was built near "Spaghetti Junction," where the highways met in St-Henri. There were lots of oddly shaped bits of land that weren't being used there. We had enough space for a hundred tiny houses. It was close to public transportation and in one of the poorest areas of town.

First, we needed to purchase up the bits of land—so Greggory started on that action. In many cases, he already found tent cities of homeless people trying to survive. So that was a good sign that the site was desirable.

Of course, that would mean we needed to relocate the people before we could build, so we did. One such tent city had about a hundred tents. That would be the perfect place to start, because each person would get a tiny house.

Greggory determined that we would need three sizes of tiny homes. The sad fact he discovered was that there were a number of families who were homeless. The families had kids. They needed a home so they could go to school.

I went back to our contractors and told them the news. We needed at least three different sizes: one suitable for singles, one suitable for couples, and another size for a family of four. For larger families, we would double up the beds and use bunks. Basically, these would be one-bed and three-bed homes. The couples home would have a double bed, while the single home would have a single bed. The family home would have three double beds. This way, if there were more than two kids, they could bunk together.

We ended up with three sizes of tiny homes: 100 sq ft, 150 sq ft, and 250 sq ft. Each house would have a kitchen, convertible sitting/sleeping area, and bathroom. The larger units would have extra loft sleeping areas.

I gave Greggory the happy task of letting the people know in our first village what was going to happen. Surprisingly, he got mixed reviews. It wasn't until he told them they would get to live in a motel while their tiny house was being built that they actually got on board.

We had planned to have the tiny houses prefabricated in a factory and then delivered to the already-serviced site, ready to plug in. To do that, we needed to clear the tent city, then clean up the ground and prepare it. We wanted the homes to have a little green around them too, so we planned for walkways and trees. We'd leave the open spaces around the homes to their owners for planting.

The first tiny homes were delivered for the families, because they needed the most space.

When the Leduc family moved in, they cried at their good fortune. They had two school-aged children who hadn't been in school for a couple of years because they had no permanent address. Now, their kids could be registered. Suddenly, the parents could get assistance and jobs, and start to make their lives better. They didn't own the tiny house, but it was theirs to decorate.

Once they no longer needed the house and had found a home of their own, it would be cleaned and given to someone else in need. The charity gave each homeless family two years to turn their life around. If they needed longer, they were put on a month-to-month basis.

We felt we needed to do this to discourage people from taking advantage of a free house, and to encourage them to become part of society again. If they were not capable of doing that, other arrangements had to be made.

Once they had jobs, they could start looking for an apartment to rent.

Our first hundred tiny houses were filled up before we had them all built. Once they were, the small village was clean, fenced in, well lit, and the residents all seemed happy. It was a success!

So now it was time to do another. This time, we wanted to go to a different part of the city. We built three more villages around Montreal, with a total of 450 units. It was a drop in the bucket, and we were still looking for more locations. It would take us two years to complete.

3—Building a Restaurant

—Rick

Now that the gala was done, Justin and I could get started on the new Escalata. It was something we had been thinking of since we opened the first restaurant in Atlanta. Now that we had a property in Montreal, we could get started. We hadn't done anything at all since purchasing the building.

A few days after the orgy, I called Justin.

"Oh, Rick, I've found the perfect architect and designer. They love my vision for traditional elegance. I sat down with them the last two days—by the way, where have you been? Anyway, we have a plan, and they are to start."

"Splendid news," I said. "Am I taking over the day-to-day?"

"Yes please. The crew will be on-site tomorrow to start demolition."

"Excellent, I won't need you up here for that," I said. "I have it covered. Do we yet have a timeframe for this project?"

"The contractor says they have about eighteen months of work," said Justin. "However, with historical sites, I've been warned delays are inevitable. Our deadline is about two years from now. They will make their deadline one way or another."

"Good, because I really want to do that soft launch in October, so we have a couple of months to work out the kinks before the grand opening on New Year's Eve," I said. "I'll make sure they can stick to the schedule."

I got off the phone with Justin and looked around the office that I was using at Falon's charity. She was good enough to loan me a place to take calls and meet people for the build.

I really felt over my head on this, but Justin had to stay in Atlanta to keep the first restaurant operating. It was my place to get this done. Thankfully, between Andrews and Mark, I was put in touch with some good people to work with.

Everyone was meeting here to go for dinner shortly. I heard Andrews talking as he walked down the hall with Gwen. Lora popped her head into my room and asked if I was ready. We walked across the street to a bistro and took a table for six in the back.

As we were eating, Lora brought up the subject of turning.

"So I wanted to talk about turning. Is there a timetable for me to be turned? And Andrews?"

"Yes, as a matter of fact, I was working on that for you both," said Gwen. "We need to get the injection from the family doctor and administer it at the right moment. For Andrews, hon, you'll have to be bitten by Mark, and Lora, you'll have to be bitten by Rick."

"In the throes of passion?" asked Andrews.

"No—in the middle of a fight," said Gwen. "It doesn't have to be a big fight, just enough to trigger his fangs."

"I can do that," he said with a smirk. "I'm used to wrestling with Mark."

"So when can we do this?" asked Lora excitedly.

"How about a Friday night?" asked Gwen. "I'm available on the twenty-third. We can reconvene here for a little nookie party."

Falon blushed at the thought, and my body responded by getting excited. I wasn't the only one, either.

"So it's settled."

4—A Time Trip

—Lora

For six months, I'd been seeing things about my body improve, like my vision getting better. I'd started healing quickly, and I was able to bite Rick. We kept that under wraps for the most part, waiting for the ceremony.

So many changes had happened! Rick was now living with me in Montreal part-time while the restaurant was still under construction. He and Justin split the time between the two restaurants, so Rick had some time in Atlanta to develop new desserts.

When the new restaurant got up and running, they'd be able to take their hands off daily operations—mostly. Rick found all the staff he wanted for the kitchen. Most of them were working already and had been told to keep their new jobs secret until the new place was ready. It makes a big difference when you can hire talent—he lined up an amazing executive chef who would bring prestige to the new place.

One thing remained consistent: our lovemaking. It became more—not just sex, but almost a spiritual experience. As we were now able to give each other the euphoric drug, we soared together. I felt wrapped in some sort of life power whenever we reached that height too, like I could accomplish anything.

I continued to work with Falon on the Tiny House Project. We were all so used to working with each other. In a year I expected we'd be a well-oiled machine. The plan was to have an annual gala event so that we could start Tiny House Projects in other cities.

But what I really wanted to do was continue the research I'd started into the ancestry of the immortals, and to find those other thirty-four groups. With the kids back in school, I had time during the day to get back to it.

I was also looking forward to the transmogrification ceremony, even though it would only make what was already a reality official. We talked at length about being immortal: whether we should be telling the kids, who needed to and know, and how we were going to deal with not getting older. We didn't have answers to many of those questions. We didn't tend to openly speak about our skills, it was too exposing, and people would not be very charitable towards us. If humans knew we existed, what we were, they'd have us locked up and experimented on. So I completely got the secrecy surrounding being an immortal.

One positive change of Rick living with us now was that I didn't have to earn a living anymore. That was a big adjustment, having a man pay for everything. I was able to quit my job and dedicate my time to research into the immortals.

I reconnected with some of my old network, and re-established ties with my supernatural underground.

The supernatural world lives under the human world, in the shadows, unseen and unheard. This makes it difficult to find. Beyond that, the resources I did find couldn't be borrowed from their owners, so it meant I was away often. That wasn't good. So whenever I could, I brought Rick along with me because we were looking for his family.

The DNA tests that I ran a year ago came back with interesting results. Rick and Mark were not related. There was definitely another group that existed that descended from those original people. Also, *Rick and I are not related*—that was a weight off my chest. No DNA shared at all. Yeah! Again, that was exciting as it meant I come from a third group descended from the original people.

I did have my family tree, but it only went back about a thousand years. That wasn't nearly far enough, but perhaps I could trace back my magical skills, if not my DNA. One small detail was very interesting: the ritual to turn a mortal into an immortal did not introduce DNA from the immortal. Falon's DNA was unique to herself, and not related to Mark's.

The book we found about Group 32 indicated they were living on the Caribbean island now known as Cuba. We found them living there from 800 BC until the late 1400s, when Europeans arrived. There were no written records in the human world for that time period in that part of the world. There used to be, but monks burned them. So this gave us a place to start looking. This was perfect. What could be better than the Caribbean?

What we learned: Group 32 moved into the Caribbean Islands between 800 and 200 BCE (our time). Some of the islands were inhabited and surrounded by shallower water. This made sharing of food and goods between them easy. It seems the immortals had trade with the humans. What was really interesting was that the native humans went through enormous social and cultural changes during that period. This suggested that Group 32 contributed to their well-being.

The native population's new use of agriculture likely came from Group 32. They introduced farming to them and taught them to form larger communities. The immortals intermingled with the natives, and the children born were either immortal or human with special talents.

The native people started experiencing physical changes as well. Climate changes further shaped the islands' inhabitants. The tropical climate of abundant rainfall turned into drought as the rains stopped and this forced them to adapt. When the oceans warmed significantly, severe tropical storms ravaged and flooded the islands, forcing the human settlements to leave for safer ground.

When the Europeans showed up in the late 1400s, the native populations scattered across all the islands and Group 32 went into hiding. They stayed away from the Europeans, who were somewhat more advanced than the natives. However, the Europeans were brutal, and only interested in killing and stealing. The immortals didn't want to get involved for fear of revealing themselves to the invaders.

Group 32 had taken advantage of living by an extinct volcanic mountain. Using its old lava tubes, they built structures underground in order to avoid bumping into the Europeans. They had no contact until it was impossible to avoid it, and then they fled.

The reason was not clear, nor was where they went. And why did they give up 693 years of development? The last entry in the book didn't say. Now we needed to find another book that would continue the story.

Where would they have gone?

I would need magic to further this research, because there was no mundane way I could get that information. So I needed to go back to the occult store.

As always, walking into that establishment was literally walking into another dimension. It always made me a little squeamish. Once inside, the experience was fine because what you were looking at didn't warp and bend strangely.

"You have returned, Lora O'Reilly," stated the disembodied voice known as Esperanza.

"Hello, Esperanza," I said. "Yes, I'm back. This time I need to find a bridge in time between the 1400s in the human world and 803. I'm looking for a woman from Group 32 of the immortals who lived on the Caribbean island today known as Cuba, twelve hundred years ago. There are no human records."

"I can help you with that, yes. Please follow the light."

Again a ball of light formed and led me off down an aisle I hadn't seen before. There were no books here, but lots of paraphernalia for performing all kinds of magic. There were vessels of different shapes, candleholders, and crystals. This side of the store smelled a little like brimstone.

"What's burning?" I asked.

"Nothing you need to be concerned about," was the answer.

The ball of light stopped in front of a huge mirror and was hovering about eye level in front of me. I touched the mirror's surface and discovered that it was fluid—like quicksilver, yet it was maintaining a vertical shape.

"What is this?" I asked.

"This is a travel mirror," said Esperanza. "It will take you to specific people in time."

"Am I supposed to go through the mirror, Esperanza?"

"Not yet," said the voice. "You need to calibrate it for the correct time and location. There are many rules about traveling across the time bridge. You must acquaint yourself with them first."

A door opened on an armoire behind me. Inside the armoire was another door to a room, probably similar to the one where we found the books.

"Same process?" I asked.

"Yes."

Saying the same spell quietly while pushing on the back of the armoire opened the secret door. The room behind was another library, not as big as the other one I was in, but still quite large.

Stepping into the armoire gave me the same sense of moving through dimensions. As I popped out on the other side, the view expanded and shaped itself into a very tall horseshoe-shaped room. The back wall was flat with a huge paned window—who knew what it looked out on.

Again, in the middle of the room stood a simple round table with a light on it. There was a book already on the table, and it was open. I entered the room and walked up to read the book. It was entitled *The Rules of Time Bridge Travel*.

The rules were listed on the page, and they were short and to the point: 1: Do not make changes in the past to events that have already happened. 2: Do not leave anything from the future behind in the past. 3: Don't get killed in the past.

"Esperanza, how would I know if I made changes to the timeline?"

"When you travel through time, the people of that time have to live their lives as they are meant to. You cannot change the outcome, you cannot interfere."

"And where is my great-great-grandmother?"

"Is that who you are trying to reach?"

"Yes."

"She lives in a pocket dimension. That is a magical place, and the rules of time travel do not apply."

"That is good." I continued reading. The consequences of breaking any of these rules were also listed on the page: "Should you break any of these rules, you may not find your own time again."

That seemed rather severe. Did it mean that you won't be able to return to your own time, or did it mean that your time would be changed when you did?

"Esperanza, what does this consequence mean?" I asked.

"If time has changed in the past, you could eliminate whatever sequence of events that were necessary to create you. Therefore, you may not exist and be able to return to your time," said the voice.

"Oh!" I cried. "I understand. Okay, so don't make changes or interfere."

"When you travel through the time bridge, your manner of dress will change to match that of the time period."

"That's handy. Can I take my phone to record things?"

"Yes, but you cannot leave it behind, Lora O'Reilly."

"Last question, I think: How do I set the time and place?"

"Simply tell the mirror where and when you want to go."

"That sounds easy."

"Be very specific, Lora O'Reilly. The mirror has a nasty sense of humor."

"Like 'on a beach on the island of X on a date?'" I suggested.

"Yes, that will work."

"Does the mirror take latitude and longitude?" I asked.

"Perhaps," said the voice.

"How do I return?" I asked. "Sorry, I had more questions."

"You need to return to the point of entry and say 'Mirror, return me to my time,'" said the voice.

Well, let's give it a try, shall we? I walked back to the mirror and stood in front of it.

Looking at the vertical liquid wall was unnerving. I had the feeling that it would spill on me any moment.

I am going to do a test first. I am going to visit my grandmother for a moment.

"Mirror, take me to summer, 1823, in Pointe Marion, Dorval, Quebec," I said to the mirror. The mirror's liquid surface swirled and cleared, and I was looking out at a river. The shoreline was lined with pine trees and rocks. It was on a spit of land jutting out into the water, so that looked right.

I stepped through and the mirror disappeared behind me. This place surely looked real, and it looked like Earth. Huh!

I was standing in a forest. First, I did a 360 degree turn to see what was around me. I recognized the gray stone building behind me to the left. It was reputed to be a summer place for nuns. This spit of land was a retreat for them. My grandmother, I don't know how many greats, lived in that convent. She wasn't a nun, but she was their gardener. Little did they know they housed a witch in their midst!

I marked the spot I arrived by dropping a scarf at my feet. It wasn't something that would normally be there, and I could grab it on my way back.

I saw the tower of the convent in the distance. I remembered being told there were gardens surrounding the building outside the walls. They grew their own food. Moving toward the convent, I scanned around looking for any movement. I nearly bumped into a wall of hedge that was in the forest. It was utterly quiet, no birds or squirrels. When I looked down, I saw that I was now wearing the habit of one of the nuns. *Good disguise, mirror*, I thought to myself.

I wondered if this hedge was one of the gardens for the convent. It seemed too deep in the forest to be able to grow food. As I walked along the hedge, I heard someone humming a tune. Up ahead, I saw what looked like an opening. When I got there, the gap was just big enough to squeeze through, so I took a step or two so that I could see inside.

What I saw made me gasp. It was a magical place! There were plants swaying to the tune, and fireflies dancing among the plants.

I stood there transfixed by what I saw. Some of the plants glowed beside the fireflies. *Wait*, they weren't fireflies at all. They were too big to be flies. I stopped and looked closer—they were faeries!

I crept forward around the corner and she came into view: a beautiful white-haired lady in a green tunic. Her smile as she hummed made her face light up.

"Lora, I know you are there, no need to be quiet," said the woman, surprising me.

"You know me?" I asked.

"Of course I do, dear. You're my great-great-granddaughter," said the woman.

"So you're Innogen?" I asked.

"Indeed I am," she said. "Come and sit with me. You have only a little while before you must return."

"How did you know I would be here?" I asked.

"Oh my, it seems our power has diminished over the years," said Innogen. "I could sense you through time, child. You have a great task ahead of you."

"Do I call you Innogen or Grandmother?" I asked.

"Call me Innogen, my dear," she said. "I couldn't stand the ceremony of being called 'great-great-grandmother.' Tell me, who was it that stopped your training? Your mother or your grandmother?"

"I never saw my mother train anything," I said. "My great-grandmother died before I was born. I knew my grandmother dabbled, but my mother always told me it was nonsense. It wasn't until I came of age and felt a strong impulse to try magic that I realized I had the ability. I started studying then, but I've had no teacher."

"Oh my dear child, you need a teacher, and I would be happy to fulfill that role. Now that you know how to reach me, come back to me again and we will begin your training in earnest,"

"Innogen, I would truly appreciate that. What is this great task?" I asked.

"You are destined to unite the immortals and bring our kind back," answered Innogen.

"Unite the immortals? Do you mean bringing the families together?"

"Yes, child. As well to bring back those of us who carry the seed of magic given to us by the immortals," explained Innogen.

"Bring them back from where?"

"From the dimension they were sucked into. Humanity mistrusted the immortals and their children who had magic. During a ritual gone wrong, a coven managed to trap themselves in another dimension. The few immortals that were left escaped the humans hunting them by hiding, and one of them descended into me and then you.

"Those human magic users that were lucky to find refuge with the immortals were saved from being rounded up by the villagers and put into a mass fire to kill them," concluded Innogen.

"Are those children immortal too? And am I immortal and I didn't know it?" I asked.

"No, I'm afraid you're not immortal. It took about ten generations until they noticed that immortality was bred out of our kind. We retained our power, but as our blood was diluted by more humans, we lost our long lives, then became human ourselves. Those children who could mate with immortal blood again passed immortality onto their offspring."

"Innogen, can I become immortal again?" I asked her.

"Yes, of course you can, dear. You just have to take a potion of agents that will alter your body back to where it should be."

Hmm, that sounded familiar. Could she be referring to the transmogrification ceremony? I thought.

"How do I 'take' this potion?"

"Well," said Innogen with a smile, "the traditional way is getting bitten by an immortal. They had another tool I recall. They stuck you with a sharp object they called a syringe. Whatever the method, it was to introduce their venom into your blood. Sometimes it requires several applications before the transmogrification happens."

"I know what that is!"

"Without realizing it, you found your mate, and he's immortal. He has fangs? Does he use them to give you pleasure?"

I nodded.

"Well, that's not all they do," she said. "They also inject you with the necessary chemicals to start the transmogrification process. The more often you are bitten, the faster the change happens. You should already be experiencing symptoms of change."

"I am. How did you know?"

"I can see far from here," she answered cryptically. "But enough talk for now, you should return to your time. Time moves differently here than it does out there. The mirror's rules cannot be broken without dire circumstances happening. Go, now!" said Innogen.

"Grandmother, I will be back!" I said enthusiastically. "I don't know how to thank you." With that, I ran back out of the garden and back to the spot on the beach where I had dropped the scarf.

"Mirror! Return me to my time!" I called out to the empty space.

Behind me, a liquid blur happened in the middle of the air. It swirled and moved until it stilled and became focused. It was the store from where I'd departed. Turning around, I picked up the scarf and stepped through the mirror.

Just as before, the mirror shut the opening with a snap, and I was standing in the store again.

"That was close! Did you achieve what you hoped?" asked the voice.

"I did achieve what I needed," I said. "What do you mean close?"

"You nearly missed your window to return. There was only a few seconds left before time ran out."

"What would happen if I am late?"

"You would not be able to return, and would be trapped there until someone found a way to open the portal again. Time flows faster here than where your grandmother is. Nearly nineteen hours have passed since you stepped through the mirror."

"Oh. I met my great-great-grandmother," I said. "She instructed me to return for training. Can I do that?"

"Yes, as I told you before you left, your grandmother lives outside of time, so you met the only person that isn't breaking the rules. There are no other beings in that dimension," replied Esperanza.

"How does she live outside of time?" I asked.

"That garden is enchanted. It is suspended in time for other witches to find. She is a great scholar of our kind."

"Can I reach that garden any other way, then? Or do I have to come back here to the mirror each time?" I asked.

"Innogen will undoubtedly teach you an alternate method eventually."

"Very well," I said. "That is enough for today, Esperanza. I think I'll exit now."

"Goodbye, Lora O'Reilly. Until next time."

I found myself outside the building in the back parking lot. It was bright daylight this time. I had a lot to tell everyone about! *And I'm starving!*

Pulling my phone out, I called the gang and asked them to meet me for a meal at Chenoy's.

I arrived at the restaurant first, so I grabbed one of the tables outside on the patio, in the corner, away from most people. The server came and took my order for a drink. I was sipping on it when the others started trickling in.

Rick was first.

"Hello, love. Good idea for lunch!" He kissed me on the lips and a little zing pulsed through me, as always. "Do you feel that?" Rick asked.

"Feel what? That little zing every time we kiss? I certainly do, and it always charges my libido!" I answered him.

"Oh good! It's not just me. I was starting to worry I had a problem. Every time I kiss you, it gets hard. Every time," he said, grinning.

"Sit down on this side of the table and cover yourself with a napkin. No one will notice what I will do," I said with an impudent grin on my face.

Rick looked at me and his fangs slowly elongated. He went to cover his mouth with his hand, but he didn't stop my hand from rubbing his cock. I felt my new fangs elongate a bit too, so I kissed him to hide them.

"Wait, do you have fangs? Did I see fangs?" asked Rick, pulling back from me. His had retracted.

"Yes, they started growing a week ago. I guess all the venom you've given me has started the change," I said.

"Oh, this is marvelous!" he crowed, and kissed me again. I could feel his fangs elongating again as our lips touched again. I couldn't help myself, I had to reach out with my tongue.

Mark and Falon arrived and stopped a few feet away from us. Falon looked at us with laughter on her lips, and Mark rolled his eyes. They sat down opposite us, and grinned.

"You know we can smell that, eh?" said Mark.

"Yes," I said. "Do you think I care?" I kept my lips closed until my fangs receded.

Falon elbowed Mark, laughing out loud. "See, I told you she has fangs now."

"She does indeed. Fun times in booths, eh?" chuckled Mark.

"Really, love, you have nothing to say on this matter, not ever!" she said.

"I guess not." He looked at her indulgently, then glanced around the patio to make sure we were alone. Mark fondly caressed Falon's breast and pinched it gently as he delivered a very hot kiss.

Our server, standing behind Mark, cleared her throat quietly.

"Sorry," said Mark breathlessly. He took his hand away from Falon reluctantly and put it in his own lap.

"Can I take your orders today?" asked the server. Her face showed a broad smile. "You four must be newlyweds."

"Well, not all of us, yet. Please may I have a medium jumbo smoked meat sandwich with fries and a vanilla shake?" Falon asked.

"I'll have the same, please," said Mark.

"Me too," said Rick.

"And I'll make that a fourth!" I said.

"Excellent! I'll be right back with your beverages."

"Oh, waitress…?" said Mark.

"Yes, sir?" She turned around and looked at him.

"You will not remember what we do at this table," said Mark, looking into her eyes.

"I will not remember what you do at this table," she repeated. And then she left to place our orders.

"I gotta learn how to do that!" said Rick.

"Compelling?" Mark asked. "I'll teach you."

"But first let's hear what Lora found out," said Falon.

"Okay!" I said. I started recounting the story of what I learned in the occult store, my trip through the mirror, and most importantly what she told me. When I got to the part about transmogrification, they all gasped.

"Wait a minute," interrupted Mark. "You mean that to turn Falon I didn't need the ritual?"

"No, I don't mean that," I explained. "I meant that it could be done either way—through injection or through bite. The fact that it didn't happen after the first time you bit her means that it just takes more than one dose of the venom. It actually did start the transmogrification. It just needed more venom. The injection they gave you was a very pure form of the venom, and would ensure the process was completed without complications."

"Well personally, I prefer the ritual. It's a lot more fun," said Falon.

"It's sure a lot more fun than the option of being bitten back in the past," I replied.

5—Searching for Group 32

—Lora

Now that I had visited my Great-Great-Grandmother (3G) Innogen a few times and had added to my magical ability, I wanted to get back to looking for Rick's ancestors.

Innogen was from an illustrious background. She was the granddaughter of Ureth and Esperanza I of Group 32 and the daughter of Aedanmar, an immortal, and Padaro, a human. From their line came great power and long life. Even though Innogen was born human, she was born with magic. She rose to be a very powerful magic-wielder. She spent a great deal of her life traveling to find other humans like herself.

Eventually, Innogen settled down in what is now Ireland, because she liked the temperate weather. The other magical humans she had met in her travels started arriving on her doorstep until there was a great group of them. They formed the first coven of witches, with Innogen as their leader. The coven had an alliance with the local group of immortal beings and together they worked to improve the life of humans in that area as best they could.

Unfortunately, humans didn't always take kindly to their 'interference'. Once the Christian church took hold, they were persecuted and hunted. So the coven and the immortals went underground and became a memory in the minds of the humans. Stories circulated about them, fables and myths surrounded the area they were last seen, but humans no longer had contact with them, as far as they knew.

Today, not much has changed. Perhaps magical people weren't hunted anymore, but humans still had no tolerance for real magic. Innogen wanted to train me some more so that her knowledge wouldn't be lost, and I agreed to do so, but this project was more pressing in my book.

She did suggest that the mirror time bridge could be used as a scanning device. Perhaps using it that way, I could find Group 32! This was a good idea: I had to go back to the occult store again and speak to Esperanza.

The last book I found there brought Group 32's history up to the late 1400s when the Europeans first invaded Cuba. Searching the library some more, I found references to other groups. The immortals had a summit meeting around that time, and the decision was that they would not interfere in the humans invading the Caribbean Islands.

Ureth, the immortal leader of Group 32, was forbidden to provide any assistance to the natives, and was instructed to go into hiding.

Okay, so now I needed to find where they went into hiding.

That could wait. I was hungry and tired from reading. So I took a break to get some fresh air. Esperanza popped me out of the store into the back alley. I walked to the nearest coffee shop to sit down, have something to eat, and to call Rick.

"Rick speaking," he answered.

"Hello, lover, it's me," said Lora.

"Hello to you too. How's the research going? I wish I could help you!"

"Actually, I've made some progress. I've located a book that told me about a summit meeting of sorts that the immortals had about the Europeans when they arrived in North America in the 1400s. They were concerned about their practice of warring with the indigenous people. When the Spaniards arrived in the early 1500s, they witnessed the greed of the Conquistadors."

"That's interesting. I guess they decided to do nothing?"

"Apparently, there was a lively debate, but in the end, yes," I said.

"Have you found anything more on the location?" he asked.

"Yes! I have a more detailed description of a set of caverns they used in a mountain. It may be worth visiting."

"Like an archeological dig?"

"Yeah, something like that," I answered. "I'm thinking more of finding a guide that may have family stories about the people that lived on the mountain. There has to be someone who keeps this memory alive."

"Good idea. When do we leave?"

"Let me make some arrangements. But first, I want to finish what I was reading to see if there are any more clues," I told him.

After I finished my meal, I returned to the occult store and the room where I had been reading. Finding another stack of books that held historical records for Group 32 was difficult, but, eventually, I found another slim volume written in a beautiful script.

For some reason, I was sure the author of this one was a female. This one was written in first person too.

I was right: it turned out that the author was the wife of Ureth, who went to the summit meeting. The account told the story of how the immortals had helped the indigenous humans until they couldn't, then fled to another island to go into hiding, only to experience a terrible storm. The account had a description of the new island, so perhaps we could find it.

Unfortunately, there were no other pages in the slim volume, leaving me wondering if I had only discovered part of the story. *Did Group 32 survive the storm? Were they still on the island?*

What to do next? Well, at least this account gave me a description of the island I could look for. It was also during the period of human records, so maybe someone had mapped the island.

"Esperanza, I need maps!" I said.

"What sort of maps, Lora O'Reilly?" asked the disembodied voice of Esperanza.

"Ancient maps—from the 1500s onward, of the islands of the Caribbean. Maps made by people on ships, preferably. I can look up modern maps on our computers."

"Follow the light, Lora."

The light took me to another room where there was nothing but maps, some of them dating back thousands of years.

The map room was organized by location, then year, so it was easier to find what I needed. I located the section on the Caribbean, and a drawer where maps from the 1500s were stored flat.

There were all kinds of maps showing islands, but many were not recorded in the same location. In fact, the larger islands had moved around, if the maps told the truth. However, I did find a few that showed a small volcanic island with lots of rocks around it for the sole purpose of a warning. "Do Not Sail

Here" was written in blood-red letters across the island on several maps.

While the island was listed at different latitudes and longitudes on each map, the shape and warnings were consistent. I took photos of the maps with my camera so that I could use them to search in atlases.

Finished for the day, I put the maps away and asked Esperanza to guide me out. My back hurt, my eyes hurt, and I needed a hug!

6—Living with immortals

—Andrews

he conversation I had with everyone a few nights ago got me thinking about my life with these immortals. I knew their secrets and not once in my association with Mark had I ever wanted to live his life. Now it was different. Meeting Gwen changed me in ways I couldn't have predicted. Not only did I think of her all the time, but I could not see myself in the future without her.

Gwen had asked me to come to her willingly, to be her human. At first, I had been offended by the suggestion, but now after the night we all spent together after the gala ... well, I wasn't offended anymore.

Now, Gwen was planning on turning me into an immortal. That was what she said a few nights ago. That she had a plan.

But do I want to be immortal?

That might sound like a stupid question. I knew it did. But I had worked with Mark for years now, so I know the problems that come with immorality. It wasn't just sunshine and lollipops. There were people who wanted to kill all of the immortals, and actively hunted them.

I don't just want to be a human sex toy either. Oh God, but the sex was inhuman. I've never had sex like that before. Never! Bar none.

Okay, Andrews, let's look at this logically, I said to myself. *Do you want mind-blowing sex for the rest of your natural life with a woman who looks like a goddess and can bring your Johnson back to life with a twitch of her finger?*

Well, when you put it that way, yes. Who wouldn't?

But is that all there would be to life?

That wouldn't be enough. I needed more. As much as I'm game for lots of sex games and kink, I need more. The kink hasn't been as exciting recently. After the hookup I had with Lora, it kind of all faded. I am no longer interested in hook-ups and games. What's happening to me? At my age—thirty-six—I shouldn't have any doubts about what my life's direction is. Why am I even thinking about this?

Working my way out of my self-reflection, I made a decision: I would go through the transmogrification, but only if there was more than just being a boy-toy in it for me.

My phone rang.

"Hello, Gwen,"

"You knew it was me calling?" she replied. I could hear her smiling on the other end.

"I remembered your number, and it came up on my display."

"Wonderful," she said. "Are you available in thirty minutes?"

"Ah, actually, no, I'm afraid I have a meeting to go to in ten minutes," I answered. "Can I call you when I'm finished?"

"Of course," she answered. "Do I get my answer today?"

"Uh, yes," I stammered.

Why do I get so nervous around her?

The meeting with the tiny house team broke by 4:00 that afternoon. By the time I got back to my office, it was nearly 4:30. I opened the door and snapped on the lights to discover Gwen waiting for me.

"Have you been waiting in the dark?"

"It's not that dark to me. I can see perfectly. But yes, I've been waiting. I didn't mind as I'm waiting for you."

I wonder if she's naked under that coat again. Those perfect breasts, that creamy skin...

Snap out of it!

"Can I get you a beverage?"

"Please, scotch if you have it."

Pouring two one-finger glasses of scotch, I brought them over to Gwen and sat on the couch beside her. We toasted to a successful future, and each took a sip. Then Gwen put her drink down on the table to the side and turned to look at me.

"Robert, I want to be straightforward with you. I am very attracted to you. I've never been attracted to a human before. They are usually too fragile for an immortal. But you are not. In fact, you're quite robust. That means you may have some of our genes. If so, that will make the transition very easy."

"I have not been able to stop thinking about you since the gala night. I know we live in different cities, and my work takes me on long trips often. But I want to ... I want ... I want to be with you whenever I can," she said with a swallow.

Was she nervous? Was this goddess nervous speaking to me?

"Where is the dominatrix that commanded me to have sex with her?" I asked. "I did not expect this."

"I came on too strongly," she answered. "I was reacting to a compulsion to be with you. That normally only happens when, well, when you find another immortal, a mate. I want to find out what it is because it's more than I expected."

"Well, whatever it is, has infected both of us," I said. Gwen let out a breath as if she had been holding one. "I have been unable to think of another woman but you, and I've lost interest in all my kink partners and the games we used to play. I'm not sure what's happening to me."

"Even after the orgy?" she asked. "You had some premium kink there."

"That was a game, and it was a human response to being scared to death, and I'm thinking it wasn't just a human response," I said. "No, that doesn't change my feelings. Strangely, I've always been able to tell the difference between sex and love. It's never really felt like just sex with you."

"Really?" she asked. "It was intended to be just sex."

"Yes, I know, but we connected on a level I've never connected with anyone before."

"I felt that too," she said. "I thought something was wrong with me, because I couldn't stop thinking about you."

Gwen had a small smile on her lips. She looked straight at me. Her lips were looking very kissable right now. Gwen unconsciously licked her lips, wetting them and making them shine and look even more tasty. I felt a little fazed. Normally very self-confident and assured of myself, I was on new ground. She glanced away from my gaze.

A moment later, I sat beside her, leaned into her, and placed a delicate kiss on her mouth.

Gwen looked me in the eyes and returned the kiss. I tasted the longing in it, as if it were mine. Our kiss became urgent and more demanding as we explored each other's mouths. Running out of breath, I broke the kiss and pulled back.

"Well, that kind of says a lot," she said. "That was nice."

"Indeed," I said. "Would you like to join me for dinner?"

"I don't have anywhere to be, so yes, please. That would be delightful."

"I know a cute little place around the corner that has wonderful food and quiet, private tables for two."

"Let's go."

The small French restaurant specialized in homemade soups and breads. Our French onion soup au gratin was hearty and authentic. Served with fresh baked baguette and a selection of cheese and pâtés, it was a complete meal. Andrews ordered a Bordeaux wine to accompany their meal.

Because we were early for dinner in Montreal, we had the place to ourselves. White linens and candles set an atmosphere comparable to Paris.

"This is my new favorite restaurant, I think," said Gwen. "It is so quaint and delightful."

"I discovered this place one day when I worked late. It's out of the way, so I don't know how they are still operating. But the food is amazing and the service is excellent. They have mastered the balance between being attentive and being invisible."

"Indeed they have," replied Gwen. "I especially like that we get water without asking."

"What would you like to do after dinner?" I knew what I wanted but was not entirely sure Gwen wanted the same.

"Would you like to come to my hotel room?" she asked. "We could have a nightcap and dessert there."

She suggestively licked her lips again, only this time she did so quite slowly and deliberately. Then Gwen looked me right in the eye and gave me one hell of a "come hither" look. I felt myself getting hard in spite of myself, so I spread my napkin on my lap and crossed my legs.

Clearing my throat, I took her hand that was sitting on the table.

"I would be honored to accompany you anywhere," I said, without stammering this time. "Let me get the check and we can go."

I motioned to the garçon to bring the check while I emptied my glass of wine. Gwen continued to sip on hers as she waited. A secret smile on her lips. *Those lips!* I was obsessed with those lips. I just wanted to eat them.

The bill paid, I pulled out her chair and gave her a hand up. Gwen tucked her hand through my elbow and we left the restaurant.

"Where are you staying?"

"The Novotel."

"That's a bit of a hike," I said. "Do you want to walk, cab, or calêche?"

"What is a calêche?" asked Gwen.

"Horse-drawn carriage," I said. "It's a civilized way to get around, and they take you on a bit of a tour too. It's quite lovely this time of year."

"That sounds romantic. I'd love to do that."

We walked over a block and found a number of carriages waiting while their drivers were talking and having coffee.

"*Bonsoir, mes hommes. Est-ce que quelqu'un est prêt à s'engager ce soir?* [Is someone ready for hire?]

"*Oui, monsieur, c'est moi!*" said a jolly-looking gent with a big handlebar moustache and a beret. "*La voiture blanche, avec les chevaux blancs.*" [Oh yes sir, the carriage with the white horses.]

I helped Gwen up into the white carriage at the end of the line and got in myself.

"*S'il vous plait, monsieur, nous souhaitons nous arrêter à l'hôtel Novotel,*" I said. [We would like to stop at the Novotel.]

"*Certainement, monsieur.*" [Certainly, sir.]

"Wow, I didn't realize you spoke French, Robert," said Gwen.

"Well, it's the primary language of this city, so it's better to be fluent," I replied. "I know four other languages as well because of my work. We travel all over the world, so it helps to have the most common languages in your bag of tricks."

The calêche ride was about an hour long. It wove around Old Montreal, and up along Sherbrooke to see some of the prominent galleries and houses of the city's founding families. The driver deposited them at the front door of Novotel by 8:00 pm. Early for an evening.

As we walked through the lobby, a gentleman called out to get Gwen's attention.

"Gwen! Is that you?" came a male voice from the lobby bar.

Gwen turned around and noticed a man sort of staggering toward her. Clearly, he'd had a few too many Happy Hour drinks.

"Oh, hello, I'm sorry, I forgot your name," she said.

"Michaels, John Michaels," he said. "We met today in court."

"Oh, yes. Hello again, Mr. Michaels. What can I do for you?"

"I would have asked you to join me for a drink, but I see you have a fella with you. Client or friend?"

"I don't see how that is any of your business, Mr. Michaels. I will decline your offer, with thanks. I have other obligations this evening," said Gwen as she turned away and looked at Andrews.

"Come along, Mr. Andrews, we should not be late for that meeting."

"Right away, Ms. Mitchell," I said with a smile.

Once they were in the elevator, Gwen dropped the snooty posture.

"Sorry about that. I needed to get away from him quickly."

"No need for explanation. He was an obnoxious drunk. Pity though, because I was about to suggest a drink at the bar."

"We can order up a bottle of something if you like. Perhaps with some dessert, for later," suggested Gwen.

"Do you prefer wine or spirits?"

"Order a bottle of Macallan, please."

Gwen opened the door to the room and walked in, dropping her briefcase and legal paraphernalia on the sofa just inside. It was a suite with a nice-sized sitting room, kitchen, and a bedroom. Picking up the room phone, I called down and ordered some strawberries, whipped cream, coffee, and a bottle of Macallan.

"I'm sorry, sir, we don't have strawberries or whipped cream, but we do have strawberry shortcake. I can add ice cream to that for you?" said the desk clerk.

"If you have strawberry shortcake, then you must have strawberries. And what hotel restaurant doesn't have whipping cream?"

"I'll see what I can do, sir. A whole pot of coffee or cups?"

"A whole pot please, with cream and sugar on the side."

"Is that all, sir?"

"For now, yes. What time does the kitchen close?" I asked.

"Midnight, sir."

"Thank you."

The room Gwen had was nice but not extravagant. It was a standard suite with a separate bedroom and a living room with a pull-out sofa and a small eating counter for two people. Still, the small kitchen had a proper coffee maker instead of those instant coffee services some hotels used.

Gwen was sitting on the sofa when I got off the phone. I went and joined her. She turned on the TV to create some noise in the room, then took the lead and pulled me into a kiss.

Leaning into her kiss, my lips were crushed by her mouth as she took me. I'd never had any issues with the lady taking the lead. In fact, in some circumstances it was nicer.

Gwen was an aggressive woman. Knowing what she wanted, she wasn't afraid to go for it. That in itself was a turn-on.

As she pulled my tie loose and started undoing my shirt, there was a knock on the door.

Breaking the kiss, Gwen called out to come in. The bellhop opened the door and pushed in a trolley with the food items requested, along with a coffee service and two glasses with the bottle of scotch. I got up and passed a twenty to the boy, poured two glasses, and took them back to the couch.

Gwen had already removed her shoes and stockings, which were discarded on the floor. Her jacket was over the back of the sofa, and her blouse's buttons were mostly undone. As I sat down, my gaze passed over her completely. I picked up details, like the fact that she wasn't wearing a bra under the blouse and one nipple was playfully peeking out from behind the fabric.

I put the two glasses down on the table and gently pushed her to the back of the sofa. Then I kissed her lips, and kissed all the way down to her breasts, until I was beside that cheeky nipple.

When I took her nipple in my mouth, she gasped and arched her back to give me more. I tugged the nipple gently using my teeth, while I sucked on it.

I took one finger, dipped it into my scotch, and then ran it around her nipple and areola. I licked off the scotch, causing gooseflesh on her breast and her nipple to become raised and very sensitive. I let her breast go and my hand went around the back of her head as I kissed her again.

My other hand was on her knee. It slid slowly up her thigh, making concentric circles with my fingertips ever so lightly as I made my way up.

Gwen was groaning into my mouth as her arousal increased. By the time my fingertips had reached her mound, her body was eager for my touch.

I discovered that she was not wearing underwear either. In response to my fingers, she spread her legs further apart. My fingers parted her fleshy petals like a flower and found a very sensitive bundle of nerves. Pinching it lightly, then pulling it, had Gwen wiggling her hips wanting more. Applying pressure on her nub and rubbing it started driving her crazy with desire. I stopped kissing her to pay attention to her body.

Gwen grabbed my belt and fumbled with the buckle. I paused what I was doing to help. Then I inserted two fingers into her vagina and started rubbing the sensitive spot inside.

Gwen was gasping now, moaning and making all kinds of noises I hadn't quite heard before. Her eyes were glowing. Her fangs elongated and she licked them suggestively. But I held on to my self-control: I wanted to bring her so high that a single thrust would collapse her like a house of cards.

She was almost there. Her breathing was accelerated and shallow as she panted in effort to not give in to the climax that was building.

I inserted a third finger and started pumping them hard, really thrusting them inside. With my second hand I was gently pinching her nipple, interspersed with kisses and licks. Her hips were pushing to increase the depth to which I was penetrating her. I could almost get my entire fist inside. But I wasn't going to do that.

Gwen was desperate for me to take her fully. It came out as a whimper as she begged me to take her.

"You're not ready," I said simply.

"I am, please, I need you to take me," she said.

I pulled my very excited cock from my pants. She gasped in delight when she saw how full I was. She started drooling. She leaned forward to grab me, when I pushed her back.

"You will not touch me."

Gwen whimpered again. "Please, let me touch?"

I tossed her over on her front, and bent her over the side of the couch, spanking her beautiful ass. One sting, one kiss. Another sting, another kiss. Gwen was squealing and gasping with the pain and the pleasure. She looked behind her and wanted to watch.

"Turn around!" I ordered.

She did so with another whimper and got spanked. I took her slit with my tongue, licking her from clit to anus and burying my nose between her legs. I inhaled her scent. It was magnificent to me, and it made me even hungrier for her. I gently licked her nether regions, scooping up the wetness. Her reaction was to lift her ass up to get impaled. I didn't though. I licked again and fingered her. From this angle, I could get three fingers easily, maybe four and the thumb in her anus.

I inserted three fingers, and then licked my thumb and pushed it in the puckered hole.

Her scream was delightful as she was impaled in two places. Now her hips were gyrating again, trying to get more. With my free hand, I spanked her again. The multiple sensations were delivering a higher arousal than ever, and I knew her orgasm was built up to a maximum point.

When I thought she would take no more without climaxing, I withdrew all the sensations. I took my hands away and stepped back so the heat from my body was not there. The reaction was instant. Gwen started to whimper from the pent-up energy that had nowhere to go. The moans were loud and hungry, like a beast that needed to feed.

I stepped back up to her and took her in one thrust, my cock reaching the end of her sheath without a problem. I held still for a moment, until her need overcame the shock of being taken and she started to whimper again needing me to move, making her wait just a minute longer.

"Do you want it?"

"Yes, please."

"Do you really want it?"

"Yes!"

"How much?"

"I will die!"

"Not enough."

"GIVE IT TO ME," she yelled. And with that she compelled me to deliver.

Pulling out and ramming into her again and again, Gwen wailed and keened as the climax took her. Her body shuddered over and over again as waves of pleasure suffused her. When I came, I poured my seed into her like I had no tomorrows left.

Gwen was motionless over the arm of the sofa, all her limbs limp and hanging. She moaned one more time, but the smile on her face was pure joy. I was unfortunately soft enough to pop out, so I went and got a towel from the bathroom.

By the time I got back, Gwen was stretched out on the sofa, her legs splayed lewdly, so I could clean her up. I dipped down and kissed her mound in reverence before applying the hot cloth I had brought. Catching most of my cum as she leaked, I dried her up and placed a clean towel under her ass.

She motioned to me to lie on top of her. I had a better idea. Instead of lying down, I scooped her up and carried her into the bedroom and laid her out on the bed. Then I lay down beside her. She rolled onto her side and smiled as she looked into my eyes.

"That was some sex," she said. "I don't remember ever being at the mercy of someone like that before."

"Did you enjoy it?"

"Uh huh, I did very much," she said. "What else do you have?"

"I have lots. I just can't keep up with you as a human."

"I know," she said. "I'll fix that."

"You think it will work? Turning me?"

"Yes, but there is a temporary fix."

"What's that?"

"The temporary fix is my venom," she said. "It will supercharge you."

"I've noticed that. How about a little of that venom now, and then I'll pleasure you again."

"Come here, lover."

7—Transmogrification

Transmogrification: the act of being turned into something else.

Lora was very excited because tonight was the night Rick was going to change her. She was going to become an immortal. She sort of knew what to expect, but they hadn't used this serum on a magical person before. So there might be some unexpected consequences.

Nevertheless, she was pumped and horny as anything. She was thinking of the act in front of her friends, and what might transpire afterward as a result. After all, six of them had combined before and it had been wonderful!

They had agreed to meet at the office because there was more space. Falon had the conference room booked since 3:00 that afternoon, and Lora didn't know what Falon was doing.

"Greggory, what is Falon doing in the conference room?" she asked him.

"Your guess is as good as mine. All she instructed was for me to have delivered six large pillows, a variety of sheer curtains, and a feast for 9:00 p.m. Then she told me I had to leave before 5:00 today or else."

Lora could tell he didn't like the "or else" part of that statement.

"Sounds very bohemian," she said. "Falon was planning a small gathering, I know that."

"Yeah, well, apparently her most important assistant is not invited."

His feelings were genuinely hurt. Oh well. Lora looked at her watch and it was 4:45. Greggory was packing up his desk and putting on his coat.

"Well, I'll see you on Monday," he said.

"Bye, Greggory," she said. "Have a great weekend."

Lora waited until he was in the elevator and the door closed before knocking on the conference room.

"Who is it?" asked Falon.

"It's me. Lora."

"Come in."

Walking into the conference room, she was astounded at the transformation. Falon had pulled the table down to one end and stacked all the chairs. In the center, six people-sized pillows were arranged in a circle and there was a large kaftan in the middle with smaller pillows. Hanging in a circle, from the ceiling to the floor, were sheer curtains diving off the pillows from the center. Surrounding the whole area were standing candelabras all with lit candles. It was a magical and seductive feeling.

"Wow, you've been busy!" said Lora.

"It's been a lot of work to do by myself, but I'm trying to recreate the room Mark and I had for the ritual. I want you to have the same. It was magical. Well, not magical, just magical feeling. I also purchased special robes for you and Rick."

"I'm kind of happy it's not just a shot and that is it."

"Nope, you are going to have the whole experience," said Falon.

"This is very nice, Falon!" said Gwen, entering the room. "You've outdone yourself."

"Thank you, Gwen. You may take a pillow. I have something planned for you and Andrews too."

Gwen walked to a pillow and sat on the floor, leaning up against it.

Mark was next to enter, and was suitably impressed. Then Andrews, and finally Rick arrived.

"Gentlemen, please select a pillow. Lora, come with me please. Mark, will you take Rick?" asked Falon.

"Yes. Come on, Rick."

Falon took Lora to an adjoining room and as ritualistically as she could manage without a gaggle of women and a bathtub, helped her through the ritual of cleaning and dressing.

"I understand what this is," she said.

"Yes, a ritual cleansing."

"I can manage that by myself. Do I put on this robe for the ritual?" Lora asked.

"Yes, then come into the circle of curtains and kneel."

She left to go take her pillow. It ended up between Andrews and Mark.

Mark went with Rick to a separate room to help him prepare.

"Rick, your job is to give her enough venom that her body won't absorb it but that it will react and start the process. I'm going to give you a serum that will boost your ability to produce venom. Then I want you to relax and enter a meditative state to center yourself."

"How will that help?"

"This is a ritual, not just sex. So you want to make sure you are in the right frame of mind. Remember, you have to give her everything you've got."

Mark returned to the main room after giving Rick his instructions. The four of them were waiting. Rick and Lora appeared at the same time and walked to the middle of the circle and knelt together.

Gwen stood and walked to the center of the circle with them. Addressing everyone, she said, "I, Gwen Mitchell, member of the Council of Elders, am here to witness the transmogrification of one Lora O'Reilly. With four immortals present, we have a council."

"Lora, you have come before this council of immortals and asked to be turned," said Gwen. "Is this what you want?"

"It is," answered Lora.

"Will you protect the secret of our presence from humanity as your life depends on it?" asked Gwen.

"I will," she answered.

"Then permission has been granted for an immortal to turn you. Who here volunteers to give this human the bite of life?"

"I do," responded Rick.

"Will you protect the secret of our presence if she fails?" asked Gwen.

"Yes, I will," said Rick.

"Then by the power granted me by the council, I, Gwen Mitchell, allow this transmogrification to happen. Please proceed."

Lora looked at Rick. He was so beautiful in that very sheer robe. She could see the outline of his muscles carved into his body, how his pectoral muscles flexed with the anticipation of what was to happen, and his very happy member saluting her.

He reached out to her and wrapped his arms around her.

"I have to drain myself," he whispered in her ear. "That means we have to make love with everything we have."

"I'm down for that," she said. So Lora kissed him, deeply, wantonly, giving him everything she was. He pulled her tightly against himself, and she could feel the energy rise in both of them. His hand came up behind her head and wrapped itself in her hair and pulled her head back and he licked and sucked on her neck a little. That stirred her body and excited it, making her wet.

His other hand snaked inside her gauzy dress and down to her mound. It found the wetness between her legs, and a groan escaped his lips as he buried his fingers in her folds. A sigh escaped hers as she felt him come home.

As he pushed his fingers into her vagina, her knees buckled and they fell to the floor. He cushioned her head as he laid her out and held himself above her.

"My woman, you are beautiful," he said huskily. His voice was nearly a growl as it strained past his lust. "Let me worship you."

Kneeling between her legs, he bent over and took one swollen nipple in between his lips and sucked gently, exciting it more. He needed one hand to prop himself up, but the other continued to rub her vagina as his mouth assaulted her nipples. Three fingers were expertly manipulating all the nerve endings in her nether regions, all the sensations swirling around and alighting her, coiling up the lioness inside and making her ready to spring. When he opened his eyes, there were rings of gold rotating around his irises. The more excited he got, the faster they spun.

She pulled her legs up so she could wrap them around his waist. This placed his fully engorged penis at her door. He rubbed himself in her wetness, the velvety softness belying the hardness of the shaft. She wanted to grab him and impale herself, but he wouldn't let her.

"Na-ah-ah," he said. "Turnaround is fair play." He was smirking.

"I'm hungry for you," she said.

"Yes, and I want you to be hungry."

With that, he teased her by rubbing his head back and forth, popping it in a little and withdrawing. This made her squirm with desire.

Sitting back on his haunches, he leaned over and took her nub in his mouth. Between his teeth, biting her ever so gently, she felt the floor fall away as the only thing she felt was completely centered on his mouth and her nub. The coil was tightening now alarmingly fast as the heat built up.

Stimulating her as many ways as possible, Rick brought her to near climax, then backed off a smidgen before bringing her back. Several times and she was about to explode with hunger for him inside her.

Finally, when he judged she was not going to be able to hold off anymore, he plunged inside her to the end, "tipping her," as Falon would say. The pain that shot through her was startling, and yet it was so erotic she very nearly succumbed to orgasm right then. But Rick stilled himself while her vagina squeezed and held on to him tightly. As it loosened, he started rocking gently, using his length to reach every corner inside her.

This brought on her orgasm so quickly she was gasping as the shudders took her. But he didn't stop, and soon she was breaching another one, this time bigger. At the peak of the wave, he bit down on her hard and the venom coursed into her like never before. His seed released at the same moment and kept going longer than normal. He was giving her everything he had.

I may end up pregnant because of this! she thought. But the thought was fleeting as the drug sent her into a euphoric state where she was floating among pink and purple clouds and every fiber of her body was singing.

She wasn't aware of anything that happened next.

Rick released all his seed and drained himself of venom, a trick that was difficult by the very nature of its design. When his body started shaking from the effort, Mark went to him and told him to stop. At which point, Gwen gave her an injection.

Rick collapsed on top of Lora, utterly spent. When he rolled off, his member limp, she had passed out. Falon got up and cleaned and dressed Lora again in the robe. Mark cleaned and dressed Rick. Then they left the couple to come back to consciousness on their own.

"Well, that was something to behold," said Andrews. "I have never watched a couple have sex before, especially one that charged."

"It's quite something, isn't it," said Gwen. "Makes you horny as hell. The power that comes with our sexual act is not only all-encompassing, but it's contagious."

"You're right, Gwen," said Mark. "In the past hundred years, our people have not gathered together at all to celebrate anything. I'd forgotten what it was like to have a group of immortals together like that. We feed off each other. I surely felt it when Lora suggested group sex after the gala."

"I remember that," said Andrews. "The four of you were glowing that night, and it didn't seem like just your eyes."

"There was a time when our people would get together in groups that allowed us to share our power. Usually, it was done sexually, because that was the best way to connect with each other on a fundamental level. We used that power to create what we needed," explained Gwen. "That hasn't happened in a long time."

"No, our 'family' has moved away from the old ways. But our tiny group here has become one, though, hasn't it, Gwen?" said Mark.

"I think so," said Gwen. "It is your turn, Robert. But I cannot turn you, it has to be Mark."

"I'd have sex with Mark," Andrews said in jest.

"Really?" asked Falon.

"Well, look at how beautifully made he is," said Andrews.

During Rick and Lora's lovemaking, everyone had shed their clothes. Everyone was in a state of arousal after watching—it couldn't be helped. Perhaps that's why the air was so charged.

"I don't know about that," said Mark. "I may be too big for you."

"I can attest to that," said Falon. "But you don't have to penetrate."

"This conversation ... well, let's continue it another day," stated Mark.

"Relax, I had no expectations," interrupted Andrews. "I figured I would be wrestling you."

"Phew," said Mark. "I wasn't sure there for a minute. And I'm not sure he cared!" Mark laughed as he pointed to his interested member.

Falon went and sat by Mark's pillow and snuggled into him.

"I'd have watched that," she murmured into his ear.

"You would have?" he asked her.

"Would you have done it?" she asked.

"Had sex with Andrews?" he asked quietly. "I don't know. I've never been inclined that way, but apparently my cock isn't opposed. So who knows?"

Falon laid her head on his chest and smiled while he wrapped his arms around her.

Andrews and Gwen were on their own pillow, heads together, talking quietly too.

Rick was the first to come back to consciousness.

"Oh fuck, that was something else," Rick said quietly as he opened his eyes. He tried to get up but stumbled. "Oh boy do I feel weak."

"You will for a while," said Mark. "You will feel dazed and sore. You have given Lora a piece of your immortality, and as such you will be weakened for about two weeks. You may also be a little bruised from the extraordinary effort it takes."

"I feel like my dick has fallen off," he chuckled. "God, I hope not!" He quickly reached for himself and chuckled again when he found all three appendages safe and sound. "Ow!" he emitted, "they hurt!"

"You were given the serum, remember?" asked Falon, "That slowed down your metabolism so your body wouldn't burn too hot. You'll have to heal the old-fashioned way, a little slower."

Lora came around a little while later. She rolled onto her side and a very satisfied crooning sound escaped her lips.

"Mmm, that was amazing," she said. "Where is that man of mine? I need to thank him."

"Right here, love."

"Rick, wow, I hope you understand just how mind-blowing that was."

"Lora, you'll be dopey for a little while more, but when you come down, you're not going to feel any soreness since you got the venom," said Falon.

"Rick is sore?" she asked.

"Yup, especially my balls!" he answered.

"Oh, my poor baby." She reached for them to caress them and kiss them.

"No! Please don't touch it at the moment," he cried. "I don't want to know if they can be roused up right now."

Lora laughed. Somehow, she imagined what he meant. She lay down beside him and rested her head on his chest. She was listening to his heartbeat and suddenly realized it was in sync with hers, perfectly.

"Wow, our heartbeats have synchronized!" she blurted out.

"Yes, that happens," said Falon. "It's a lovely feeling."

"I'm famished!" she cried. "You want some food, Rick?"

Lora jumped up and grabbed two plates of food, brought them back to the circle and sat down beside Rick. His arm encircled her ass as she sat beside him. Lora fed him some food as she popped a grape into her own mouth. *We are now permanently linked together, forever. What a feeling!* She thought.

"Andrews, you're next," said Gwen. "Please make your way to the center."

They had moved Rick and Lora to the outside circle, and removed the pillows and kaftan from the center, and removed the curtains as well. Now the center of their circle was a gymnastics mat. Andrews got up, naked as the day he was born, and walked to the center and sat on folded legs.

Mark got up, also naked, and walked into the center. He remained standing.

"Robert, you have come before this council of immortals and asked to be turned," said Gwen. "Is this what you want?"

"It is," answered Andrews.

"Will you protect the secret of our presence from humanity as your life depends on it?" asked Gwen.

"I will," he answered.

"Then I, as a member of the Council of Elders, give permission for an immortal to turn you. Who here volunteers to give this human the bite of life?"

"I do," responded Mark.

"Will you protect the secret of our presence if he fails?" asked Gwen.

"Yes, I will," said Mark.

"Then by the power granted me by the council, I, Gwen Mitchell, allow this transmogrification to happen by combat. Please proceed."

"Andrews, attack," said Mark.

"I think, considering what we're about to do, you can call me Robert now."

Robert got up from his heels and started circling Mark. He knew that he couldn't defeat Mark, but he had to fight well enough to get his aggression up. His first attack was Krav Maga, and it was meant to sweep his feet out and take him down. Unfortunately, Robert was the one on the floor. Mark let him up.

Robert's second attack was to come at him with some judo moves designed to catch his neck with his legs and take him down. While he caught his neck, Mark was able to turn it back on him and wrestle him to the ground.

This time he didn't let him up. Robert struggled and they wrestled on the floor for a few minutes. When Mark's eyes started glowing red, he knew the bite was coming.

Mark was on top of his hips, keeping his legs from moving, while his hands were isolating and holding his head and arms still. Mark bit down on Robert's shoulder with everything he had, pumping venom into him, counting the seconds to give him the right dose. After seven seconds, he released his bite and licked the puncture wounds clean so they would close. Combat-induced venom had a different composition, and didn't require a boosting serum to be given to Mark. That's because the combat venom was more potent and designed to kill, and he had to be careful of the amount he gave him.

Robert had already passed out as Mark stood up. Gwen ran over and gave him a serum injection and then covered his body with a blanket.

"Now we wait," she said.

"What's happening to him?" Lora asked.

"Similar to you, he's been given a euphoric drug, but it has a different chemical property. Because it was generated with aggression rather than arousal, it's designed to kill. Mark gave him enough to render him immobile and slow his heart down to near death. Now the serum will prevent him from dying, as the venom will alter his DNA and remake him from the inside out—just as it will you."

"The process is not without pain and discomfort. As your bodies are changed, your cells are remade, things are repaired. Your bodies will be returned to the peak of health and the moment in your life when that was. Your features will change somewhat, and perhaps you will even grow again."

"Grow, as in get taller?" asked Lora.

"Yes, taller, broader, your skeleton will become stronger, reinforced, and your muscles will become more capable."

"Cool. I may get taller!"

"Now, remember, guys," said Mark. "These changes will take up to six months to finish. Since you are going to be growing fangs, your mouth will be very painful. I have some painkillers that will help. I suggest rest for all of you for a couple of weeks."

"I'll keep Robert in bed with me," said Gwen.

"Rick and I are just fine being holed up for a few days, right, hon?" Lora asked.

"Well, not too long I hope. Weren't we going to start a Tiny House Project in Atlanta, right?"

We all laughed, because Rick was so driven.

"That may be put on hold," said Mark.

8—Getting to Cuba

Sunshine, palm trees, turquoise waters, *sigh.*

Lora was having lunch at her neighborhood coffee shop when she discovered that she could read the newspaper headlines at a newsstand across the street. *Wow! This new vision is amazing!* Then she read one of the headlines and gasped. Oh my goddess, can I be so lucky?

She let the waitress know she was just going to get a paper, and not to clean up her lunch. She then darted across the street and brought back the newspaper.

The headline was spectacular! *New Caves Found by Miners in the Sierra Cristal National Park, Cuba.*

Lora read the story and discovered that some caves had been found deep in a mountain by some illegal miners. The system of caves was vast, but the unique thing about them all is that there was the residue of a huge fire. All the caves had been scorched with soot on their ceilings.

In the record from Group 32, she had read that the immortals burned all organic matter in their caves before leaving to make sure nothing was left behind.

Could these be the same caves?

A tingle of excitement ran though Lora. She had to tell the group what she had found. She called Mark first.

"Mark, I hope I'm not bothering you," said Lora.

"Nope," he answered. "What can I do for you?"

"I've had a big breakthrough on my research to find the ancestors," she said excitedly.

"Really? What kind of breakthrough?"

"There was a headline in the newspaper today about a cave being discovered in Cuba by some miners. I think it may be the very cave that Group 32 was living in for six hundred years before they left after the Spaniards arrived."

"Oh wow, this is a breakthrough if it is the same cave. What gives you the idea?"

"Well, one important detail that was in the story was that the caves' ceilings were covered in soot. In the record written by the immortals of Group 32, they mentioned burning everything in their cave before leaving. That would have left charcoal residue on the ceiling, no?"

"Yes, you're right. That would have blackened the insides of the caves," he said. "That is exciting. What do you want to do about it?"

"I want to go to Cuba and explore those caves. But I need help getting there and establishing a cover story. Can your council help with that?"

"They might. But I would prefer to help you with that first," Mark offered. "We could easily go down to Cuba as

Canadians on vacation. In fact, it's common for groups to go together and rent villas."

"Oh, that is a smashing idea," said Lora. "That could be our cover after we see the caves."

"I would start with Falon, Gwen, Andrews, Rick, yourself, and me," he said.

"Clever, that way we have all the angles covered," she said. "I like it."

"Organize the details and let me know when and how, and what it will cost. I'll make the arrangements financially and get Gwen working on visas for all of us."

"Okay! Thanks, by the way. This is huge," said Lora.

"It's a big deal for me too. I want to learn more about us."

Lora went to work finding out who had control of the cave site, how to get access, get accreditation, and get there. There were a lot of hurdles to jump over, but eventually she cleared them all and received written permission from Cuba to visit the site and research it. Her group was going to be accredited through a Canadian university archaeological society. Of course, because the university didn't have to pay anything, they were delighted, and provided a letter of reference right away. The stipulation being, that if the group found anything significant that had an impact on Canadian history, they would share the knowledge.

Their passage was booked and their hotel was reserved. They found a reasonable hotel on the beach about a hundred kilometers away from the site. It was the closest they could get to the caves.

The group rented three vehicles at the airport and drove the scenic seventy-five kilometers to the hotel from the airport. When they got there, they were given three adjoining rooms with a view of the ocean. It wasn't a fancy place, but the beds were clean and the view was spectacular. The beach was the best.

Falon and Lora couldn't wait to change into swimsuits and go to the beach. The guys just shook their heads as they flew out the door. Andrews, being Canadian, understood, and he was close behind the two girls. Gwen, Rick, and Mark, being southern Americans, didn't get it. Canadians don't have beaches in their country, not like this with warm tropical water. So the only way they experience this is to leave home. Americans have so many places to be at the seaside that they're much luckier than Canadians.

Falon didn't stop running into the waves until she was waist-deep, at which point she did a dolphin dive into the water. She surfaced five hundred meters away, and the smile on her face could have lit up the night sky.

"Oh my God! It's so warm!" she screamed.

Lora was right behind her, jumping in and swimming out to meet her.

"Isn't this heaven?" Lora asked.

"It sure is. They'll have to drag me out by my hair!"

Eventually the rest of the group got to the beach. Andrews was the only one who went in the water with the girls. The three Americans just sat on the beach on their towels.

Falon got out of the water, strode up to Mark, and shook the ocean water from her soaked hair all over him.

He shrieked in a very unmanly, un-immortal way. "Why did you do that?"

"Come on, silly, come in the water. It's amazing," said Falon.

"I don't swim," he said quietly.

"You don't know how or you're afraid?" she asked.

"Both," he answered. "Our parents never encouraged us to learn how to swim, and instead yelled at us for approaching the water."

"Oh my, that's a terrible shame," Falon said. "Come with me, I'll keep you safe and teach you how to swim." She grabbed his hand and pulled him close, and they walked to the water together. Mark tentatively approached the waves as they crashed and raced inland. The first one that hit him he yelped. But then he realized it was okay. It didn't take him long to learn how to wave jump and he was standing in waist-deep water. Falon held his hand the whole time.

Andrews approached Gwen next. She had the same reason for not being in the water. Andrews did the same thing for her too, with the same positive results. Soon Gwen was diving face first into the waves, having learned from Falon how to dolphin dive.

Rick was the only one left on the beach. He got up on his own and walked down to the water's edge and watched Lora jumping up and down. He was up to his knees in water before he realized it, and Lora was swimming back to him.

"Do you know how to swim?" she asked him.

"Not well. I got swimming lessons when I was a kid, but I was always afraid of the water."

"Well, walk out to me. I'm actually standing on the bottom," she said.

Rick walked out to her and realized that the water only came up to his chest. The waves weren't as big this far away; they gently rose up and down.

"Relax, let the water lift you up and set you down again," she explained.

Rick tried. He tipped his head back and let the tension leave his body—and he started floating! He was floating in the sea! A gentle swell came and lifted him up and settled him down on his feet.

"Oh wow, that's amazing. I float," he said.

"That's the magic of salt water, people float easily," she explained. "The problem is that if you're not paying attention, you can float away on the current and end up quite a distance from where you started." She pointed to the beach. They were at least a hundred meters away from where they entered the water.

The six of them played in the waves some more, then lay on the beach until almost dinnertime. The hotel chef came out to tell them that food would be served in about thirty minutes.

This was a different kind of hotel. They had set dinners at set times. But it was kind of like being in someone's home too.

The group picked up their towels and went back to their rooms to shower and change for dinner. When they came downstairs to the lobby, the maître d' was waiting to seat them in the dining room. They had a large table set for them near the windows overlooking the sea. It was a special table with a cooking surface on one side, and they were all seated around the chef.

The dinner that night was barbequed boar. It was served with fresh seafood caught that afternoon, and a beautiful fruit salad made from local fruits. It was fun watching the chef sear the boar portions on the open flames of the cooking table. He skewered shrimps and scallops and set them on the flames too. There was a spicy seafood sauce to dip them in.

Everyone was so stuffed that they turned down the special dessert that the chef had made for them. Feeling bad, Falon suggested they all take a walk on the beach first and then come back to enjoy the wonderful dessert.

The chef appreciated her suggestion and said that he would serve coffee and dessert on the beach for them. The gang of them then took off, enjoying a spectacular sunset while they walked westward along the coast. It was very romantic.

"This is good enough to be our honeymoon," said Mark as he snuggled Falon into his body.

"It is," she answered. "I'm glad we're doing this as a group, it's interesting. But I'm glad for these moments with you too."

"Hey, guys!" called Rick. "Guys, we're heading back to the hotel."

"Okay, we're coming!" yelled Mark. "Well, I guess we should join them."

When they got back to the hotel, they discovered the staff had set up a tent with chairs and a fireplace for them on the beach. The wait staff brought their coffee and dessert there, and told them to take whatever time they wanted.

"Would you like anything else, señor?" the maître d' asked Mark.

"Does anyone want an aperitif?" asked Mark.

"I'll have a cognac please," said Gwen.

"I'll have a Tia Maria please," said Lora.

"And I'll have a Grand Marnier please," said Falon.

All three guys wanted single malt scotch.

"I'll be right back," said the maître d'.

"Wow, this has been a great place so far," said Andrews. "I'm impressed with the service we're getting."

"It helps that they don't have many guests—perhaps we're the only ones right now," said Falon.

"I don't think so," said Lora. "I saw some other people here earlier."

Rick got up and added a log to the fire. The hotel had left them a small stack of wood too. Lora was curled up on Rick's lap and they were cooing at each other.

Gwen and Andrews were in their own chairs, but close, and tête-à-tête in conversation.

Falon was sharing Mark's chaise as he wrapped his arms around her.

"This is perfect," she said.

"This is perfect," Mark agreed.

Staring into the dancing flames, Falon soon was asleep on his chest. He chuckled at the quiet purr of a snore he heard, but he didn't disturb her.

"I think we're going to go up to the room," said Rick. "Goodnight, all, we'll see you for breakfast."

A chorus of "Nights" followed them up the beach to the hotel.

"Gwen and I are going to turn in too. Goodnight, Mark," said Andrews.

"See you tomorrow, Andrews. Goodnight, Gwen."

A little later, Falon woke up. The fire was very low, almost just coals, and everyone else had left.

"Are we alone?" she asked.

"Yes. Just us and the dolphins," said Mark.

"Mmm, kiss me, then."

Falon reached up and met Mark's lips as they took her mouth. He pulled her up and put her arms around his neck. She swiveled her hips and straddled him on the chaise lounge. As his arms wrapped around her and pulled her closer, she rubbed herself along his quickly hardening shaft.

A gentle groan escaped him and tickled her lips. Her tongue sought out his fangs and stroked them gently. His groans became more hungry.

"Let me carry you inside before this goes too far out here," he suggested.

"Nah, this is nice here. No one can hear us," said Falon. "Besides, we have this nice chaise instead of being on the sand. You wouldn't believe where sand ends up after sex. It's not fun!"

Falon reached into his pants, took hold of his cock, and Mark's eyes glowed in response. As she stroked him, his fangs elongated. She stood up and removed her panties, then straddled him again. This time, she pulled his pants down enough so that she could free his cock. She bent over and kissed its head, and watched as it happily twitched. She then stroked it the whole length while she wrapped her lips around the end of his cock. A throaty groan escaped Mark's lips as Falon kissed and licked him. When she was happy with her work, she positioned his cock at her vagina and rubbed it in her wetness. His head was so soft to the touch, and yet so hard. It was like velvet-covered steel.

Mark's hips were moving up and down as he became more eager to be inside her. After lining him up, Falon sank down on his shaft, taking him all inside. She sat with him inside, and felt her body adjust to his size. He had nearly reached the end, but not quite. Her sheath tightened as she squeezed him and was rewarded by feeling him fill her a little more.

Falon started gently rocking back and forth on his cock, while Mark used his fingers to separate her petals and find her nub. Applying pressure and pulling on that sensitive bundle of nerves made Falon move even faster as her body started riding a wave. Pushing down on Mark's cock and rocking back and forth were building up a nice head of steam, but it wouldn't be enough to achieve orgasm.

"Take over," she commanded.

Mark pulled out, flattened the chaise, and indicated for Falon to lie down. Instead, she kneeled on all fours in front of him. Mark growled and stepped behind her. In one thrust, he impaled her again to the end of his shaft. He wasn't tipping her yet, but with each thrust, he got longer and harder, and three strokes later he was hitting her end. The pain caused Falon to cry out his name. He stilled for a moment.

"No! Don't stop!" she cried.

Working together, they increased the force of the thrust until it was hammering her. She whimpered in pain and screamed in ecstasy as he rode her. When he knew she was about to burst, he reached around, touched her clit again, and her orgasm exploded like fireworks.

Mark finished off himself as she was climaxing, pounding into her at a fast rate until he too exploded. He felt his seed pour into her as she tilted her head to offer her neck. The bite was the icing on the cake. It threw her into another orgasm, but not before she took his hand and bit him too. The two of them rode a series of orgasms that made them shudder helplessly. They then collapsed on the chaise, soaking wet from sweat, and delightfully blissed out of their minds.

9—Spelunking

—Lora

Breakfast was served out on the patio the following morning. It was amazing! Between the pancakes, fresh fruit, great coffee, and everything else, I was soon stuffed again. I didn't think I had digested the big dinner that we had eaten last night yet, but who was going to turn down this amazing food?

Luckily, my newfound immortality meant I wasn't putting on weight. How wonderful was that? Rick was an immortal garbage can too. My, could he put the food away! So could Mark. Those two must burn so many calories it's not funny. Falon's appetite was bigger than it was before, but not in the same league as the guys.

After everyone came down—Gwen and Andrews were last—and had heaping plates of food placed in front of them, I decided to get into the job for today.

"How did everyone sleep?" I asked.

A few mumbles of wanting more, but I think they were all boinking last night. I know I was.

"Okay, gang, today we are going spelunking."

"Huh?" said Mark. "What's spelunking?"

"Glad you asked," I said. "It's the activity of cave exploring. I've got a driver hired for the day that will take us to the cave site that was recently found. After today, we can drive ourselves there if we want to go back."

"Oh, that sounds like fun," said Falon. "Do we need gear?"

"Yes, and I have arranged with a local company to outfit us. We can rent the equipment by the day, the week, or the month."

"I think we'll need it for at least a week, no?" asked Mark.

"Yeah, I think so too. Can we rent it for a week, and then see if we need more time?" I asked.

"Of course."

"Are we all going?" asked Gwen.

"Today, yes. Then, if you don't want to after that, you can skip out. But I'm hoping that with six of us, we'll be able to cover more ground. These are natural caves, but former dwellings of Group 32 of the immortals who came here originally."

"What's that?" asked Gwen. "Dwellings of Group 32, did you say? I was reading something about that subject a week ago. There was an old council ruling that was called into precedent, and I had to read up on it because I wasn't familiar with it."

"I'm sorry, Gwen, I didn't explain much to you yet," I said. "I've been researching our history, and discovered that one of the groups of immortals that left the ark ship, settled in the Caribbean Islands." And then I launched into an abridged explanation of what I had found and why we were in Cuba.

"Cool!" she said. "Okay, I'm in. This is interesting."

"Our driver is meeting us outside at 9:00. I've ordered a picnic lunch for us through the chef. They should be bringing that out right away."

"Good. Let me go brush my teeth and grab hiking shoes," said Falon.

"Me too," said Rick and Andrews together.

We dispersed to meet at the front door ten minutes later. The drive out to the national park was interesting. We traveled through beautiful countryside speckled with extremely impoverished houses and villages. It was painful to see how little some of the people had. Everything was extremely old.

Once we got into the mountains, the weather cooled off a bit. The canopy of the tropical forest was quiet due to the density of the plants. It was like wearing mufflers on your ears. You heard birds, but they seemed far away.

Our driver took us almost the whole length of the lake that was between the mountains. He was approaching the end of the hills, where it looked like a face or perhaps a wall socket had been carved into the rockface.

A deep crevasse had opened up on the side of the hill and rubble could be seen lying on the ground in a puddle. When we got up to it, it wasn't a puddle. The pile of rock stood several stories tall. It would be a difficult climb to get into the crevasse.

We all piled out of the cars to await our site guide. He came along in a few minutes in your typical khaki-green Jeep. I walked over to his vehicle and introduced myself. He told me to get hard hats out of the back, and light kits with batteries.

"Hey, guys, come over here and get your hats and lights."

As I distributed them to each of us, Manuel, our guide, checked that they were fitted correctly and working.

"Everybody, my name is Manuel. I'll be your guide for this spelunking expedition. There are some rules I need you to obey without question.

"Rule #1: Do not go off on your own.

Rule #2: Do not go off on your own.

Rule #3: Do not go off on your own."

At which point we all chuckled.

"Seriously, the most dangerous thing you can do in a cave system is to isolate yourself. If you want to explore a section, ask me. I will be able to determine if it is safe and we can all go together."

"If you feel you can break the rules with impunity, please take a buddy with you. If you get into a jam, the buddy can find me. I will laugh at that point and perhaps come to help you. Or not."

We roared with laughter.

"These caves are pretty new, we haven't been inside very far, nor have we mapped them," Manuel continued. "So it's very easy to get lost. The government of Cuba forbids us to touch the walls where the blackening is. This is potentially a sacred site, and we have yet to interpret the meaning of the markings inside."

"If you find anything, please hand it over to me at the end of our tour, as it belongs to Cuba."

"The only other rule is to make sure you have good shoes and water. Both of those become a necessity when you get stuck somewhere. I will give each of you a radio. Keep it clipped to your belt at all times. Do not use the radio unless you have an emergency."

Manuel gave out the radios and showed each of us how to turn them on and use them.

"Okay, are you ready?" he asked us. *"Vamonos!"* [Let's go!]

The climb up the rock pile was difficult for Falon and I because we were shorties. The others practically zipped up the rocks. At least our new strength helped us. Thank God Mark and Rick stopped to lift us over the really big steps. That part alone took about an hour.

Once we got to the mouth of the crevasse, I felt tiny, insignificant, like an ant. It towered over us like a skyscraper so high you could barely see the top. Walking through that opening was like walking through a time portal, which of course it was, but our guide didn't know this. Only the six of us did. It was more impressive than walking into Notre Dame Cathedral. There were no columns, no supports, just a vast open space that soared higher than it would seem possible. We were so small inside, it barely registered an echo.

I was frozen in place with a gasp on my lips as I stared into the void. It was so dark in spite of the fact that they somehow had installed lights.

"Manuel, how do they have lights in here?" I asked.

"Gas generator—similar to mining lights. They are strung up along the walls, and the generator is outside the cavern," answered Manuel. "But the lights don't go everywhere, and not that far inside."

Manuel started moving forward, and I had to run to catch up because all I wanted to do was swivel my head and look. It was awe-inspiring to think that our ancestors were here in 800 BCE living and teaching the local humans.

As we passed out of the first chamber, there were tunnels that went off the side. One or two of them were lit, but most were not. Manuel kept going forward though, taking us deeper into the mountain.

At the back of the first chamber, the floor started to tilt downward. It became a spiral hallway that ended in another chamber. This one was well lit. There were spotlights pointed upwards to the ceiling as well.

What we saw there was startling. The ceiling was darkened with soot, and in the soot were drawings of people doing things such as plowing, planting, harvesting, giving birth, getting married—everyday life things a person would have done. However, there was a reverence to the drawings, as if they were to memorialize something instead of just the activities.

For instance, there was a tableau where there were two people sitting in tall chairs giving an audience to more people kneeling in front of them. It looked more like a Medieval depiction of a king and queen over their subjects, except the chairs were oddly intricate and detailed.

I went to take a closer look at the drawings. The chairs looked more like something from a modern car. They were bucket seats, and the people sitting in them were strapped in with five-point belts like a race car driver—or an astronaut. I took photos of this tableau to capture as much detail as I could.

Falon was taking photos of the other depictions as well. Between the two of us we were trying to photograph as much of the site as possible. Manuel said we could spend some time here looking at the frescos. I walked around with Rick and looked at more of the images. Some of them had characters under them similar to the characters I found in the volumes written by the members of Group 32. Were the immortals teaching the humans writing? We took photos of that too.

After ten minutes, Manuel told us that we were moving on. At the back of this room there was another spiral hallway going down. This one ended up in a great wide hallway. Maybe it was a hall for people to gather.

There were drawings here too. They depicted groups of people sitting together on the floor and sharing meals. Could this be the room that they gathered to eat? At the end of the great hallway, there were pictures of people giving out food for the people who went and sat down to eat. Those people were dressed in loose-flowing robes and had elaborate headdresses or hairstyles on their heads. It was difficult to tell which. Again, I was shooting photos of everything I saw.

This time Manuel took us down a wide tunnel—a lava tube?—that was on the same level to another large room. This one was narrower but long and very peculiar. In the walls, alcoves had been carved into the rock. They were no bigger than bushel baskets, and were smooth and gently curved. They would make perfect containers for food. Was this a store for the eating room?

There were images on these walls at the entrance behind us and I only saw them when I did a 360 degree spin to take the whole room in. The pictures here had babies drawn in the alcoves. Was this a nursery? Or a hospital?

We backtracked to the great hallway and went the other way, again down a tunnel on the same level. The next room was similar to the alcove room, but the "baskets" were much larger, deeper, and wider. There were several stacked one over the other too. The images on the walls here showed food storage in the alcoves. That made sense. In a way, it looked a little like a supermarket—shelving and bins for products.

We exited the market room at the end and found yet another spiral hallway down.

"Manuel, any idea how deep we are?" I asked.

"Our estimates are about seventy feet at this point. That is the equivalent of four and a half stories or thereabouts."

Wow, these people were quite the builders!

The next chamber we saw had very exciting artwork. There were drawings of what looked like constellations on the walls.

One of them was recognizable to us—it was our solar system. It was easy to pick out Earth being the third planet from a large sun. As well, there was a picture of Saturn, recognizable with its rings. But clear across the other side of the room was another constellation that I didn't recognize at all. It had double suns and planets in a configuration I hadn't seen before. Between these two constellations were drawings of objects that can only be guessed at as spaceships. How the primitive natives of the 1400s drew spaceships is a mystery. But there they were, clear as day. Snapping lots of photos, I wanted to catalog this space the most.

We know this was done after the immortals left in the 1500s. The Cubans didn't know this, so they had all kinds of crazy theories. This room seems to tell the story of how this group of immortals had come to Earth. Did they tell the natives that they were from another planet? Did the natives guess? Were there existing stories still being told to explain these images?

"People, please come closer," called Manuel to gather us together. "This is the last room we have installed lights. There are other rooms to see, but we will need our headlamps. This is when it becomes dangerous to get separated. You cannot imagine how dark it is down there until you've experienced it. At this point, we are going to tie ourselves together. Please wrap the rope around your waist, tie a knot, and pass it to the next person. Leave six to eight feet between to give some latitude."

Manuel started by tying himself off first, then handed the rope to the next person. Once we were all tied together, he moved on.

In the middle of this room was an opening. It was smaller than all the others we passed through, clearly designed for only single people and not multiple people to pass through at a time. Once we went through that opening, the darkness felt like a thick blanket pulled over my head. It was absolute and a little terrifying. I heard Rick's voice in my ear, calming me down.

We were six immortals, and we could all see in this darkness. The new ones just had to adjust our eyes more. I glanced back at Rick, who was behind me, and his eyes were glowing. Good thing he was the last one on the rope train.

"Are my eyes glowing too?" I asked.

"A little. As they adjust to the darkness, they will get brighter."

Falon glanced back at me and her eyes were glowing too. I had to assume that Mark's, Gwen's, and Andrews' were as well. That left only Manuel not able to see in the darkness. Somehow that was very comforting. We all turned on our headlamps and started following the leader. The lamps didn't spill too much light forward though. I could barely make out Falon in front of me and she was only eight feet away.

The corridor we were walking down had a slight upward tilt to it. We walked for what felt like five minutes when I bumped into Falon in front of me.

"Oops! Sorry, didn't realize you had stopped," I chuckled.

"That's okay," said Falon.

"¡Hola! ¡Hola, amigos! We are now in front of what we think would have been a living quarters. On the left is a small opening and a chamber to explore."

We all shuffled into the chamber. It seemed to be about thirty by thirty feet in size, with a twelve-foot ceiling. This was confirmed when Manuel turned on a floodlight and pointed it upwards. The light didn't reflect off anything on the top, but we were afforded more ambient light to walk around. There were depressions in the back of the chamber on the floor. Toilets? There were also lots of alcoves carved into the walls at different heights and sizes. Over the "door" opening, I discovered small holes in the rock. Where they hung a covering over the door perhaps?

There were also images on the walls here. Images of people lying next to each other, sleeping, and copulating. Clearly, this was a chamber for personal use. What was interesting about these pictures was that the immortals were shown as quite tall people. The men were very well endowed too.

Huh! That was genetically passed down. Good to know.

Some of the natives might have lived with the immortals, formed family units and had children. Stories of their endowments would have spread among the women, so that they would all have wanted to sleep with an immortal. I knew from the texts that they did take human wives and did have children. How did the human males stack up?

"There is only one other place that may be of interest to you, but it is quite a hike in the dark," said Manuel. "There are lots of these chambers and multiples of the other ones we have been in too. The one I'm speaking of seems to be a transportation center of some sort. It will take about thirty minutes to walk there—in the dark. Who is willing?"

Without hesitation, we all were game. We knew what we would find, or at least suspected what we would find.

"Manuel, as part of our study, do you mind if we spatially mapped these caves? We have small handheld devices with us," I asked.

"If it was part of your field permission, who am I to say no?"

Rick shrugged off his backpack and took out the small LiDAR device he had and started it up. He would walk at the back of our group and scan as we walked.

"We cannot go any further here, but let me take you to another part of the complex that is amazing. We have to return to the great hallway to access it."

Manuel reversed course and walked back as far as the great hallway. There he chose another large opening in the wall on one of the sides. It exited into a wide spiral hallway that angled down fairly steeply. Clearly, it was going under the other chambers we had been inside. Without handrails to grab on to, it was a little disconcerting because you felt like you were supposed to run. Of course, that would have been suicidal.

After ten or so minutes, we finally reached the bottom of the decline and the hallway flattened out. We started walking in a straight line. In fact, it was remarkably straight. Rick mentioned to me that the LiDAR showed amazingly straight tunnels. He was also able to let me know that we were 152 feet underground at this point.

After another fifteen minutes, the floor started angling up. Rick let me know we were still going in a straight line but that we were rising three inches every fifteen feet. At this rate, we would break the surface in roughly an hour.

However, long before that, we came upon a large doorway that was closed. Manuel found a lever of some kind in the wall and pulled on it. The door swung open away from us. The door was wide enough for all six of us to stand side-by-side. As the faintly lit chamber beyond us was revealed, we issued a collective gasp. It was humongous! Bigger than a football stadium in Texas!

Frozen in place again by awe, the six of us stared. Manuel had a big smile on his face, knowing that the reveal was indeed impressive.

"Welcome to the space port!" he cried. "At least that's what we're calling it until we discover its actual use."

I wanted to tell him he was correct, but couldn't.

"This chamber measures over sixty thousand square meters. We had to use lasers to measure it. There are three other doors in the side as large as this one coming from three different directions. That would suggest that the underground city was three or four times larger than what we have uncovered so far."

There were a few gasps and sounds of surprise when these details were revealed.

"There is a raised platform in the middle of the chamber. We do not know its purpose, but it looks remarkably like a landing pad. We have not found evidence yet, but we suspect it may rise and lower. This alone suggests an advanced race of beings made this facility. We have not carbon dated anything yet, but we haven't found any objects anywhere. The only evidence of people is the drawing in the blackened ceilings."

"Manuel, there is some light in here. We can all see how big this place is, yet it is not open to the sky. So where is the light coming from?" I asked.

"Good question," he answered. "I don't have an answer, yet. We have been looking for the source of light and have not yet found it. We suspect it is being brought in from outside using some sort of refraction system."

"Manuel, do you mind if we wander around here for a while?" asked Rick.

"I can give you an hour if that is okay," he said. "We need to head back up to the surface soon or it will be too dark."

The group conferred. Mark and Falon would go to the left, Gwen and Andrews would go to the right, and Rick and I would go to the center. Photos and GPS measurements as often as possible.

Rick and I started toward the platform in front of us. It didn't take long to get to the edge because it took up most of the space in the chamber. I swiped my hand along the vertical surface of the stone. It was smooth as silk, no nicks, no curves, no divots, just like a piece of manufactured steel.

"Rick, I agree with Manuel. I think there is some sort of lift system on this platform. Feel how smooth it is. There is no reason to carve something this perfectly unless it has to move and you don't want friction."

"Let's follow the edge. Maybe we can find some sort of device or structure," said Rick.

Running our hands along the smooth wall, we walked in a counterclockwise direction. Eventually we came upon some sort of a structure in the ground at the base of the smooth wall. Rick's vision let him see it perfectly. I could see better than a human, but my immortal vision was still developing.

"Lora, there are gears here. There is a large gear system encased in a huge well. The gears interlock and get smaller the further away from the platform," described Rick.

"I'm not an engineer, but that sounds like a multiplying force, or a reducing force. I've got a night vision camera on my phone. Take some photos for me of what you can see."

"I wish we had seen something that gives us clues to who these people were," said Rick.

"I think I know who they were, and we have clues about where they came from now too," I said.

"Are we sure this was Group 32?"

"Yes, I'm positive it was them," I said.

More exploring of the platform found a staircase carved into the side leading to the surface. I ran up the stairs and was at the top before Rick noticed and could stop me. He followed me up to the top. Once we were both there, we could see different things. The light was coming from up top, and we could see that it was an opening in the side that was exposed to daylight. We couldn't see that from the floor. Also on the top we discovered writing and markings on the floor of the platform. Instructions? Line-up points? Graffiti? Who knows.

Rick took some more photos with the night vision camera, then used it to get a shot of the opening at the top of the chamber. We explored more and found two more flights of stairs going down to the main floor. It looked like the ceiling was in fact some sort of cap. Perhaps it was the part that went up and down, and the platform simply was the point at which it stopped.

I was considering this idea, and looking for supporting evidence, when Manuel called us all back to the doorway we came through. The acoustics in this chamber were seriously good. I hope he hadn't heard our conversation.

"Okay, folks, we need to return to the outside now. There is only an hour of daylight left, and we should exit the crevasse before then. They shut off the gas generator at sundown."

We were all a little disappointed we couldn't have more time, but we put our big kids' pants on and followed.

"Vamanos!" called out Manuel. He set a blistering pace to keep up all the way back. We entered that very first chamber just as the lights blinked out. We all snapped on our headlamps again and continued out of the cave system. As we crossed the threshold of the crevasse, the jungle around us suddenly came alive with all kinds of sounds as the sun disappeared. It was creepy just how dark it was outside too. But we had six—well, four—apex predators in our group, because I doubted Falon or I could go after a large predator. I wasn't worried, but still old habits are hard to quelch.

Our car ride back to the hotel was quiet. Falon and I fell asleep on our guys' shoulders. Gwen and Andrews sat together whispering. It was very late by the time our ride dropped us off at the hotel. We all said our goodnights and staggered to our rooms to sleep.

10—Cruising the Caribbean

—Lora

Sexuality is fluid. What turns us on changes with our experiences. The more we experience, the larger the variety of things to turn us on. Why stick with vanilla when there are thirty-one flavors? Although if you really love vanilla, then by all means go ahead.

Personally, I loved vanilla, but I also loved to throw in some nuts once in a while, or turn it really upside down and try a flavor I'd only heard about but not yet tasted. Sometimes, it was exciting to introduce someone else to something new.

After the sex party that spontaneously happened the night of the gala, Rick expressed an interest in exploring other flavors together. This was new for me—I'd never had a partner, a permanent partner, willing to do things with me. Having an immortal to play with added another layer on top. Not only were they basically insatiable, they were better endowed than average human males. And there were those glowing eyes and the fangs—which eliminated anyone who wasn't an immortal as a playmate, as far as I was concerned!

When thinking about additional playmates, my selection wasn't big. There was Mark and Andrews. I already knew Andrews was into kink, and Mark and Falon seemed to enjoy the multiple-person orgy.

After spelunking in the caves, I had an idea of what game I wanted to try next. Rick returned from getting coffee in the lobby and found me musing on the bed. I hadn't bothered getting up yet, feeling lazy; I was just relaxing in bed. I had a book in my hands, but I wasn't reading. My mind was too busy thinking about sex.

"Hey, love, shall I join you, or are you going to get up?" he asked.

"Come and join me," I said. "I have been thinking about flavors."

That comment received a throaty growl from Rick as he stretched out on the bed beside me. His irises were swirling, indicating the first step of arousal had begun.

There was a knock on the hotel room door just as Rick was about to molest me some more.

"Who's there?" called out Rick.

"Mark and Falon."

"Is everyone up?" asked Rick.

"Yup. We're meeting downstairs for brunch."

"Okay, we'll be down in fifteen minutes," answered Rick. "Damn, I was hungry for you," he murmured.

"We should meet the others so we can talk about what we saw yesterday," I replied.

"Ah, but your body is so much nicer to have," he said, pouting a little.

"I promise you can blindfold me later and do what you wish."

"Huh ho ho," came the sound from his lips. He kissed my lips and rolled off the bed. His prominent erection led him to the bathroom.

"That's a problem we women don't have to deal with," I chuckled.

"And you are very lucky about that too!" Rick called back from the shower. "Eeek, it's cold!" he screamed.

I laughed but was grateful that I didn't need a cold shower to shrink my body parts. Not that our group of friends would care that Rick had a raging erection. Hell, they'd all appreciate it. But we didn't want the staff to feel uncomfortable. After all, we were the only over-sexed immortals around.

Rick and I arrived in the dining room about twenty minutes later. The others were all smirks and smiles.

"We did not have more after the knock!" I cried. "We just had to relax from almost having more!"

"Oh, so Mark's knock was a 'just-in-time' stoppage?" roared Falon.

"Or a JIT interruption," added Andrews.

"You guys, next time I'll just leave him happy, okay?" said Rick.

"Fine by me, as long as we get to play," said Gwen suggestively.

"Ooooh, one point for Gwen!" cried Falon.

"It would be a shame to waste a good erection," said Mark, who grinned from ear to ear.

"I sense another group effort on our horizon at some point," I said.

That drew interesting smiles from the other five. Were they all thinking about that? Falon was the surprise responder.

"It's definitely something to talk about," she said.

The guys cleared their throats a bit awkwardly, while the three girls glanced at each other, smiling. Conspiracy time!

"Okay, let's discuss why we came to Cuba," I said.

"Right! Wasn't that an amazing cave?" asked Falon.

"Are you positive it's our missing link?" asked Mark.

"Yes, absolutely," I said, "especially after finding the gears and levers in the space port."

"What is the next step?" asked Rick.

"I now need to find the island. With evidence to support the existence of Group 32, we know they moved to an island off the edge of the trench.

"How far do you think it is?" asked Mark.

"By boat?" I asked. "Don't know. It took them over an hour to fly there, but there was no indication how fast they were flying."

"We have three more days booked here. Is there anything else we can do with our time in Cuba?" asked Mark.

Everyone looked like they were biting their tongues off! And then everyone burst into laughter at the same time.

The servers came and poured more coffee for us as we were catching our breath.

"Now that we have that out of our system, seriously folks, is there anything else we can accomplish here?" asked Mark.

"Can you see if you can rent a boat?" I asked. "Perhaps we can cruise the islands?"

"Oh, that's an amazing idea!" said Falon and Gwen together.

"Let me speak to the hotel management. Maybe they know of a place to get a yacht by the week, which sleeps six."

"Meanwhile, I'm going for a walk on the beach. Anyone want to join me?" asked Falon.

Nearly everyone agreed, so we all finished off our meals and got up to go to the beach. Mark told us he'd meet us out on the beach later.

11—Booking a Cruise

Approaching the concierge's desk, Mark signaled he needed a moment of his time.

"¿Si, señor?"

"I was wondering if you knew if it was possible to rent a yacht that sleeps six around here."

"A yacht? Oh, a ship, yes, there is a marina not very far that has small ships available for rental. They come complete with crew. I can phone ahead for you if you like."

"Really, that would be wonderful. Could you get me the cost for say three days please? All six of our group will be coming. We would need to be back here in three days to catch our flight home."

"Of course, señor." The man picked up the phone and made the call from memory.

Huh! Maybe they get a lot of tourists requesting such an excursion, thought Mark.

Twenty minutes later, the concierge motioned Mark to return to the desk.

"I have your numbers, señor. The marina does in fact have a yacht available for the next week. It sleeps six guests and has a crew of four. The cost for a week is 3,200 euro."

That is nearly five thousand dollars Canadian. Not bad for six people for a week!

"Please book a charter for us. We'll go today. No need to refund anything to us from the hotel. This was a last-minute change, and I understand how important income is. Keep it. Your service has been amazing," said Mark.

"Oh! Señor, that is too kind! I cannot do that."

"Yes, you can, señor. I won't accept a refund," insisted Mark.

"¡Señor, *muchas gracias*! I will call the marina right away and book the passage. They will want a deposit."

"Señor, you have my credit card information. Please pay the whole thing up front."

"¡Si, señor!"

Mark was pleased that the task went without a hitch. Now to collect his friends and get packed. Walking out to the beach, he spotted them playing in the shallow waves close to where they had dessert the other night.

Falon saw him walking toward her and stopped to wave.

"Great news," Mark said as he got there. "There is a marina not too far from here, and apparently yacht excursions are quite popular. They have one that sleeps six, with a crew of four. The weekly rate is five thousand dollars. Not bad for food, board, and fun for six for a week. That's only $120 per person!"

"Wow, that is a great deal. Shall we book it?" asked Rick.

"Already taken care of. We can leave when we're ready and take off as soon as they are ready to leave port."

"Wait a minute, what happened to we have three more days?" asked Falon.

"I can change the flight back," said Mark. "This is too good an opportunity to cut short."

"Okay, everyone go pack and be back down here in fifteen minutes," Lora said. "Falon, pack for Mark too so he can change the flights."

Mark went back to the front desk and enlisted the concierge again to help with changing their flights. They'd end up being closer to the airport from the marina. Moving the flights a week further was a little tricky mostly because there were no flights on that day. They would need to come back to the hotel for two nights and then go to the airport. Not a problem!

The gang was back downstairs right on time. Mark gave them the news about the flights, and they were all happy to have an additional week in paradise. They all piled into the courtesy bus for the hotel. They would be driven to the marina, and then picked up after the cruise.

The marina was very big. There were lots of yachts and some cruise ships docked as well. The commercial dock was on one end while the private docks were on the other. Their group made their way to the commercial dock, where they located the correct slip.

"¡Hola!" called Mark. "Is anyone on board?"

"Hola, señor. Is this Señor Mark Chisholm?"

"Si, señor, and these are my guests. May we come aboard?"

"Si, señor."

Mark motioned to Falon to go first, then himself, then Rick and Lora, and Gwen and Andrews bringing up the rear. Once on board, the crew introduced themselves and showed them to their cabins.

"This is a catamaran! I've always wanted to sail on one of these ships," said Falon. She was really excited about this.

The cabins were not large, but each had a queen bed. Considering it was a catamaran, it was pretty impressive. The girls changed into bathing suits and the guys changed into shorts and tees. Back up on deck, the captain insisted they all wear life vests. They were also given a short lesson on sailing cats and what to watch out for when they were moving in windy seas.

The captain asked us where we wanted to go. Mark asked to see a map, so the captain took him up to the bridge. Lora went along to point out the general area and explain what we were looking for. We just didn't know which one. The captain said that he could sail around those islands so we would see two sides. He warned us that many were uninhabited. Lora told him the one we were looking for was not supposed to be there.

The captain notified us that they would set sail in thirty minutes. We were welcome to sit on deck in the guest area, just to be careful and watch out for the sails and the crew.

12—Sandbars and Shipwrecks

—Lora

Being at sea is an uplifting experience. The wind off the water is pretty much constant, so too is the sound of the water on the hull of the catamaran. It made a pleasant *shush-shush* sound, like being sung a lullaby by the sea while you were rocked in a cradle.

Overnight, the captain made short work of getting us into position on the outer limits of the islands we were going to look at first. In the present-day Bahamas chain, there were hundreds of islands. Most were used by either hotels or private citizens. But some of them were still uninhabited.

I wasn't sure if having people on the island necessarily disqualified the island or not. After all, the immortals would have adapted to modern times, and perhaps they were living in plain sight now. If they were living in plain sight, their community would be housed underground somehow. That alone would dictate a minimum amount of land required.

My first thought was to look in the areas where the most shipwrecks happened over the past five hundred years. That would indicate that the ships ran into the rocks off the coast. So the first thing to do was to survey all the islands, and search for ones with very shallow water and rocks close to shore.

The captain had positioned our yacht just off the coast of Antigua. The small archipelagos south of there didn't seem likely, so we went northward next. There was a very deep-water trench that split off the Dominican Republic from the Turks and Caicos. We would follow that trench up as far as the Bahamas, looking for uncharted islands. Because we were in no rush, the normally four-and-a-half hour sail took us most of one day. We stopped frequently to compare what was in front of us to the maps of the area.

It wasn't very likely we would find an uncharted island, but it was possible. More likely was finding a charted but uninhabited island. There was also such a thing as phantom islands. These are islands that are found by someone, recorded, which then disappear. Sometimes sailors find them, sometimes they don't.

One thing was for sure: there were a couple of places where hundreds of shipwrecks kept happening. There must have been a reason. I believed it was because there was an island there that wasn't on the charts and maps. Only a satellite photo would show it, as long as the satellite was over the area. Duffy had that technology, but it was not on board our yacht. And right now, I didn't have a friend that could help us on that score. I wonder if Mark's council could?

Sailing on the yacht was a vacation in and of itself. The crew kept us well fed with gourmet food, and was constantly serving something to imbibe. We three girls spent most of our time sunbathing, and the guys took to deep sea fishing with the crew. The crew didn't have a lot to do in so far as driving the yacht. It had an autopilot of sorts, and we could cruise along slowly using the engines instead of sailing.

The captain raised sails between the islands for the sensation of it, but when we got close, he'd switch to engines.

We dropped anchor from time to time, to go swimming and snorkeling off the back of the yacht. The coral reefs were quite beautiful. Because the catamaran rode high in the water, we were able to get very close to shore. One afternoon, we even put in at a small beach. It was wonderful because there were no other humans around.

The crew made us a picnic and took us to shore. It was divine. A private beach with no one else on it but the six of us. The crew set up the meal, tables and chairs, then returned to the yacht to leave us for several hours.

"Anyone want to explore this island while we're here?" asked Falon.

"I'll go with you," I said.

So we put on some shoes and walked into the edge of the palm forest. It was a remarkable forest, all palms and some ground dwelling flowering plants that looked so exotic. I hadn't seen most of them in person, except at a florist. Hibiscus was one of the common ones, but we saw orchids and towering plants called the Dagger Log. While there was evidence of lots of birds living on the island, there was no sign of people at all. So we returned to the beach.

The next day, when we got to the spot where all the shipwrecks happened, we could see them like ancient skeletons on the bottom in the shallows. It was a little creepy. But there was no island anywhere. The captain didn't want to tempt fate and sail across the water in between the rocks and reefs sticking up. I couldn't blame him. So I asked him to drop anchor here and let us explore this reef. My theory was that there was something here, we just couldn't see it.

The six of us got into wetsuits and scuba gear. One of the crew members took us into the water and gave us two hours of instruction on how to use the equipment. It wouldn't be enough if we ran into a problem, but it would get us in the water. He warned us to not go deeper than twenty feet, given our limited training.

We left the yacht behind and started surface swimming toward the reef and rocks. We stopped as a group when we reached a sandbar that we could stand on. Now that we were away from the crew, we could speak freely.

"What are they talking about?" Falon asked Mark as he was watching the yacht.

"Nothing of note, really. They are discussing meals and the direction they will go next," he answered. "They have no idea what we are looking for."

"That's good," I said. "I wouldn't want to create a curiosity in them."

"Okay, Lora, now what?" asked Gwen.

"Well, as far as I can think, we need to make our way discreetly across this reef and around the rocks and see if we bump into anything," I said.

"Bump into something?" asked Rick.

"Yes, like a landmass that is shrouded or invisible," I suggested. "According to the text I read, they managed to hide the island by projecting an image of water dangerously filled with shallow reefs and rocks. Ships wouldn't want to pass through the opening between the islands, because of it. Just like our captain refused. His charts indicated dangerous shoals for any ship with more than one meter draft. That pretty much eliminates any ship. Only dinghies would be able to navigate that, or swimmers."

"Beautiful. Hence, we are swimming," said Rick.

Looking around, the three older immortals tried to see something with their better vision that would suggest a direction to go.

"Look at that over there," said Gwen, pointing to a dark looking section of the water that appeared to be shadowed but had nothing above it.

"That looks suspicious," I said. "That's exactly the thing we should investigate. Gwen, why don't you take Andrews and check that out?"

Mark's sharp eyes spotted another anomaly, so he and Falon swam over to that one. Rick then spotted something underwater that was anomalous. So we started with that.

Before swimming our separate ways, we had all agreed that we would meet back on the sandbar in thirty minutes.

Rick and I dove under the water and headed down about fifteen feet. The water was so clear that we had perfect vision. The reef was truly beautiful, and we had lots of company in the form of fish and eels.

The anomalous object looked like a cave. Not really odd for a cave, but the location was interesting. We hoped it might be an underwater access point. We swam slowly in case our yacht's crew was able to see our progress. We didn't want them to think we were doing anything other than being tourists.

When Rick reached the cave-like shadow under water, he swam right in and disappeared. I panicked for a second or two until he reappeared in the same spot. By the time I reached him he was looking around at the rocks without realizing he had vanished. I got his attention and told him to surface.

We followed our bubbles to make sure we didn't surface too fast, like instructed. On the surface, we tapped on our heads, to indicate everything was okay.

"Rick! I said excitedly. "You vanished for a split second while you were swimming!" I was trying not to be loud.

"What do you mean I vanished?"

"You were swimming toward the cave, vanished, then reappeared two seconds later!" I screamed quietly.

"I must have swum into their shroud, then," he said, equally excitedly. "You know what that means?"

"Yes!"

"That it's still active, which means they're still there!"

"Yes!" I screeched quietly. "So now, let's methodically go back to that opening. I want you to watch me as you go in and come out. As soon as you see me do this—I made an X with my hands—stop, and I'll swim toward you before proceeding."

"Okay, let's go."

Rick did just as I asked. He swam toward the cave then stopped, turned around and faced me. As he back pedaled with his hands and feet, he watched me. Only in one spot did he vanish, and I made my X. He moved forward again so that I could see him. Then we swam together into the shroud.

Behind the shroud was more of the same, rocks and reefs, which is why Rick didn't notice he had swum into it. We went about twenty feet in, then I suggested that we surface and look above to see what we could see.

It took a few minutes to surface with our bubbles like before. When we broke the surface, we were facing the yacht. We tapped on our heads, but they didn't seem to notice. Rick turned around first. I heard him gasp behind his mask.

I turned around then to face the same direction, and in front of me was an island. An island that had not been there before. It was lush, green, and had a mountain in the middle. Just like the description in the book.

Rick looked at his GPS and noted the coordinates of the island. I turned back toward the yacht and waved my arms frantically. They didn't notice. So we were behind the shroud too.

"Rick, do you want to swim up to the shoreline and check it out?" I asked.

"I want to get a GPS reading from the shoreline, yes. But I don't know how much exploring we want to do without an invitation."

"We won't get an invitation if they don't know we're here," I mentioned. "Let's go and at least touch the sand to say we did!"

We swam to the shore and walked up the beach. We stopped about five feet from the tree line, and Rick took another GPS reading.

"Okay, let's get back to the rendezvous point and tell the others," he said. Clearly, he was as excited as me.

As we were putting our masks back on and getting into the ocean, I heard something behind me. I turned around, and standing on the beach were people, immortals, watching us go back into the water.

"Halt!" cried the one in the center.

Rick turned around and nearly fell over.

"Hello!" he called.

"Who are you and how did you find our island?" asked the one in the center.

"Let me answer that," I said. "Hello, my name is Lora. We are descendants from your people. We are both like you. I found you because I went searching for you and found ancient texts written by your people describing Group 32 and where you moved to. We came looking for you, but we have made sure to cover our tracks, and not let on to humans what we were doing, or why."

"Lora, I am pleased to meet you," said the man who had spoken. "My name is Ureth, and I am the leader of our group."

Oh my God. This was the same man who was written about in the volumes!

"I am very pleased to meet you, Ureth," I managed to say calmly. "We were about to regroup with the rest of our team and let them know we found the island. May we do that?"

"Unfortunately, no. We cannot let you leave. Your friends have also found their way onto our island, and they have been taken to the village. Please come with us."

"You don't understand!" I cried. "If we do not reappear, the humans who brought us will wonder where we went and there will be a search. The best thing for you is to let us go. As immortals, we understand the need for secrecy. We keep the same secret."

Ureth conferred with his other people on the beach for a moment. Rick could hear them and related what they were discussing to me very quietly. They were scared that we were yet another group of treasure hunters who'd accidentally happened on their island. But if we were treasure hunters, why would they keep us here? Rick filled in the answer: to wipe our minds of finding them.

"Lora, let me talk next," said Rick.

"Lora, we have spoken together and—"

"Ureth, I apologize for interrupting," said Rick. "I am an immortal too. In fact, we're both immortal. I heard your discussion, and there is no need to wipe our minds of the memory of finding you. We are not treasure hunters. We are seeking our family, our kind, our ancestors. My mate, Lora, has only recently gone through transmogrification, but she carried the genes and skills carried down from her ancestors. Her abilities came from you. We came with two other immortals, siblings, who are from the same family. We believe they may be descendants of Group 35. Both of them have mated as well, and the mates have also gone through transmogrification. So, we will all keep our secret and yours."

"And what is your name, young man?" asked Ureth.

"Young man, huh? It's been a long time since anyone has called me that!" said Rick. "My name is Ricardo Benal. I was born in Cuba and my family has a long line of 'special people' with skills that humans don't possess."

"We will let you go … on one condition," said Ureth.

"If we can meet this condition, we will do it willingly," I said.

"Hmmm," said Ureth. "Yes, the condition is that you return without humans and stay with us long enough to give us news of the world."

I was so shocked by this offer, I literally just collapsed in the waves and knelt there weeping.

"Did I say something offensive?" asked Ureth.

"No, not at all, Ureth," responded Rick. "I can sense my mate has become overwhelmed with joy at your offer."

"Hmmm."

"When can we return?" I managed to get out of my mouth. "When may we return, Ureth?" I asked more politely.

"Whenever you are able."

"Will you bring our friends to us, please?"

"They are already on their way to this part of the beach," replied Ureth. "It wasn't until they came into close proximity to us that we realized they were a group of immortals. We have given them the same invitation."

"I don't know what to say!" said Lora. "Thank you seems so inadequate."

Rick and I dove back into the water and made our way out to the sandbar. The others were not there yet, so we got out on the sandbar and sat down in the water to wait. The yacht noticed us there and hailed us. We waved back and let them know we were okay.

Mark appeared first out of the water. His expression was extreme excitement. Falon popped out of the water and ran toward us.

"We found them—or rather they found us!" said Falon excitedly.

"Us too!" said Rick. "They wanted to prevent us from leaving at first."

"Yes, they made us get out of the water and follow them. Eventually, one of them looked at Mark and asked him if he was an immortal. He was very surprised that we were not human."

"They got Gwen too, so they should be back soon."

Like magic, Andrew's head popped out of the water and he pulled off his mask.

"They found us!" he yelled across the water.

"We know!" we all chorused together. I signaled them to come join us on the sandbar.

Gwen swam faster into the sandbar and was out of the water in a jiffy.

"They thought we were treasure hunters at first. They were defending the island as a claim and wouldn't let us go any further," explained Gwen. "They received some sort of communication that had them taking us to a village to be detained."

"It was probably the fact that there were three pairs of us showing up in different places," I said. "It made them nervous. We got the treasure hunter thing too. I had to tell them we were immortals and weren't going to blab."

"Ah! That's why they were sniffing me," said Andrews. "They asked Gwen if I had turned yet."

"Okay, now that we have made contact, what's next?" I asked the group.

"I think we should go back to the yacht, finish our vacation, and plan the next stage very carefully. They now know about us too. To return here, we need to do so without human assistance," suggested Mark.

"That makes sense to me," said Andrews.

"Well, our first step now is clear. Let's go and enjoy the rest of our holiday. We have four more glorious days on the yacht and a couple of days on the beach."

"I second that!" said Falon. "I've got some lovemaking to catch up on!"

"Me too," I said.

"Me three," said Gwen.

The guys looked at each other, smiled, and sighed. Oh, the life!

13—Food Seduction

—Lora

There was a wonderful breeze bringing the sensual fragrance of tropical flowers through our hotel room's open balcony door and windows. I was lying on the bed, letting the breeze cool my skin. Rick had gone out somewhere and left a note that he would be back shortly. Until then, I was just enjoying being naked.

I heard the hotel room door open and close quietly. I didn't bother opening my eyes, because I recognized my mate's smell.

He stood at the archway to the bedroom and watched me enjoying myself.

"Hmmm, should I be jealous?" he asked with a very sexy voice. I could hear that his fangs had elongated a smidgen because there was a subtle lisp.

"Of my fingers?" I asked. "Oh, no, they are just a standby for you. They are not nearly as skilled."

Rick continued watching me as I played my fingers across my skin. I was following the patterns of the breeze as it brushed across me, swirling my fingertips like the wind across my breasts.

I listened to his breathing getting shallow and fast as his arousal increased, until a small groan escaped his lips. I opened my eyes a crack to witness him adjusting himself in his jeans.

Grinning to myself, I upped the ante by snaking my left hand down to my mound and twirling my finger in the short-cropped hair just above it. Rick sucked in his breath through his teeth. I let my finger explore my folds and spread them to rub myself. My hips automatically started rocking back and forth in response. A moan escaped my lips too, as my own arousal started to build.

"You're not doing that right," he said from the doorway.

"Oh?"

"Let a master show you the proper technique," he said, approaching the bed. I heard a rustle as he put whatever he had been holding down on the desk, and then I heard his jeans drop to the floor.

He got close to me on the bed, and knelt on the floor.

"Oh mujer, me pones tan caliente. Déjame darte placer," he mumbled in Spanish.

He pushed my legs apart enough to get his mouth on my nub and started flicking his tongue. His lips encircled my nub and he sucked me into his mouth, with a little nip of his teeth.

I gasped at the contact; it was so hot in contrast to the cool breeze. His mouth was scorching hot, and it warmed me up everywhere.

He licked and kissed and sucked on my folds until they were swollen and ultra sensitive. Then he pierced my vagina with his tongue, almost making me climax, lapping up the juice that had soaked me, and licked his lips.

"Oh, I love your flavor, woman. I could feast on this all day."

But then Rick got up, leaving me hanging there almost ready to climax!

"Hey, where are you going? You cannot leave me here like this!"

I opened my eyes fully in time to see his erection walking by. It was magnificent. There was a slight curve to it today that would help touch my sensitive spots inside. Oh Goddess, let that man take me now!

Rick came back with a tray that had a dish of strawberries, a cup of whipped cream, and a bottle of something brown—chocolate sauce perhaps?

Hmmm, whipped cream can be used in so many ways.

"So, what's all that for?" I asked.

"I thought fruit for breakfast would be nice," he said. "But I need a serving dish."

With that he scooped up some whipped cream and placed a dab on each of my nipples. Then he licked and sucked the nipples clean.

Oh God, I'm not going to last long playing this delightful game.

He scooped a finger into the chocolate pudding as it turned out, put it in my mouth, and let me suck it off.

Wow! Some delicious pudding that had a complex blend of coffee, Tia Maria, crème, and cinnamon. It was light and just the right amount of sweetness. But I digress!

Rick took another two fingerfuls, brushed the pudding all over my nipples, then he played popsicle by putting them in his mouth. He licked them off noisily. Then he picked up a strawberry and dipped it in the chocolate, and brought it to my lips. I took a vicious bite and he smiled. He dipped it in chocolate again, and this time I licked it off the strawberry lasciviously.

Rick finished off that strawberry, then took another. This time he used it to paint my body with chocolate, all the way down to my mound and inside my folds.

He carefully lapped up all the pudding, using his tongue to clean me like a cat—interspersing licks with nibbles and kisses.

My belly button became his favorite dish as he filled it with chocolate and whipped cream. He dipped strawberries in my belly button and fed them to me. He had a veritable dessert ready to go. He had lots of fun with that one. In fact, that vessel was used a few times. He licked me clean too.

"I want to taste a bellybutton pudding, so lie back, mate," I said. I was tired of watching and wanted to play too.

I filled his bellybutton with whipped cream, and sucked it out and licked it clean. He groaned as my tongue dove in and swirled around, licking it all up.

Next, I covered his cock in whipped cream too. I licked it off like an ice-cream cone. His member twitched in my hand, then I kissed him on the head, enveloping him with my lips, drawing him deeply into my mouth, and then with my teeth lightly scraped him all along his shaft as he pulled out.

He growled and pushed me back on the bed again. Taking my mound with his hand, he spread me and then punched his cock into me, taking possession.

His eyes were aglow, and his fangs fully extended as he looked down on me like a predator. Strangely, I felt no fear, but I certainly had the arousal factor turned up on high. My own fangs came out too as something in me responded to this animal that had me in its grasp.

I wrapped my legs around his hips and drove myself further along his shaft, pushing him into me more.

His growl became a groan of utmost pleasure as he reached the end of my sheath. That spot, at the end, isn't for everyone though. It hurts a little too.

"Come on, beast, take me, make me yours," I whispered into his ear.

The beast did indeed take me. Rick's thrusts were monumental as he pulled out almost completely and then impaled me over and over. Each time, the hit at the end drove a little exquisite pain into my arousal until I thought I would explode.

"I cannot hold back any longer," Rick growled at me.

"Let go."

With that, his slow, steady, pace became fast and furious as he pumped into me. He arched his back and howled as he released his seed and came crashing in on my neck for the bite that would release my spring too. I bit him at the same time and we climaxed together violently. Waves of pleasure carried me away as he flattened out on top of me. I unhooked my legs from around his hips, and they splayed as my body turned to gelatin.

Rick licked the spot where he bit, and lifted himself up to gaze down at me.

"I never know what will happen, or what I will find with you."

"Makes it interesting, no?"

"I was an animal. Sorry," he said.

"Why are you sorry?" I asked. "You don't hurt me, Rick. There is nothing you could do to me sex-wise that would hurt me. Besides, I love it when you're rough. I don't know why, but there is something about being taken by you, being possessed by you. It's fulfilling in an ancient way."

"What shall we do today?" I asked.

"Let's go to the beach and build sandcastles," suggested Rick.

"I need a shower first," I answered.

"I'll join you."

14—Fighting Neptune

—Lora

Showered and dressed for the beach, I gathered some essentials like suntan oil, towels, hats, flipflops, and a coverup, and went out to reserve some chairs on the beach. Luckily, it was not busy at all. Maybe half a dozen couples were out, and there was ample space between. The hotel even provided those fabric cabanas to put your chaises into for privacy.

Grabbing one at the far end from everyone else, I set up six chaises and three umbrellas. The hotel staff immediately came over to offer assistance, and set up three cabanas for us as well. Then they brought over some tables, with pitchers of ice water and glasses.

I sat in the middle cabana chaise and set up my beach. I wanted to sunbathe first, so I laid out a big towel and flopped down on my stomach to relax with a glass and a book.

I was four chapters along by the time Falon showed up, and then Gwen. We three were into the sun. The guys, when they showed up, went and hid in the cabanas. They moved an extra chaise lounge there so they could all talk.

Around lunchtime, the wait staff came and took orders for drinks and meals on the beach. We got fresh-caught lobster and salads, plus a pitcher of margaritas.

"Hey, let's build a huge sandcastle!" I suggested.

"Sounds like fun," said Gwen.

"We need some tools," said Mark. So off he went in search of tools.

The rest of us picked out a spot above the tide and started blocking out the castle.

"I'll work on the moat," said Falon. "Every castle needs a moat, especially by the sea, to carry away the water safely."

"Robert and I will work on the walls," said Gwen.

"Okay, Rick and I will start on the citadel."

Just then Mark returned with several pails, shovels, and some molds.

"They have a whole store for kids' toys to build sandcastles. I bought a whole bunch. There should be enough for everyone."

By the time the tide turned, we had a huge structure built with turrets and crenelated towers and Falon was busy digging a large moat around the entire castle. I got photos of it with all of us sitting inside the walls. It was a lot of fun.

Then the tide started attacking our castle. We swung into high gear rebuilding the structures and digging ditches to protect the walls and take the water away.

We fought valiantly against our foe until the waves finally overtook us and crashed on top of our castle. Mark stood in the middle of the castle shaking his arms at the sea.

"Come on, Neptune! Do your worst!" yelled Mark. At which point a great big wave came in and smashed the castle, soaking Mark where he stood.

Rick ran back to pick up our things off the sand so they didn't get soaked. The rest of us, laughing like crazy people, started dancing on the castle's ruins and applauded Neptune for his victory.

The other guests must have thought we were nuts, but we all had a great time. Then the hotel staff asked if we wanted dinner on the beach or on the patio. We opted for the beach because we could talk freely there.

They set us a beautiful table with candles and fabric walls surrounding us that were sheer and gently moved in the breeze. We had a wonderful view of the ocean, and nothing else.

During dinner, I brought up the elephant in the room.

"Okay, guys, what are we going to do next about Ureth?" I asked. "I mean, he's the same individual I read about in those ancient texts. He's one of the original Group 32 members. He can fill in so much information for us, maybe even help us find your family Rick, and more of my family too. In general, he may have a better idea of where the different groups went."

"Did anyone else think they let us go a little too easily?" asked Mark.

"I thought it was odd that we were basically under guard, then we weren't," said Andrews.

"Maybe that's because Lora was talking to the leader and letting him know who we were," suggested Rick.

"Ya, but how did our groups find out?" asked Gwen.

"Maybe they can speak to each other's minds?" asked Falon.

"Did anyone make physical contact with any of them?" Andrews asked.

"Not us," said Falon.

"Neither us," said Rick.

"And not us," said Andrews. "Which is strange. We all went calmly with them and without being touched. What are the chances that there weren't actually people on the beach, but some sort of a projection?"

"Interesting concept, Andrews," said Mark. "It's entirely possible."

"Are you suggesting that they were … uh … holograms or something, and they got us to willingly go with them?" I asked.

"I'm wondering why we all started to follow them without objection," said Andrews. "Normally, that would not be something any of us would do."

"Well, let's put that under the category *Huh?* and keep going," I said. "What are we going to do next? Do we want to see if we can return and actually meet with them?"

"I vote to take another trip out there on our own," said Mark. "I believe we can get there without a captain."

"I remember the heading we took. Once we get to the islands, we'll be able to find the right spot," said Rick.

"Well? Is it settled?" Gwen asked. "Are we going back out? And when?"

"Let me see if we can get another yacht," said Mark. He got up and walked back to the hotel to speak to the concierge.

"Andrews, do you really think they may have been holograms?" I asked.

"Lora, I'm not sure, no. But it was weird that none of us thought twice about following them. So we either didn't pick up any vibes at all, or we were compelled somehow."

"And the only way we wouldn't pick up vibes was if they weren't actually there. I get it," I said. "It's handy having these immortal skills."

"Rick, did you pick up anything?" asked Falon.

"No, nothing. Like Andrews, I think we may have been compelled. But they didn't order us anywhere. And they were touched by Lora's response to their invitation."

"How so?" asked Gwen.

"Well, Lora became overwhelmed by emotion when they asked us to return to stay with them long enough to bring them up to current times. They expressed concern that she was upset."

"Maybe our newness in being immortal makes a difference," I said.

"You mean you may not smell like us?" asked Gwen.

"I don't think so. Perhaps the older you are, the more obvious it is to others?" I asked.

"Mark is 156 and I am almost 330 years old, so perhaps that makes a difference."

"You're 330?" choked Andrews. "You mean to tell me you've been alive for 330 years?"

"Yes, my love. And most of it was very lonely until I met you," said Gwen.

"Wow, just wow."

"The rest of us are really babies in comparison," said Rick.

Mark returned at that moment. "Babies?" he asked. "Are we talking about babies?"

"Only that the four of them are in comparison to us, brother," said Gwen.

"Oh, you divulged our age, did you?"

"It was contextual. We were talking about the greeting party on the beach."

"Oh, yes."

"Andrews, do you have any contacts that can set us up with scientific equipment?"

"Yes, absolutely. And he's in Key West, so a hop, skip, and a jump from here. Let me fly back and set it up. I'll be gone for a few days."

"Okay. I'll get another yacht rented for a week—say, in two weeks from now? Will that give you enough time to set things up?"

"Duffy will probably bring the equipment to us via ship."

"Duffy, the same guy you worked with in Switzerland?"

"Yup, the one and the same," said Andrews. "I'll contact him on the way to the airport, and let you know what happens."

"Always the cautious one," smiled Mark.

15—Someone's Getting Married

—Lora

"I think we need a plan that identifies a goal and how we are going to achieve that goal," said Andrews. "Since we're all on this journey together, let's make a list of what we want to achieve together."

"I'd like to get more information on transmogrification and the technology that the immortals have," said Mark.

"I want to see if they have known the descendants that lead to me," said Rick. "I would like to know who I'm related to, and if my mother is alive."

"I want information about the other groups, where they went, and if they still exist for our family records," said Gwen.

"As a new immortal, anything I can learn is great," said Falon.

"I'd like to learn what they did, and how they did it—to learn their technology," said Andrews.

"I want to learn ancestry too, specifically to match what I do know of my genealogy with actual people," said Lora. "I want to learn more about my abilities and where they came from."

"So we have a starting list," said Andrews.

"Tomorrow, we'll need to provision the yacht and make plans. Let's get some sleep tonight," I said.

Chuckles escaped from most of my friends as we all joined in on the joke. Immortals have a lot of sex and normally it doesn't tire us out. On the contrary, it invigorates us.

Living in paradise has an effect on you.

Bright and early, the sun came flooding in our room. I nudged Rick away and he rolled over and gathered me up in his arms.

"Hey, none of that, Mr. Benal," I murmured into his ear. "We have a lot to do today."

"Oh yes, we have shopping and provisioning to do. That should only take a couple of hours. Plenty of time for making love to my mate."

"Rick, would you marry me?" I asked.

He sat up startled and looked at me wide-eyed.

"Did you just propose to me?"

"I think I did," I said. "It's been on the tip of my tongue for days now. I think this paradise is influencing me."

"Do you want a wedding?"

"I've never had a wedding. I've actually never been married officially," I said.

"No? None of your children's fathers wanted to marry you?" he asked, offended for me.

"None of them asked. Neither did I," I admitted.

"My love, my true love, my mate, I want to spend eternity with you. Yes, I will marry you. It would be an honor to take you as my wife. I would be proud to give you my name too if you would take it. I would adopt your wonderful children too if you would let me."

"You have been thinking of this for a while too, eh?"

"Yes. This paradise has influenced me too. I was planning on shopping for a ring for you when we got home," he admitted.

I jumped up and flung my arms around his neck and he held me closely to his heart. We stayed that way until I heard a quiet knock on the door.

"Hello?"

"Good morning, you two. Are you awake?" asked Falon.

"Yes—I just asked Rick to marry me!" I blurted out.

Falon came running in. "What? You asked him to marry you? Rick, your answer had better be yes!"

"Of course it is. I was planning on getting her a ring once we got home and asking her!"

"Eeeeeeek! Mark, we're going to have a wedding!" screamed Falon out the door.

Gwen, Andrews, and Mark all came out into the hallway.

"A wedding?" asked Mark. "When? Who?"

"Rick and Lora—they just proposed!"

Everyone came running into our room and were hugging us and clapping us on the back, congratulating us.

"This is wonderful news! We will have our first wedding," cried Gwen.

"First? You guys don't marry?"

"No real reason usually."

"So when do you want to tie the knot, guys?"

"How about before we leave this beautiful paradise?" suggested Falon. "There's no rush, but we are here. We're having the honeymoon first after all."

Rick and Lora looked at each other and smiled.

"We want to come back to get married here, but let's wait a few months. We really want to see this trip to its conclusion first."

"Sounds like a plan," said Mark. "Okay, everyone back to their rooms. Get dressed, there is a lot to do today. Falon and I will meet you down at the patio in fifteen minutes."

16—Ship Ahoy!

Plans for returning to Canada got scuttled in favor of renting another catamaran and going out to the islands ourselves. With the help of Duffy, a friend of Andrews, we would have the technology with us to perform some scientific studies on the area. Hopefully that would bring us closer to finding what we wanted.

Duffy's ship arrived overnight at the port where the catamaran was launched. Andrews let the group know that he was back when they all met for breakfast.

"Okay, folks, there is a lot of equipment to move from the ship to the cat," said Andrews. "We won't be using all of it. Even with splitting up the jobs, it will take a couple of hours to shift. I recommend that Duffy captain the yacht for us. He has the experience to read the charts."

"Will he be a security risk for, you know, us?" asked Gwen.

"No, he's solid, and anything he sees, he'll keep to himself," said Andrews. "But we need a crew of two to manage the yacht. We can do the cooking ourselves, but we need experienced hands piloting the ship through the islands."

"Okay, agreed," said Mark. "We'll send the girls to get food and provisions again, while we help Duffy move the equipment to the yacht. Where can we store the equipment?"

"The yacht is designed to carry ten, six passengers and four crew," said Andrews. "We'll be eight. That leaves two crew berths for storage. If we keep our clothes to a minimum, and store all the food in the galley, we'll be fine."

The dive platform on the back of the yacht had room for scuba gear to be stored, plus a Jet Ski lift. They were able to tether the underwater scooters to the lift normally used for jet skis. All the other equipment that they would need—cameras, sonar and LiDAR, mapping technology, extra tanks, and a couple of drones—was packed very tightly into the crew berths.

"Duffy, this is Mark and Falon, Lora and Rick, and Gwen," said Andrews, introducing everyone.

"Folks, I'm Captain Duffy, and this here is my crew: Wendy is cook, and this is Bertram, Fields, and Sparks. These three gentlemen were my tribe in spec ops."

"Duffy, we'd like you to captain the yacht for us," said Andrews.

"Okay, I'll bring Bertram with me, and the others can stay on-station here in dock until we need them."

When they all assembled with their gear at the yacht, the rental company operator shook his head at how much they were bringing.

"Do we have too much weight?" asked Mark.

"No, señor, not too much weight, the boat can handle much more. Just why do you have this much?"

"Ah, we have planned an expedition of sorts. It will take us at least a week. I cleared it with your office that it would be okay if we didn't return on time," said Mark.

"Si, señor, no problema. Do you have all the charts you need?"

"Duffy, do we have all the charts we need?" asked Mark.

"I took a brief look and yes, we're good for that," said Duffy.

"Perhaps we should keep some of the larger equipment here until we need it?" asked Mark.

"That may be a good idea," said Duffy. "I'll get Fields to bring back some of it and he'll be on standby if we need them. I'll bring a tracking device on board so that they can find us quickly in open water."

In the meantime, Falon, Lora, and Gwen started packing away the food in the galley, while Rick and Andrews started stowing the gear they were taking in the spare berths and the on-deck storage. They dropped everyone's bags on the berths being used by each couple.

The others overheard Mark and Duffy going over instructions with the rental operator for the motor, safety lights, procedures, and such too. There was a manual in the bridge and separate manuals for all the different equipment as well. A lot of reading! They were all eager to shove off, so some of them were pacing.

Mark finally exited the bridge and said goodbye to the operator. "Duffy, let's go."

Duffy turned to Bertram and said, "Make ready to shove off."

"Aye-aye, Captain."

Falon got the aft ropes, Lora got the forward ropes. Andrews went up to the bridge. Rick pulled in the buoys. Mark did a tour of the deck to make sure everything was tied down and ready to go.

"What do you want me to do, Mark?" asked Andrews.

"Andrews, start reading that safety manual, please. I want someone to know those procedures completely. In the event we run into trouble, you will be in charge to get us to safety."

"Sure thing." Andrews picked up the heavy book and started reading while seated in a co-pilot's chair. "Wow, this little ship is loaded with amazing technology."

As the yacht pulled away from the wharf, the gang collected on the bridge to watch their progress going out to sea.

"Duffy, once we clear the island and are at least fifty kilometers off shore, please shut off the engines and drop anchor," said Mark.

"Okay."

It took about half an hour to clear the traffic from the harbor and make way for open water. Duffy cut the engines and dropped anchor as instructed.

"All stopped!" called Duffy.

"Okay, gang," said Mark. "We are now well away from everyone and anyone who could overhear us. Andrews has done a full sweep of the yacht to ensure that we have no listening devices."

"Is that important?" Falon asked.

"Just being prudent," said Andrews.

Mark carried the map over to the large kitchen table that shared the same covered space as the bridge.

"Come look at this map, please."

The group and captain gathered around, discussing and pointing.

"That is the location our GPS gave us where we found the hidden island," said Mark, pointing to a black spot on the surface map. When he changed from it to an underwater topographical map, the spot was no longer blank. There was a significant seamount in that spot that appeared to break the surface.

"As you can see, there is an island there," said Mark. "It rises up from the seafloor, and we think the surface area is at least a few square kilometers. It's not a big island."

"Is that where we are heading?" asked Lora. "I mean, we don't have an exact location for the island we found, because it's hidden."

"Yes, that is our first destination. It's as close to the spot we were when we discovered them."

"Mark, I will set these coordinates, then," said Duffy. "It will take roughly six or seven hours to reach that spot."

"Andrews and I will take turns at watch, if you need," said Mark.

"The rest of us can make up the berths, and get food on the table," said Gwen.

Lora and Falon started on dinner, while Rick and Gwen made up the berths.

Scouting through the food that was brought on board, Falon discovered that there was a lot of meat, plus a good amount of bread, veggies, and dairy. Whoever did the shopping was at least thinking meal-wise instead of generally.

She found some large racks of ribs and decided to barbeque them on the deck. There was a good grill on board that would serve as the main cooking surface.

Inside the ship's galley there was a coffee maker, microwave, and a hot plate. The fridge was a good size, and the freezer was the same size as the fridge.

Falon started prepping the meat and Lora worked on the rest. She squealed in delight when she discovered a fully stocked bar and wine fridge too.

"We're going to eat well tonight, people!" she announced. "Ribs, veg, potatoes, and some lovely bottles of red."

"Don't forget our crew!" said Gwen.

"I won't. We have enough for everyone to enjoy."

The yacht was cruising nicely on course on a reasonably calm sea. There was a warm breeze coming from the south, and the sun was setting behind Cuba. Falon was contentedly slapping BBQ sauce on the ribs as she cooked them, smiling to herself enjoying the sun, sea, and air.

Mark walked up behind her and wrapped his arms around her waist.

"Something smells wonderful."

"The ribs will be done shortly," said Falon.

"I'm not talking about the meat," he said suggestively.

"Later, my hungry man. We eat dinner first."

The others were collecting in the dining area. Gwen was setting the table, Lora was pouring the wine. Rick was preparing some sort of dessert for everyone, while Lora changed jobs to plating out the sides.

"Okay, ribs are ready! I need a platter, please," Falon called out.

Rick handed Mark a large platter. He held it as Falon sliced the ribs apart and served them on to the platter. Then Mark carried the ribs to the table as everyone sat down. Falon shut down the grill and closed the lid. Walking over to the dining table, seeing all her friends sitting around chatting amiably and sharing plates, gave her a special feeling.

"You know, I really love you guys," said Falon, sitting down.

"Not like family. I hope," said Rick.

"Almost, but closer than that," said Falon with a suggestive smile. "There's an energy I get when we're all together like this, close. I can't quite put my finger on it."

"Guys, I think we need to read-in Duffy and Bertram," Lora said. "If we're going to openly speak about this, then they need to know what we're doing and be sworn to secrecy."

"I agree," said Andrews. He called Duffy and Bertram to the kitchen.

"Duffy, Bertram, we're going to read you in on some very sensitive information. You and Bertram will be sworn to secrecy, on threat of very serious consequences. It is unavoidable, I'm afraid, due to the close proximity of all of us on this yacht."

"Andrews, you know me and my men. We all served together. Your secrets are mine, and we'll take them to the grave."

"Thank you, Duffy," said Mark. "You see, we are not human."

Mark began the story of who and what they were. The two men were captivated by the story, and their faces reflected their emotions, ranging from awe to terror. When Mark was finished, he asked if they had any questions.

"Ah, just one," said Bertram. "Can you prove you're this … creature?"

Mark took out a penknife and sliced his palm open in front of them. They watched in horror and amazement as the blood stopped almost immediately and the wound closed, leaving absolutely no mark at all.

"Okay, you got me, sir," said Bertram. "I'll be back to my job now."

"Duffy, you okay?" asked Andrews.

"Well, I've got no words, son. That is truly amazing. You have my support and loyalty," said Duffy.

"We just need you to keep the secret," said Mark.

"Oh, not to worry! I'll keep your secret. No one would believe me anyhow! I'll be on the bridge if you need me."

"Well, that went well," said Falon, after Duffy had left. "Now what were we talking about? Oh yeah, the energy we all feel around each other."

"I know what you mean," said Lora. "I have felt that energy several times. In fact, right after the gala it was so strong, I felt like it influenced what I did and said."

"That makes perfect sense," said Gwen. "When the six of us are together, we're feeding off each others' sexual power. Especially now, with all of us being immortal, there is a power that comes off of us because we are mated. Our hearts are synchronized with our mates, but in a group setting when we are working close, you discover that all of our hearts will synchronize. That's when the magic happens."

"Is it sexual magic?" asked Lora.

"It is a form of magic, yes. It's life magic. Sex creates life, so it's the most powerful magic there is," explained Gwen.

"Let's eat!" said Lora, as she glanced around the table at her immortal friends. All of their eyes were glowing in arousal. "Then we can have another party."

"I'm down with that," said Rick.

Mark came back to the table with another bottle of wine and picked up his glass. "This is going to be a momentous adventure for us. Not only have our friends decided to tie the knot, but we're going to be meeting our ancestors," he said.

"I want to make a toast to us—a group of disparate souls who have come together like no others. We have become closer emotionally than I've experienced in hundreds of years. True love has brought us together, and it gives us power. It gives us life magic that we can use to create as our ancestors did. To the true love that binds us, and to our long future together!"

"Hear, hear!" said everyone.

"Dig in!" Falon declared. The group ate in companionable silence, with occasional compliments to the chefs who did the work. When they were done, they all went and lay on deck together, staring up at the stars.

"I wonder where our home planet was?" asked Rick.

"That should be in the records," said Gwen.

"Don't talk about that, I'm feeling too tingly right now," said Lora. "Can anyone else feel that?"

"I'm feeling something," said Falon. "It's like I'm being zinged up my spine. Hey, look at this!" She was holding up her hand. "There are swirls of gold light around my hand!"

They all looked at her hand and saw the gold light swirling around her fingers. Some of them gasped.

"That is magic," said Lora. "That is magic!" She took Falon's hand and the swirls increased to go around both of their hands. Then Lora grasped the hand next to hers and the swirls enveloped her entirely.

"Oh my goddess," said Lora. "This feels like I'm having an orgasm."

Lora got onto her knees. She was beside Mark's head. Falon smiled at her, giving consent. So Lora bent down and gave Mark a kiss, a deep kiss. He reacted by pulling her on top of him. A moan escaped his lips as her weight settled on top of his cock and she started grinding on him. Lora still held Falon's hand to maintain the connection.

Andrews was next to Falon, so he took her other hand and the energy engulfed him as well. Falon was sitting on the floor beside Mark, so Andrews pushed her gently to the deck and straddled her, holding her hand over her head. Balancing on his knees, he kissed her deeply, and she squirmed as her arousal ramped up. Falon released Lora's hand and slid it down Andrews' jeans, taking hold of his hard shaft. He groaned into her mouth.

Gwen beckoned to Rick from the other side of the deck. He went to her and picked her up and sat her closer to the others, where he planted a deep kiss on her mouth. Nipping at her lips, she moaned as microdoses of venom entered her body. When Rick pulled back, and sucked on her neck, she shuddered with delight.

The pheromones were flying, and as the immortals became aroused together the energy fuelled a type of magic that had not been used for eons. As the couples changed hands, and heightened each others' arousal, the swirling magic light changed hue and intensity. It went from being just around the couples to surrounding all six of them, then encompassing their entire yacht.

They shared their bodies, and their hearts synchronized. They bit each other to raise the level of excitement, and the magic grew. They were totally unaware that their shared love experience was having this effect. All they could feel was each others' bodies touching, caressing, and penetrating. They were like six batteries hooked up in series.

Rick was deep inside Gwen, and she was stimulating Falon's breasts. Andrews was deep inside Falon, while she was tweaking Lora's breasts. Mark was deep inside Lora while she was playing with Gwen's breasts. With their heads close together, they could all touch at once. The guys were thrusting in unison now, and the girls were holding each others' hands as they all gasped and screamed while their collective orgasms built. The energy around them grew and grew until there were great swirls of gold magic encircling them all. They were all panting and keening as the thrusts got harder, each man completely engorged and hitting the end.

As their orgasms came to a climax, all six let a scream loose as their bodies shuddered and shook from the effort of cresting that wave. The magic exploded out from them in a seismic wave in all directions like a tsunami. If they had seen it, they would have seen their energy kick up a wave in the sea and push it 360 degrees outward from the boat. On some distant shoreline, that energy would disperse, but it would create something before it does. Because this was life magic they had created.

The guys collapsed in between their partners and bit the girls, which they reciprocated. Then they all rode the second wave together too, which was just as strong as the first one.

"Ah … ah … ah, ah, oh my!" screamed Falon.

"Oh goddess, yes!" cried Lora.

Gwen screamed, "Ah, fuck me, that was good!"

All six were spent and sweating as they collapsed on the yacht's deck in a heap of bodies, all breathing heavily from the exertion, smiles on their faces.

"What the fuck was that?" asked Mark.

"I don't know, but I want more," said Rick.

"Give me a minute, will ya?" asked Andrews. "Always so demanding!"

They all laughed at the innuendo.

"No, seriously, Gwen, what was that?" asked Mark.

"I believe we've just experienced what our ancestors would call the spontaneous group generation of life magic," she answered. "Did anyone happen to notice at some point our hearts were all synchronized?"

"I did," said Lora. "I was acutely aware of the magic building. I felt it like the hairs rising on my neck. It was very powerful. I presume that the synchronization is the point at which you cast a spell if need be?"

"That's what I understand, yes," said Gwen. "But I'm no magic wielder."

"I am, and I'll tell you the focus of the casting was immense. It exploded out of us like a detonation and went 360 degrees around us," said Lora. "I've never experienced such power."

"Can anyone move?" asked Falon.

Crickets…

"I'm so hungry!" said Falon.

A few more moans, and the knot of limbs started undoing as people reclaimed their body parts.

It was completely dark, the sea was calm, and the breeze had died. It didn't look like their position had changed much. Mark was first to stand and walk over to the railing naked to look out over the water.

"All looks peaceful," he observed. Mark then went back to the pile of naked bodies and lay back down with them, curling into the group.

Falon's head was on his stomach and her legs were over the top of Rick, while his head was lying on Gwen, and Lora's was on Andrews.

They fell asleep there together, intertwined and content.

A seagull cawing overhead woke Lora first. She was accustomed to hearing them in Montreal but hadn't seen any when they were on the yacht. Opening her eyes, she discovered she was in the middle of the pile of friends where their hands and legs were all entangled. She looked up and saw it was bright daylight, but they were lucky the canopy on the yacht had covered them. *Do we get sunburned? That would have been bad.*

Lora checked where her head was and found someone's cock next to her. It was a happy cock, standing up and waving around. She pulled her hand out from between someone's legs and grasped the cock that was so provocatively close, brought it to her lips and gave it a kiss.

"Mmm, not yet, please," murmured Mark.

"What a lovely cock you have, Mark," said Lora.

"Mmm thank you, I think."

Falon found a cock near her and similarly handled hers.

"Ah, no, I've got to pee!" cried Rick.

Falon laughed and let him go. "But, Rick, he's so happy!"

"He may be happy, but he doesn't know what's good for me," he chuckled.

"Anyone know what time it is?" asked Andrews.

"It's around 6:30 a.m. I think," said Gwen.

Again, they untangled their limbs and stood up, the guys going to the port side to pee off the side, and the girls taking turns in the bathroom. When they got back to the kitchen, they set about the task of making breakfast for everyone.

"Duffy, do you and Bertram want some breakfast?" asked Falon.

Duffy poked his head down the hatch from the bridge, and when he saw naked bodies he quickly looked away. "Ah, that would be nice, thanks. Are clothes optional?"

"Of course," said Falon with a straight face. "Clothes are always optional around us."

She heard him mutter, "I've got to get me a woman like that."

"I'm eager to ask those islanders some questions," said Mark. "I want to know if they experience what we just experienced."

"I can always approach the council too after we do this," said Gwen. "They may know something."

"Probably, but when was the last time you heard of any of those elders doing anything like this?"

"Never."

"How much farther do we have to travel?" asked Falon.

"We should make the island by this afternoon. We have time to have a relaxing play day," said Mark.

The six immortals spent their time sunbathing, reading, and hanging out together. After sundown, they ate a small meal together.

"Tomorrow, we will make land on the island for the second time," Falon announced. "Everyone needs to be sharp! So everyone have a good night! I want some alone time with my husband!"

"Hmm, I like the sound of that," said Lora to Rick.

"What's that?"

"I'm looking forward to saying 'my husband,'" said Lora.

Falon pulled Mark up onto his feet and they walked down to their berth. The sun had set but you could still see an afterglow in the sky at the horizon. It was like the horizon glowed pink for just a moment and then it was gone. The night sky was a brilliant tapestry of stars. Out on the sea, you could see everything. The Milky Way took up a big part of the sky; the far side of it spiraled away from our solar system. The most spectacular sight of all was the sea reflecting the sky. The calm sea was a mirror, and it made you feel like we weren't even on the planet but floating in space.

"Come on, Robert," said Gwen quietly. "Let's make the most of the yacht's motion." Andrews got up and followed her to their berth, leaving Rick and Lora sitting there on deck overlooking the water.

She crawled into his lap and snuggled into him as he wrapped his arms around her.

"It's going to be difficult to go back to reality after being here for so long, isn't it?" she asked.

"Yes, it will. But we haven't left yet. Let's just stay here for a while," he murmured.

Lora was listening to his heartbeat calmly thumping in his chest. She fell asleep against him. Rick picked her up and carried her to bed.

Rick laid her down and then slipped into bed behind her, sliding up against her body. She scooched herself back against him, feeling his response to contact with her skin.

"I'm just going to hold you, *mamacita*," he whispered into her ear.

She was a little disappointed, but was so tired she couldn't move a muscle. His cock slipped between her legs and just nestled as she held him there. His warm presence was more comforting than arousing.

17—Looking for Islands

—Duffy

Hidden from view, the island could only be seen underwater.

The swaying and bobbing of the yacht in the waves was relaxing, and it felt good to be out to sea again. I had been on watch since a little before dawn. It was nice to have the boat to myself. All the others were still asleep, but I expected them up on bridge again at dawn.

I started a pot of coffee so they would have some go-go juice to wake them up. Sure enough, Andrews was up on bridge first, yawning, but awake and dressed.

"Morning," he said. "Has it been quiet?"

"Good morning, sunshine," I said. "Quiet as a mouse. No one has been on the water."

"That's a good thing, I guess," said Andrews.

"Better than pirates!"

Mark and Rick were walking up the stairs together. Mark looked refreshed, and Rick looked tired. Funny how differently people sleep on a ship.

"Coffee's ready, gentlemen," I announced.

"Oh, you're a godsend," said Rick, pouring himself and Mark cups. "Thank you. Do you want a cup?

"Please and thank you," I said.

The three of them sat at the galley table and started speaking in hushed tones. They were planning what they would do today. Just then, Falon came upstairs to join the group.

"Oh, give me some of that coffee please!" said Falon.

"Sure, here you go," said Rick, handing her a steaming cup.

"Mmm, this is delicious, thanks," she said. "Who made?"

"Ah, that was me," I said.

"Great coffee, Duffy," she said. "It's fragrant and rich."

"It's a little chilly on deck," I said, noticing she was only wearing a bikini. "So you may want to put some more clothes on. It will warm up once the sun gets higher."

"I'll be fine," she said, wrapping her fingers around the cup to keep them warm. "So what's up? Where are we?"

"About an hour from our destination," explained Mark.

"Cool, do you want me to start on breakfast for everyone," Falon said. "We should not start this expedition on an empty stomach." She got busy in the galley, making scrambled eggs, hash browns, and toast.

Pretty soon the other girls were up and everyone was talking out on deck.

"Breakfast!" Falon called.

"Hey, someone go get Bertram too." Andrews padded off to the bridge and returned ten minutes later.

We all sat down and passed food around until we all had some. Since we were approaching the immortal's hidden island from a different direction, we didn't want to run into any shoals. I had set an "auto-pilot" before I sat down to eat. Andrews got up frequently to check overboard for obstructions.

"Hey, Mark, what is that?" asked Andrews, as he was pointing out the starboard side.

Mark got up and took the glasses from Andrews and looked where he was pointing.

"I'm not sure. I'm interpreting it as something to avoid, but I don't know what it is. Check the map."

I got up and went to the charts. "There isn't anything on the chart that indicates anything is there."

"Huh!" said Andrews. "We're almost upon it, whatever it is."

We all stood at the railing and looked out to sea, scanning the water.

"Hey! I see it!" said Lora pointing off the starboard side. "There is something sticking out of the water."

"It looks like something metal, and pipes—perhaps some type of structure?" Falon asked.

"It's a conning tower," said Mark, looking through the glasses again. "From a submarine."

"Oh, the part that sticks up when a sub surfaces?" Falon asked.

"Exactly," said Andrews. "So there must be a wreck there. It's awfully shallow there, apparently."

"What are the depths marked as on the chart?"

"Several thousand feet," said Andrews. "But that doesn't look like several hundred."

Falon ran down to the dive platform and stared overboard. The sea was turquoise here, and that usually indicated shallowness. "Duffy, stop!" she yelled.

I cut the engine but the yacht was still moving forward. So I put the engine in reverse to stop the boat's forward motion. We came to a full stop in a few meters.

"I am not positive, but the water looks quite shallow here," said Falon. "The only way to know for sure is to dive. Let me take a look."

Falon dove into the water without scuba equipment to freedive. In a few moments, she was back on the dive deck.

"The bottom is very close to our hull," she reported. "Perhaps a few meters only. If we had proceeded further, we would have grounded the yacht."

She dove down again and swam to the far side of the yacht where the water looked deeper. She surfaced again. "It looks deeper on the other side of the ship."

"Can you get an idea of how deep?" I asked her.

"Yeah, I will use a freediving technique I learned." She dolphin dove into the water and swam straight down. Twenty seconds later, she was back at the surface. "I was able to count ten seconds to reach the rocks."

"That translates to what about fifty feet?" asked Duffy.

"About that, maybe less because I don't have fins on. Say forty feet," she answered.

"What's down there?" asked Mark.

"Mostly rocks and corals. It took me ten seconds to reach the rocks swimming straight down. It was about twenty feet on the other side," Falon reported.

"Damn, that was close. The draught on this yacht is shallow, but it would have been a serious problem," said Andrews. "I recommend we drop anchor here and explore."

I started the engines and the craft slowly moved away from where it was and then drifted to a stop. Falon had jumped back in the water and was enjoying it.

"The water is wonderfully warm here!" shouted Falon. She dolphin-kicked her way around the shallow water, and looked like a mermaid swimming in the shallow sea.

Mark was watching her from the deck and his eyes gave away his feelings. They were slowly swirling.

"You make a beautiful mermaid," he said. "I want to get in there with you."

"Let's finish breakfast first," she said, getting out of the water. "Then we can play merpeople."

After breakfast, Mark and Andrews got into scuba gear and grabbed a scooter to go explore the submarine wreck. Lora and Gwen joined Falon for a swim in the warm shallows. Rick decided to join the girls.

I of course stayed on the bridge to maintain our position.

Andrews and Mark took off toward the wreck with the scooters to check it out.

"Mark to ship."

"Go ahead, Mark," I said.

"This is a German U-boat from WWII!"

"Really? What's it doing here?"

"Don't know, but we'll make a complete circle of the craft, then return."

"Roger that," I said. Consulting the charts, I discovered a number of wrecks in the area. I looked up a book of wrecks and found there were quite a few WWII subs. However, in that particular position, there was nothing marked. No wreck at all.

I broke the silence: "Mark, I just looked up U-boats sinking in the Caribbean and there were a number of them. However, the charts don't list one in that location. In fact, there is no wreck marked there."

"Roger that," he said. "We've almost completed our tour."

It took another ten minutes before they surfaced with the scooters. They made for the yacht immediately, and got out and stowed the equipment before coming up to the bridge.

"Any other information?" asked Andrews.

"The Nazis staged serious attacks on Florida and the Gulf of Mexico, sinking nearly seventy ships and killing about seven hundred people," I said. "They lost a number of U-boats, but none were reported to be lost in this location."

"Curious," said Mark.

The girls were still playing in the shallow waters. Andrews grabbed a pair of binoculars and was scanning the horizon.

"Are you watching the girls swimming?" I asked.

"No, I'm looking for the island," said Andrews.

"What's wrong with you?" Mark kidded. Then, getting serious, he asked, "Where is this?" pointing to a land mass on the map and then looking out to sea. "I cannot see it and it should be there.

"According to the map, it's called Great Iguana Island," I replied. Standing up, I scanned the sea for the island. When I was facing the direction the coordinates said it would be, there was nothing but a mirage.

"Look, there is a large mirage over the water where the island should be," said Andrews.

"It's a very low-lying island, barely above the waves," I said, assessing the chart. "The open water around it is also shallow. Mirages are not uncommon out at sea. A lot of sailors see them."

Just then they heard the chatter of the girls as they came aboard again with Rick.

"What did you find?" asked Mark.

"Lots of shallow shoals and rocks. Nothing particularly interesting," said Lora. "What about you guys?"

"It was a submarine, World War II era, and we saw the letter U on the hull, so I'm pretty sure it was a German U-boat," said Mark.

"Why would it be in such shallow water?" Falon asked.

"Who knows. Maybe they were looking for immortals."

"Can we navigate around the U-boat and the shoals to get to our coordinates?" asked Lora.

"Yes, I think so," I said. "What say we map the area for ourselves using the sonar and LiDAR we brought with us? That way we'll have a more accurate map of the area."

I moved the yacht out to deeper water and took a GPS reading. Andrews set up the LiDAR on the starboard side of the hull, and the sonar on the port side of the hull. The ship first stayed in place and then started moving in the most likely direction to have clear water.

The sonar uses sound waves to create a very detailed map of the sea bottom as far as the waves can reach. The LiDAR shot out millions of laser points and, based on the distance the laser beams traveled, it was able to create an even more detailed map of the seabed. The LiDAR could see around corners and into caves that the sonar might miss.

I sailed the yacht around the wreck and through a narrow channel that passed on the north side of Haiti. The low-lying island came into view when we got close enough. It was really low, almost concave, and much of it was water filled.

"That's not their island, is it?" asked Rick.

"Nah, it's in the wrong place," said Andrews.

As we sailed past the island and the wreck and out into the more open sea, I kept watching our position. When Mark called a halt, I took another GPS reading and marked it on the chart. With the engines shut down we were bobbing in the water again.

"We won't be able to hold this position long because of the ocean currents," I said. "But we are almost on top of where we took the GPS reading before."

We looked around us and there was nothing to indicate an island was hiding here. Not even shallow water.

"Let's look at the LiDAR data," said Rick. He pulled the LiDAR up to the deck and stowed it in the crate after removing the data storage device—which was basically a compact flash drive. He handed the device to me.

"Here you go. You're the IT whiz of the group," said Rick.

Popping it into a laptop, the software I had installed started reading the removable memory microSD card and running an analysis. Within a few minutes, a picture started appearing on the screen of the seafloor in beautiful detail.

"Wow!" Falon said. "That is amazing!"

"Look at how those shoals curl there," pointed out Gwen. "It's like they curl around an opening or something."

"That could be an entrance to a cave," I said.

The detail on the sub was spectacular. We could see that a whole section of the vessel had blown out, leaving a gaping hole.

"Ah! They seem to have sunk themselves," said Andrews. "See that hole? That is the weapons storage compartment. It would have contained explosives, mines, warheads, dynamite, and fuel for the ship. Something caught fire and blew up the sub."

"Yeah!" Lora said.

As more data was read from the card, more details got filled in; including a vast underwater cliff that seemed to connect to the surface. The mysterious mirage island had the same almost vertical cliff rising from the depths to the surface.

Looking at the images forming on the screen for the area where the immortal's island should be, we saw that there was a sea mount that reached the surface. In addition, the LiDAR showed there were vast underwater caves and mountains that reached above the waves. It should have been visible. The fact that we could see the island underwater with the LiDAR proved it was there, and that the immortals had the technology to hide it from plain view.

"Now that's some tech I want to get a hold of!" said Mark.

"You and I both," said Andrews. "Imagine if we could build a compound to live in that was hidden from prying eyes, like this."

"Now that we have proof, let's check the satellite images to see if they can hide from satellites."

"Right-o."

Meanwhile, the girls had become bored with the tech talk. So they poured themselves cocktails and went to soak up the sun on deck, leaving the guys to analyze the data from the LiDAR and sonar.

A couple of hours later, Mark asked everyone if they wanted something to eat.

"Yeah, I could eat," said Lora. "After swimming in this beautiful water, I've worked up an appetite."

"The swimming was fun. The water is so warm here," Falon noted. They had jumped in the water several times and swam all over the place, exploring the rocks and crevices, looking for interesting sea life. Gwen pulled out the scooters to cover lots of ground.

"Okay, sandwiches are made and drinks are being served, ladies," called Mark.

Dropping our books, we went up to the bridge to join the guys for lunch.

"So do you have any conclusions after poring over your data for hours?" asked Gwen.

"Yes, we do in fact," answered Andrews. "First, they are capable of hiding even from satellites, which is quite the feat. They have really made themselves invisible, and even our LiDAR cannot penetrate their defenses. The best we can do is detect where the land comes up out of the water."

"So they are quite powerful," I concluded.

"Yes, they either have tech that is much better than ours, or just very different."

"So what's next?" asked Lora.

"Well, as far as I see it, we continue to use LiDAR and sonar in the area, while working to the location that we marked the first time we were here," said Mark. "We know that we will physically bump into something if we try to sail that far, so we'll need to anchor somewhere and swim in again."

"Let's go, then!"

By early afternoon we were sailing just off the coast of the island of the immortals. There was nothing but water as far as the eye could see. No islands were visible—even the ones on the standard maps. Us immortals, though, could see something different. There was a slight shimmer to the air.

"There it is!" cried Lora. "That is the shimmer I saw the first time we were here. That's the spot we can go through."

"Our depth here is about a hundred feet, so we can drop an anchor," I said. "I'll do that and help you on the dive deck."

The rest of us went to the dive deck to gear up. We didn't need wetsuits because the water was so warm, but we put on lightweight ones to protect ourselves from sharp shells and rocks. We each had a double tank for air and a scooter for mobility.

"I will hold this position waiting for you," I said. "Any idea how long you will be? When should I get alarmed? Will there be a signal for me to rescue you?"

"We don't know how long we will be. Let's set a limit of three days. If you haven't heard from us before that, send up a flare."

"Okay, seventy-two hours. Good luck."

"Thanks."

They each checked each other to make sure all the scuba equipment was correct, functional, and put on properly, then they jumped in. A quick refresher for everyone was done to make sure they all used the same hand signals, and then off they went.

This time they didn't split up but dove in the same direction.

I knew about where they were going, as Mark had briefed me. I was watching through the glasses. It looked like the opening that Mark and Falon had found the first time was difficult to find this time. Probably because they were looking for it, whereas before they just discovered it.

18—Landfall

—Falon

It took at least thirty minutes of hunting around to find the sandbar. We all walked up on it and sat there staring across the water. I finally spotted the opening again that Mark and I had discovered the first time we were here.

"There," I said, pointing to an overhang. "That is the place Mark and I found the entrance." We all swam toward that overhang, and followed Mark when he went through.

We ended up facing a pristine beach of pure white sand. As we hauled out and stripped off our gear, putting it out of the way under some trees, one of the immortals from the island appeared.

"You're back!" he said. "Welcome again. You can bring your gear with you if you wish. Follow me, please."

Mark and Andrews paid attention this time to see if the immortal who greeted us was a hologram or a person. They were whispering in the back of the group together, when the immortal turned around and started walking into the forest.

"I didn't feel anything from him at all," noted Mark.

"Neither did I," said Andrews. "I think it may have been a holograph."

"But that technology doesn't exist!"

"No, not in human terms. But, perhaps they have it—or something like that."

"Okay!" said Lora. She led by picking up her gear and taking off after him. Rick, not to be outdone, quickly followed her. The rest of the group started to follow too, because we didn't want to get lost.

The immortal led us through the forest on a path that was difficult to see. There were no spaces that were obvious to see the direction, and we were fighting against vegetation to get through. Again, the thought crossed my mind: *He may be an apparition or hologram because he doesn't fight anything, but just appears to glide.*

Finally, an opening in the trees was ahead of us and we came into the village. It was a collection of fairly primitive people, apparently, and not the immortals.

We put down our gear to rest a few minutes while the village people gathered around us. They were grunting and gesturing toward us; some were nodding their heads in recognition. They held no weapons this time, thankfully, but they did surround us.

"I'm still not feeling anything," said Andrews.

"I am. There is a very faint buzz in the air," said Mark.

The immortal who had brought us here disappeared behind a thatched roof for about fifteen minutes before reappearing with more immortals.

"Lora, Ricardo, you have returned," said Ureth. "Welcome back!"

"Thank you, Ureth. I've brought our friends too," said Lora. "We bring news of the world as you asked for, and hope to learn from you in exchange."

"Just one thing," interrupted Mark. "Our boat is stationed outside. The captain will wait for us for seventy-two hours before sending up a flare. If we are here longer, we need to let them know we're okay."

"Understood," said Ureth. "Follow me, and we will see you to some quarters for you to settle into."

"Now I feel it," said Andrews. "Yeah, there is a very strong energy here."

We followed Ureth behind the thatched roof hut and walked through another shimmering doorway. On the other side we found a fully modern looking building. It was a huge dome made from materials that didn't look like they had come from the island.

"Wow! This place is beautiful!" I said.

"Thank you, Falon," said Ureth. "We have limited source materials here, but there is lots of sand, so we can make glass. It's our primary building material. All other materials we have to create."

"This is all glass?" I asked.

"Some, yes, we have many ways of creating glass, even structural glass," said Ureth. "Ah, here we are. Our 'guest' building." He chuckled.

"You have a guest building?" asked Lora.

"Well, not until we met you," said Ureth. "In hope and anticipation of your return, we decided to make you some quarters to sleep in and be comfortable. I hope they are adequate." He walked under an arched doorway that glistened in the sunlight. It was like stained glass, except it wasn't. All the colors refracted out of the glass and created a colorful dance on the floor. Inside we found a common area with chairs and a table. There was one wall with three doors to the back. In the middle was a feature like a fireplace, but it wasn't clear how it would work.

"There are three sleeping rooms," said Ureth. "I hope I figured that correctly. You look like three couples. Each sleeping room has a place to wash and defecate. I'm sorry if that is indelicate, but I do not know what you would call such a place."

"We call it a washroom," said Lora helpfully.

"Ah, yes, a washroom," said Ureth. "We will be eating before the sun sets in our main hall. You will find it another ten minutes to the west of here through the forest. Please join us at your leisure."

Ureth left then, and we stood there like kids who had just been assigned our bunks at camp.

"Does everyone feel that?" asked Lora. "I feel a very strong magical buzz—very strong. It's almost overwhelming."

They were all nodding their heads.

"It's as if it's what we felt on deck but multiplied a hundred-fold," said Andrews. "Maybe they are using that sort of power too."

"Well, let's check out the sleeping quarters and unload our gear," said Rick. "I could use a shower to wash off the salt."

Rick and Lora chose the farthest door, and Gwen and Andrews took the middle door. That left the closest door for us. Mark and I walked to the door and noticed no handle, but as we got close, it shimmered and disappeared. We walked through, and it solidified behind us.

"That's a neat trick!" I said. Looking behind me. "This whole building has power radiating through it."

"Indeed." Mark's attention was taken by what was in front of us. When I turned around, I gasped. It was a huge—I mean gargantuan—bed covered in all kinds of colorful fabrics. They were hung gracefully from a floating structure above the bed that seemed to have no supports. The fabrics were translucent, letting light through, but not transparent. Come to think of it, where was the light coming from? There were no visible windows.

"Oh, Mark, remember the caves? They had light too, and we didn't know from where."

"You're right. They are using the same technology here too. It also kind of reminds me of the chamber where we had you turned."

"Yeah, a little, you mean with all the fabrics hanging down. Yes, I can see that."

I walked around the very spacious room and found comfy chairs and places to store clothes. Of course we had no clothes with us, just the wetsuits and swimsuits we were wearing. I found the washroom behind a door that was behind the bed.

Entering made me gasp in wonder again. The space was tall and bright. There was what looked like a showerhead behind a glass wall, and a sink on a rock pedestal. The commode was a tube that was chair height. When I looked in the tube, I saw nothing at all, and wondered at how it worked. I took off my wetsuit and swimsuit and sat down.

As I let go, I felt a gentle wash happen and then a breeze dried me off. Fun, and clean! When I stood up, a quiet sweeping sound occurred, but it was unclear what it did.

I stood under the showerhead, and water fell from the ceiling. It was a perfect temperature too—hot but not scalding. It felt so good to rinse off the salt water. As I was stepping out of the shower, a strong downdraft of warm air blew on my head, and then another came up from the floor to dry my legs and torso. Efficient!

Returning to the sleeping area, I found Mark sprawled across the bed. Mark looked at me naked and his eyes started swirling.

"Go use the washroom. You'll love it, both the commode and the shower. Trust me, I'll wait."

He came back a little while later, so he must have really enjoyed the commode. When he joined me on the bed, he was already excited. A little hanky-panky was welcome since we hadn't really had privacy on the yacht. The bed was very comfortable, and my lusty husband took good advantage of it.

I couldn't help but think of the ritual sex we had, with the draping sheers surrounding us. It made you feel totally cut off from everything, alone in your own little bubble.

He took me powerfully, and owned my very soul, just the way I like it. I returned his hunger by opening deeply and bringing him to a climax that drained him. My bite sent him into oblivion as did his for me. We clung there, together, joined, by teeth and body, one in soul and mind until we came down together. I no longer blacked out from the venom, and instead felt every wonderful moment of my high. We stayed that way for a while, until the breeze in the room started to chill my sweaty back. Mark suggested we get under the covers. Pulling apart was difficult, but once under the covers, he connected us again, and spooned me in his arms.

We lay there contentedly.

19—Alien Technology

Rick and Lora walked into their room and stood there mesmerized by the beauty of the chamber. They also took advantage of the enormous bed and the washroom facilities. They stripped out of their wetsuits and went to have a shower together—taking off each other's swimsuit and making the most of the space.

Rick knelt down, taking Lora's breasts in his hands and buried his nose in her cleavage as she held his head in place. When he pulled away, he was ready to take her. Lora sat down on his lap, impaling herself on his cock, connecting them and rocking her hips in a delicious rhythm that rubbed him fully inside her channel. He became so long and hard he was gasping as he touched the end.

Lora wrapped her legs around his waist to pull herself hard against him, pushing him deeper and making him hit the end of her insides until her moans became yells of pleasure. They climaxed together as they bit each other and sent themselves into euphoria. Lora wasn't blacking out anymore, and they were able to ride the wave together.

When their lovemaking was complete, Rick carried Lora out of the shower, and experienced the air-drying system.

"Oh, just like I have at home!" he said.

"Yes, now is that a coincidence?" Lora asked.

When they moved to the bed, they discovered robes were laid out for them on chairs. The robes were made of thin fabric that was quite transparent. Lora put on her robe and jumped onto the bed. It sank in response to her weight and hugged around her, cradling every part of her.

"Oh my God, this is comfortable!" she called out.

"How so?"

"It hugs every inch of me. There are absolutely no points in which my body isn't supported. Now that is what a bed should be!"

Rick joined her, and the bed adapted to the weight of the two of them, remolding itself around them, causing them to spoon together.

"Clearly, they designed their furniture to encourage sex," he said, grinning.

Over in the third chamber, Andrews and Gwen had a similar reaction to the grandeur of the room. Although, when Gwen saw the bed in the room, her first thought was sex. She initiated a favorite game they played by turning around and demanding Andrews strip in an imperious voice.

Andrews, knowing the script, had the answer just right. "No, you do not order me," he said. "Down, woman." Gwen immediately became submissive, kneeling on the floor, and begged to be punished.

Andrews stripped himself slowly, making her watch. Her eyes were glowing purple with excitement. But he wouldn't let her touch him. He teased her with his cock by rubbing it all around her face, leaving a small trail of liquid behind. When she went to lick his cock, he spanked her. Gwen whimpered and he spanked her again.

He bent Gwen over his knee and spanked her butt. She moaned in pleasure. He teased her by lightly inserting his fingers into her anus and her vagina, but without using any force, and she started to squirm. So he withdrew and made her wait. The waiting was ramping up her arousal; he could smell how excited she was. He spanked her again, as his cock was so eager to take her. Gwen reacted to the sting of the spank, and cringed slightly, so he caressed the sting away. She moaned in pleasure.

Andrews changed their positions again and bent her over the back of a chair. Exposing her completely, she had to remain quiet and compliant, something she didn't like doing. The waiting made her more excited and she wanted to move. She liked it when he punished her; the sting was pleasurable in small doses.

He was teasing her now, by twisting her nipples and caressing her ass. Gwen's libido was on fire and her arousal was pouring off her like water. She was almost ready for him.

A few more spanks and a couple more caresses and she was mewling like a kitten, begging him to take her.

Every time she opened her mouth, he spanked her again and then made her wiggle as he plunged his fingers into her core, building her anticipation. He was teasing her with his fingers, playing with her flower and caressing her opening but not going in.

Andrews knew Gwen was about to climax, so he stepped behind her and took her in one thrust. She shrieked at the intensity of his invasion, because the spanking had made her very tight. His cock parted her flesh with force, driving into her to her very end. As he tipped her, he could feel her jerk in pain and then sigh in pleasure. Her climax came shortly thereafter on his fourth thrust, and he was climaxing right alongside her.

She stood up and gave him her throat, and he bit down delivering another orgasm as the drug hit her blood. To reciprocate, she took his arm, and bit him on the inside of his bicep, flooding him with her venom and letting them both float together.

They slid to the floor still connected, and Andrews wrapped his arms around Gwen, making soothing noises and petting her head. "Good kitten, there's a good kitten. I love you, Gwen."

Purring, Gwen said, "I love you too, my master."

By the time the sun looked like it was setting, all six were well satiated and happily snoring in their rooms. They never noticed the time until the next morning, when the immortals sent someone to wake them up and take them food for breakfast.

20—Ureth and Esperanza

"Good morning!" called out the porter. "Is anyone awake?"

"Mark, someone is here—outside the room. Did we sleep the whole night?"

"I don't know, but I'll check." Throwing a towel around his hips, Mark left his sleeping area and went out to the common. There were three people standing outside, each carrying a large platter of food.

"Oh my, did we miss dinner?" asked Mark.

"I'm afraid so," answered the porter, with a smirk on his face. "Clearly, you were tired after your journey here," he smiled knowingly. "We've brought you some food to break your fast today. You'll find fruits, eggs from some of the birds here, and some bread made by the villagers. There is also meat and juices. If you would like anything else, please let me know, and I'll try to get it for you."

The porter clapped his hands. The others set down the platters of food and left quietly.

"Oh, we thought you may need some clothing. One from our community will bring you some clothes a little later. Take advantage of our facilities if you haven't already," he said, again with a smirk on his face.

After he left, Mark called everyone to wake us up.

"Food! Get up! I don't care if you're fucking right now or not!" he yelled.

All of them were standing around the table looking at the spread of food. None of them were dressed. Lora and Falon had wrapped the transparent robes around their bodies. Gwen was just naked along with Andrews, and Rick had done what Mark did in wrapping a towel around his hips. They were all glancing at each other, and burst out laughing.

"We seem to get into these situations more often now, don't we?" Mark asked.

They all agreed and sat down to eat. The food was wonderful.

"Well, the only thing that would make this perfect would be coffee."

"Oh," groaned Lora. "Coffee."

By the time they had finished eating, a woman had arrived with all kinds of clothes to put on. Most were like what they saw Ureth wearing, a type of robe made from colorful yarns. They were surprised that the clothes all fit perfectly, especially for the guys, who were all very tall. Their robes actually covered them down to the ankles.

"Excuse me," asked Lora of the woman. "My name is Lora. Thank you very much for bringing these clothes to us."

"You're welcome," said the woman. "I am Cyntia."

"Cyntia, what are the social rules about nudity amongst the immortals?" asked Gwen.

"Oh, we don't care about nudity. In fact, we only wear robes when we approach the village or outsiders. Many of us are nude most of the time. It's prudent and practical."

"Hmm, practical for what, may I ask?" asked Lora.

"We immortals are a lusty species. It's practical when one wants to couple as frequently as we do," said Cyntia. I believed she was expecting us to be offended by that.

"I like these people!" said Lora. "So would you prefer we go nude or wear these robes?"

"Suit yourself. You are welcome in any manner you feel comfortable in. We will follow your lead." At that, Cyntia retreated out the door of our building.

"Well, who votes for naked?" asked Gwen.

"I'm game," said Lora.

"I'm self-conscious," Falon said.

"Why ever for?" asked Mark. "You're beautiful, and your body is perfect."

"I've just never walked around naked!" Falon said.

"We can all go together," said Rick.

So they decided to forgo the robes and go native immortal. They walked out of the building, as couples, holding hands, and followed the path through the forest. The sunshine filtered through the canopy and lit the way perfectly. Surprisingly, there were no biting insects that bothered them. When they got to the end of the path, more of the immortals' city was visible.

Again the buildings were round, topped with domes, and made from the same materials. In the distance, there was a very large structure that looked more like a spaceship. As they walked out of the forest, immortals who were nearby, and naked, turned and greeted them. The immortals came over and introduced themselves, then walked everyone to the grand hall.

It was clear that when some of them saw the newcomers, they became quite excited, with both their eyes and cocks showing their arousals. The ladies were eyeing the guys too.

"Do you feel it?" Falon asked Mark.

"Most definitely," he said. "The place is electric with sexual energy."

Still, not one of them approached the newcomers, keeping a respectful distance. That was very polite. They were led into the grand hall and there they saw Ureth again. He was wearing a robe, but once he saw the lack of clothing, he disrobed and threw it aside. Sitting beside him was a beautiful woman with Latin features.

"I'm happy to see you have adopted our manner of undress," he said, laughing. "We do not like wearing coverings. They restrict us, and itch."

"When in Rome, do as the Romans do," said Lora.

"I'm sorry, I am not familiar with that expression," said Ureth.

"Ah, it means, when you visit a new place, follow their customs," said Lora.

"When in Rome … a good expression," said Ureth. Turning to the woman at his side, he said "May I present to you Esperanza, my wife."

All six of them bowed in greeting.

"Come, let us sit!"

He brought everyone to a large round table where they could all sit. There were pillows on the chairs to make their bums comfortable. Glasses and plates were distributed, and a beverage that was pink in color was poured out.

Several immortals from their community joined the table, until there were as many as twenty sitting.

"Welcome, everyone, to our first-ever summit with the outside world," said Ureth. "We have six guests with us who have journeyed from their part of the world. They are immortals. They seek others like themselves, and to learn of their own history. As I say your name, please stand and acknowledge everyone. Lora O'Reilly, Ricardo Benal, Gwen Mitchell, Robert Andrews, Falon Roberston, Mark Chisholm. Thank you."

"We understand that you have specific areas that you would each like to address," said Esperanza. "Please state that now."

Mark stood and replied: "I am interested in your technology and how transmogrification works, and the techniques for achieving it."

Falon stood. "I am a new immortal, so I am open to learning everything." The others chuckled as she sat down.

"We'll have to narrow that down a bit, Falon," said Esperanza.

Rick stood and said, "I am from Cuba, which I understand is a location that your community settled in for a while. I would like to find my ancestors, and specifically my mother. I was given up for adoption to humans, so I didn't know what I was until I met Lora."

Lora stood and said, "I am a witch, and as part of the supernatural world already, I have an understanding of how I came to be. I would also like to meet my ancestors and know where they came from."

Gwen stood and said, "I am part of the council for our family. We have extensive historical records, which we never really pay attention to anymore. However, I know our family would love to know if there are any other immortal communities still surviving around the planet."

Andrews stood and said, "I too am a new immortal. I have an interest in security. I run a company that offers protection. The immortal family I know has been running from an enemy for millennia, and so I am interested in how you keep yourselves secure."

"Very good, and thank you for that summary," said Esperanza. "I can break you out into groups, for you to each go with someone in that area if you wish. Or we can just address these questions as a group for everyone to hear. What would you prefer?"

"I'd like to stay together," said Mark. "But first, let us tell you of the world beyond your borders."

Mark started with recent history, describing the world and what was happening there. They asked lots of questions. Many cried at some of the news, and they laughed when he told them silly things humanity had done. When he had exhausted our current history, we all took a break.

"Why don't we give you some of the information you're seeking now?" suggested Ureth.

"Let's start with the closest question. Rick, you want to know who your family is," asked Esperanza.

"Yes, ma'am."

"Give us a sample of your blood, and we'll match it very quickly." A technician walked up to Rick and drew a vial or two of blood. "Anyone else, before I go to the lab?"

"Yes please, I would," said Lora. So the technician drew two vials of her blood too.

"I'll be back in about fifteen minutes," said the tech.

"Now, Gwen, you asked about other groups. As far as we know, there are thirty-five groups living on the planet. There were thirty-five who left during the exodus from Antarctica, and there were still thirty-five when we had a summit about five hundred years ago—it would have been during your 1400s. Since then, we have lost touch with them. I believe that the family you have are the descendants from Group 35. I had heard that 35 may have splintered, and another group formed, but I don't have data on that.

"You will find a group of us on every continent, in every corner of the world. We touched just about every culture that rose up, and some that failed. Our hand is on just about every advance humanity made. We were not supposed to interfere, but it was impossible sometimes to sit and watch people destroy themselves. However, since the 1400s, we, as a group, have stayed completely out of humanity's way. A few humans, over the centuries, have found us, received wisdom, and took it back to their lives. We don't know what became of them. Most of those who found us were considered adventurers by their society, and ne'er-do-wells that were dreamers. What they didn't know was they were on a much higher level of thinking than the rest of their society. Unfortunately, we cannot speak for the rest of the groups who left the ship."

"Then I have a lot of reading to do," said Gwen. "Thank you."

"If you wish, Gwen, you are welcome to access our knowledge. The entirety of our knowledge is kept here. I can have someone show you how to access it."

"Please!" said Gwen, her eyes lighting up with excitement.

"Now, Mark, you are interested in our technology and how we handle turning humans," said Ureth. "Well, we don't turn humans; at least not intentionally. We are a lustful species, as you probably are aware. We exercise sexual play frequently, and participate in many erotic games. Our sexuality is part of us and we are proud of it. There aren't always enough partners for everyone. We are very careful about being with people from the same lineage. When our groups were devised, people were carefully selected so that not one person came from the same line as anyone else in the group. This was to allow everyone to have sex with anyone.

"Since we started laying with humans, we have been tormented by them calling us gods. They have slain each other for the privilege of sleeping with us. They have built temples for us, and enslaved young women to 'keep us satisfied.' Little do they know that they are generally inferior, and we would rather not sleep with humans. But sometimes it has been necessary and sometimes it produced offspring. Very occasionally, one of us has met an extraordinary human to whom they were immediately connected. We did not understand this connection, but it was unbreakable. Our sexuality, in its violence and aggression, ultimately either killed the humans, or in the case of these extraordinary ones, they became one of us. It seems that our venom, when given in a particularly high dose, breaks down their mortality, and remakes their DNA.

"Through experimentation, we isolated the element in the venom that alters the DNA of a human, and changes them into an immortal. We realized that we could simplify the process by developing a pure injection. This gave the humans who wanted to be with us a clear path. Those that chose to turn stayed with us instead of returning to their human world. Unfortunately, many of them were young women, who had become addicted to the drug in the venom. That led the humans to believe that we did something to the virgins. We eventually synthesized those active ingredients and created a simple injection."

"So, if I'm hearing you correctly, it's only a component of the venom that does this?" asked Mark.

"Yes, in high doses. The natural way required frequent doses to start the turn."

"That explains a lot!" Falon said.

"We also distilled a toxin from the semen and thought it was part of the process too," said Ureth. "However, further experimentation showed it was just the drug in the venom that was needed. I take it that all three of you are mated couples?"

"Yes, we are," said Mark. "As you say, extraordinary humans with an immediate connection."

"I will say one more thing," said Ureth. "This knowledge took us thousands of years to work out. We believed that turning males would need a serum based on semen to aid in the change. We stopped doing that when we isolated the toxin in the venom. It subtly changes and is a different chemistry when males battle. It becomes more potent, to kill, and therefore is more effective to change, but it requires a measured dose and only one."

"We kind of figured that out accidentally," said Mark.

"As far as our technology is concerned, I'll have one of our people give you a tour, and you can ask as many questions as you like."

"Thank you, Ureth."

"Robert," said Esperanza. "You were interested in our security? How so?"

"How do you keep yourselves hidden?" asked Andrews.

"That is best answered by our science team. They will show you our tech for that."

"For now, let's eat!" Esperanza clapped her hands, and a dozen people laden with trays walked in and laid them down on the table.

"Dearest visitors, our customs are unusual to most humans, but seeing as you are immortal like us, we invite you to participate with us," said Esperanza. "As a lustful species, we embrace the act of coupling whenever and wherever two or more people share a connection. Connection to us is paramount. The deeper the connection, the better the sex. When we are lucky enough to find a mate, we like to share that deepest of connections."

People just started taking food off the platters and eating. Some were feeding the person sitting next to them. An immortal next to me turned to me and asked if he could feed me. I heard Mark growl a bit, so I placed my hand on his arm. First, I fed Mark a grape and watched him enjoy the experience, then I turned to my other side and was fed the same way.

The man popped a grape in my mouth with his fingers, letting them brush my lips. He smiled at me and licked his own lips. He popped a grape in his own mouth and leaned over and kissed me, sharing the grape.

It was more intimate than I expected it would be. The grape slipped into my mouth; I bit it in half and licked the juice from his lips as he held the kiss.

"You have beautiful lips, Falon," he murmured as he placed another grape in his mouth to share.

On my other side, Mark was now being fed by a beautiful woman who was sitting on his lap, also feeding him bits of cheese, breaking off bits and holding it in her lips while kissing him. The cheese slid between them while she caressed his cock.

Mark and I weren't the only ones getting such attention. Lora was being enticed by two men, while Rick had a young thing straddling him. Gwen and Andrews were entertaining two others as well, and I wasn't sure who was doing what to whom.

It appeared that mealtime was also a time to couple, as people wandered away from the table in couples or groups. Lusty people, indeed!

"Would you like to come back with me, Falon?" asked the man feeding me grapes.

Mark had already been pulled from his seat and was following the woman out of the dome.

"Yes, I would like that very much," I said. I got up and followed him out of the common area to his dome.

All of us were taken by the village immortals to have sexual play. Some went in groups, others in pairs. It wasn't until much later in the evening when we all got back to our guest dome refreshed but tired from our endeavors.

"Did everyone have an interesting day?" asked Mark.

"Oh yes," I said, with everyone nodding in agreement. "Very interesting."

"They love to have sex, every which way possible."

"How do we feel about this?" he asked. "I'll go first. When I saw those guys going for you, Falon, I thought I would lose my mind. But after our experience together, with the energy we create and the power that happens, I realized it was not about love, and then I was distracted. So I'm good with this." He was smiling.

"I had similar feelings," I said. "But then I was distracted too."

"We are lustful people," said Gwen. "Always have been. It's why we sought out humans because we needed lots of sex."

"I for one don't feel jealous or put out," Lora said. "The more I experience, the more I want. So I am okay with this, and I say bring it on." She put her hand in the center. "Who is with me?"

One by one, we each extended a hand to hers.

"This has nothing to do with how much I love you, Lora," said Rick.

"Nor I you," said Lora. "I got a triple-pen, I couldn't believe it."

"I definitely want some of that action!" said Rick.

"It hurts just thinking about it," I said.

"Ah yes, it does. But it's fleeting with the bite," said Lora.

"Tomorrow, we have tours, and more sex I expect, so couple up and get some rest, or not," said Andrews. "Your choice." He grabbed Gwen's hand and they walked into their sleeping room.

"Mark, now that we have these experiences, I'm not opposed to sharing our two, if you're interested," said Rick.

"I think I want Falon to myself tonight. But next time we'll curl their toes, okay?"

Mark took me to our room, and Rick took Lora to theirs, both of us smiling like crazy at the thought of having our "toes curled."

21—Island Day Two

—Lora

Waking up refreshed was nice. The beds were really comfortable.

"Rick, I want to see if we can get some time with Esperanza today, while the others are doing their own thing.

"Sounds like a plan," Rick said.

Dressed, we met the others in the common area and made plans.

"I'm going to go visit that library and see what I can learn and take back to our family," said Gwen.

"I'll accompany you, and then we'll speak to the engineers about their security veil," said Andrews.

"That will be interesting," said Gwen. "Meet you guys back here for dinner?"

"I want to follow up on some of their technology too and see if I can learn more about their process for making the injections," said Mark. "Falon, why don't you come with me and then we can see what else we can learn."

"Sounds good to me," said Falon.

"We have a specific task," said Rick. "You remember the occult store entity is called Esperanza?"

"Yes," they answered collectively.

"Well, we want to speak to Esperanza about her and find out more about the witches," I said.

"All settled, then. We'll meet back here at dinner."

Nods all around happened, and then they went their separate ways. Rick and I set out to find the government building, or whatever building Ureth and Esperanza worked in. To our surprise, there was no government. On asking the villagers, they were all puzzled by our questions. But we got directions to where they worked most of the day.

We got directed to a building that was just off the center street near the middle of the village. It was another dome, and inside it was filled with a luscious garden. All the plants and trees bore fruit, and some of them I didn't recognize at all.

"Lora! Rick! Welcome to my dome!" said Esperanza.

"This is beautiful, what do you do here?" I asked.

"I take fruits from around your world and attempt to grow them here, and if I cannot, I modify them until they thrive. This provides us with a bounty of food. But I never have more than one tree of each fruit. It would be too much for us."

"Fascinating," said Rick. "Do you do the same for vegetables?"

"Why, yes. Ureth works with them in the next dome," she said. "What can I do for you?"

"We came here to learn from you about a specific period in time," I said.

"Let's go and sit under the trees. There is a lovely, shaded bench not too far that way. Then we can speak." We followed her back into the garden, and sure enough there was a set of benches and tables arranged in a courtyard under some very large fruit trees. The shade was fragrant and cool. Surprisingly, there was a nice cool breeze whistling by.

"Okay, what do you want to know?" asked Esperanza.

"Back at home, there is an occult shop that I have access to. There is a supernatural soul who presides over the shop and is there to guide visitors. Her name is also Esperanza."

As I heard Esperanza's gasp, I turned to look at her.

"I see you know who I speak of?" I asked.

"She was my granddaughter," whispered Esperanza. "She was the result of a coupling between my son and a mixed-race human. My son was immortal."

"Did she have your name?"

"Yes, she was given my name," replied Esperanza.

"Do you know how she came to be a disembodied spirit?" I asked.

"Yes. As you say, it's a long story," said Esperanza.

"I'll tell the story," said Ureth, joining us in the courtyard. "Of all the people who survived the journey to this planet, and then survived the cold of Antarctica, only about two thirds survived leaving the ship. We divided the population into thirty-five groups, each with a shuttlecraft capable of bringing us back to the ark ship if needed. Each group was given a different destination on the planet, to give us the best chance of surviving. Unfortunately, not all of us made it, I'm afraid.

"Our group was sent to settle around the area between the two large continents. There were enough islands that we could select one to turn into what we needed. We spent a great deal of time on and around the land bridge between two great landmasses. There were many groups of humans who passed through the region, each with their own culture, although many had commonalities.

"When we could, we helped them, teaching them agriculture, building. Occasionally, we'd meet an extraordinary individual who learned much more and was curious about many things. Many of these people thought we were gods and worshiped us. We tried to break them of that belief, but we never succeeded. Once we were sent young, beautiful, virgins for our pleasure—for us to play with. When we sent them home to their village, they were killed because we had 'rejected' them. We couldn't let that happen again.

"We would disappear from their lives, and move away, but eventually there was another group of humans that found us. So the next time we were sent a selection of women, our men had sex with them. The human females received our venom and became pregnant immediately. They all returned to their village with huge bellies. The girls would keep coming back to us for sex, because they wanted more venom. When their babies were born, the girls died, but their babies survived. We kept the babies, suspecting they were born immortal. Testing proved that.

"Some of our men went and lived with the humans. That resulted in all the women becoming pregnant. But the women didn't have more sex, so they didn't become addicted. When the women gave birth, some died, some lost a child, some lost both, some didn't. We kept an eye on the different babies and watched them. They lived longer than their siblings and grew stronger and taller. But they still died young.

"Soon the men of the human villages wanted access to the gods too—to be selected to lay with the gods. Their bravest, most accomplished warriors would compete to be chosen. Our women took on some of these men as lovers, but rarely did they become pregnant.

"Some of the babies born to human women started to display a talent when they hit puberty. The humans became afraid of those children, and they would be sacrificed. We felt the only way we could put an end to this was to stop all contact with their society.

"The human leaders got angry that we left and blamed the mixed-race children, unreasonably saying they had been blessed too often by the gods so they had left them. Of course, this was utterly wrong. We were sickened by their willingness to slaughter their own offspring.

"Even in our absence, the humans continued to worship us, in spite of our effort to tell them we were not gods. They again believed they needed to make sacrifices to get our attention. We watched in our isolation as they held ceremony after ceremony, throwing away the lives of their youngest girls. They would tie them to the top of a mountain they knew we used to visit so that we could have a choice body for sex. It was all very terrible.

"Eventually, we moved to an island in the archipelago and settled where there were no humans. That didn't last very long. Before eight hundred years had passed, we watched as humans crossed the water and started to populate the islands around us as well. We retreated into a volcano and disguised our presence. We watched the people spread out across our island. At least they seemed to have lost the notion to sacrifice their young. We introduced ourselves again, and built a relationship with them. Many of our people found comfort in the arms of the humans, and had children.

"When the ship-filled humans arrived from across the oceans, we watched. They came with the intent on slaughtering and stealing what they could. When they learned the humans here could work gold, they became obsessed with looting every single item they found with gold on it. It was terrible to watch. We wanted to save the villagers—the children especially, but a council among my people forbade it. We could not interfere any more in the progression of time on this planet.

"We ran away under the cover of darkness to this island. Here we have stayed. Few have found us. There are many shipwrecks off the shore of this island because of the shallow reefs. It provides a natural barrier," explained Ureth.

"The humans continued to worship us," said Esperanza, picking up the story.in spite of us no longer being present. "We heard tales that they visited the caves we inhabited and held ceremonies and sacrifices. After a few decades, their love of us turned into mistrust and hate. One among them gifted with extraordinary skills, not unlike yours, used her skills to try to call us back. Unfortunately, it backfired on her, and instead many gifted humans were banished to another dimension. The ones who were left behind shunned any other people who exhibited any extraordinary ability. Those were labeled witches and the Europeans slaughtered them."

"Do you know what happened to the gifted witch whose spell backfired?" I asked.

"That was our granddaughter, and she was living in our former volcano when it erupted and most of the people were killed. She died in the fires trying to save her people. On her death, her soul was taken and trapped. The individual who trapped her would have been a great magic wielder."

"Your granddaughter, when did she become trapped?"

"That would have been about 1470. My granddaughter was at the peak of her power. She had lived about two hundred years at that point."

"Where did these magic wielders come from?" I asked.

"The magic wielders all came from the other side of the ocean," said Esperanza. "They had a network. Many were called on to help with the spell that they wanted to cast to bring us back."

"My great-great-grandmother was a very powerful magic-wielder. Was she one of those that were called?" I asked.

"Perhaps, what was her name?"

"Innogen."

"I remember an Innogen. She was in conflict with another of her order.

"I'd like to free those witches from the dimension if we can. Perhaps I can get more information from the occult world on how to do that."

"That is surely nothing I can help you with," said Esperanza.

"We'll add that to our goals. Right now though, I'm hungry. Let's go meet everyone for dinner."

22—Final Tour

—Lora

Dawn broke on our third day with the sun rising low on the horizon, making all the birds sing. The cacophony was something to behold. By the time we got out of bed and into the common room, there were platters of food left for us again.

The immortals came to fetch us for our tours. Andrews went off with scientists to learn about their security. Mark went off with other scientists to learn about their technology. Rick made his way over to the kitchens to investigate their culinary skills. Gwen was taken to their library of sorts, and Falon and I were invited to live a day in the village.

We learned their cooking, garment making, and medicine. They were so far advanced beyond us, even now, it was silly. We walked around their compound with our jaws dropped open. They really had a small city here with all the amenities you would find in a human one.

When they showed us their pod, the lifeboat craft they took from their mothership, it was huge inside. I could not imagine how large the actual ship would be. While moving around the village, we were invited to have sex over and over again. We didn't always participate.

The immortals were not stopped by any apparent inhibitions. They would put their cocks anywhere any time, between immortals. They were not into animals. They would have as many partners as you wanted. Somehow that cheapened it a bit, even for me. Whatever we took away from there, the six of us became very close as a group.

Before we left, I wanted to check up on the DNA test results they promised. Making my way to their laboratory, I found the technician who drew the blood.

"Hi there, I've come for the results of the DNA test," I said.

"Oh, pity, I wanted to have sex with you."

"First, what are the results?"

"Well, we found Ricardo's family. In fact, his mother is still with us and is living in our compound."

"Oh wow, that's wonderful news!" I squealed.

"Her name is Shonia. She is one of our food growers. You'll find her in the southeast corner of the compound, under the farming domes."

"Thank you," I said. "Now, did you get any results for me?"

"Yes, we traced your DNA to a woman in Group 12 who went to what is now Western Europe. The last we heard, they had settled near the spot now called Stonehenge."

"Excellent! That gives me lots to work with," said Lora.

"Can you do mine? I was turned, but we suspect that perhaps there may be some history because of the strong attraction we had," said Falon.

"Sure, give me your arm please." The tech took a blood sample, prepared it, and ran it through their machines while we watched. Their machines were incredibly fast, spitting out the information in a matter of minutes.

"Okay, let's look at the results, shall we?" said the technician. "Hmm, oh, this is interesting. Yes, you do indeed have some immortal DNA. I will see who this matches within our genome."

"How long will it take?"

"About five minutes. Wait right here."

"Who do you think it will come back with?" asked Falon.

"I suspect it will come back with connections to Europe like me."

We wandered around the lab looking at all the strange devices while we waited. True to the tech's word, he returned shortly.

"I have your results," he said, as he walked through the door.

"So?" I asked impatiently.

"It seems Falon is a descendant of someone in Group 12 like you," he said.

"So we may actually be cousins?" asked Falon.

"Very possible, but at least you are related."

"Cool!"

Later that afternoon, the six of us regrouped in our dome. We decided to keep to ourselves and discuss what to do next.

"This is our third day here, so we need to check in with Duffy," said Andrews.

"Yes, but let's figure out how long we'll be here," said Mark.

"I have a name to follow up on and the group that settled in my ancestral area," I said. "So now I need to go back to the occult store and do some more research."

"I was given the name of my mother, Shonia. I would like to visit her before we leave," said Rick.

"That's great news, Rick," said Falon. "I have some exciting news too!"

"What's that?" asked Mark.

"They did a DNA test on me too, and I am a descendant of Group 12 like Lora!"

"So we may in fact be cousins, but at the very least, we're related," I said.

"I am not surprised," said Mark. "I have seen enough around here for now."

"I've still got lots of questions, but I suspect I won't get direct answers," said Andrews.

"I too have a good direction to look after seeing their archives. There should be at least a dozen more groups out there," said Gwen.

"So we can leave tomorrow?" asked Mark.

"Yes."

"Good, I will ask Ureth if I can alert Duffy."

"It's still a few hours to dinner, so Rick and I are going to look for his mother," I said. "We were told she can be found in the southeast domes, where the farming happens."

"Good luck!" said Falon.

We walked that way, asking for directions as we went, until we found the farm. It was a huge, domed area, with clear ceilings to let in light. Basically, it was a greenhouse. We entered and were assaulted by the heat and humidity. Barely able to breathe, I coughed a bit.

"Wow, it is hot in here!"

"Hello?" called Rick. "Anyone here?"

"Come to the back, please," came a distant voice.

It took us about fifteen minutes to reach the back of the greenhouse.

"Hello, may I help you?" asked the woman without looking up.

"Hello, I'm looking for Shonia," said Rick.

She looked up at that name and stared into his eyes for a minute, then glanced at me.

"Who are you?" she asked.

"My name is Ricardo Benal," said Rick. "But I think I'm your son."

She looked like she was hit by a bomb. Stumbling backward, her hand felt for something to sit on. Lowering herself in place, she continued to stare at him.

Rick realized she had been standing with crutches.

"My son," she said.

"Um, yes. You did have a son, no?"

"Yes, many, many years ago," she said wistfully. A tear loosed itself from her eye and tracked down her face. "I did not know he survived."

"I did."

"How?"

"I was adopted by a human family and raised as a human. I only discovered I wasn't human about the time I was a teenager. Lora, my mate, helped me piece together who and what I was, and we found you together."

"You had a good life?" she asked.

"Yes, my life has been good."

"Oh my goodness, I'm so glad. It would not have been among us."

"Why not?"

"It's a long sad story, I'm afraid," she said.

"I have all night to listen."

"Well, when I was a young woman, not more than forty-five years, an immortal man took me. I hadn't wanted to be taken, I was not interested in men. But he needed to copulate, so he took me. He was rough and barbaric, and I was humiliated. That's not usually the way of our kind. We are aggressive lovers, but always consent, always.

"It wasn't long until I felt a baby moving inside me. At first, the wonder of it was amazing. I would sit for hours just feeling you inside me moving around. I would talk to you and pretend you answered me. He found out I was with child and promised to take the 'rat' from me and kill it. I couldn't let him do that, so when I was close to delivering the baby, you, I made my way to an island of humans. I stole a boat and made my way without telling anyone. The humans took me to a hospital, where I had you. A month later, I left the human island and returned here. Everyone wondered where I had been, but I didn't tell them what happened."

"Why did he want to kill me?"

"Because you were evidence of rape. He knew that me having a baby would bring about questions, and he would be held responsible."

"But didn't people know you were pregnant anyway?" I asked.

"No, I stayed away from everyone. Back here in the greenhouses, no one bothers me. I live my life alone and quiet. The only time I get visitors is when they want to grow something specific we are not growing yet," said Shonia. "I wouldn't have been able to keep a baby secret, though."

Shonia fell silent for a few minutes, obviously reliving that part of her life. A silent tear fell down her cheek. She finally looked up at Rick, wiped the tears from her eyes and smiled.

"But enough of this! You live, my beautiful boy. You live. Tell me about yourself, please!"

"I am a chef," said Rick. "So I work with food too."

"Perhaps you inherited that from me," suggested Shonia.

"We," said Rick, holding up my hand clasped in his, "are getting married. Lora is my mate, and she is now an immortal. She's also a witch."

Shonia looked at me seemingly for the first time and smiled. "You are a beautiful woman, Lora," she said. "Another time and place, I would have wanted you for myself. You will make beautiful babies with my son. I hope you will bring them here and let me get to know them."

"Do you have a way to communicate with the outside world?" asked Rick.

"No, we are completely isolated here. For good reasons," she said. "But you now know how to reach us."

"Yes, we do," said Rick. "Well we shall leave you to your work."

"Before you leave," said Shonia, as she came out from behind her counter. It was then that we saw she had no legs. "Please give me a hug."

Rick got down on his knees and scooped her up off the wheelchair and hugged her. They both had tears running down their faces as they reconnected physically. They stayed like that for several minutes.

"Okay, put me down please," she said. "I can still feel that connection I once had with you. Remarkable," she said in wonder.

He placed her back in her wheelchair carefully.

"How did this happen?" he asked tentatively.

"That man did this to me so that I couldn't run from him," she said simply. And they understood her reasons better now.

"How did he get away with that?" I asked.

"He didn't," she answered. "When the community discovered that he had made me lame, he was put on trial and executed for his crime. But that happened after I had you and had returned to the island. I had been able to sneak off, but coming back was trickier. They saw me approach. When they realized I couldn't walk, he was immediately arrested. Until that day, he would come and take me whenever he wanted. I was a prisoner to him."

I could feel Rick's anger building. I placed a calming hand on his shoulder, and he glanced at me with frustration in his eyes.

"Mama, I would kill him for you if he were still alive today."

"Son, do not waste yourself on a thing like him. I am free now."

"Bye, Mama," he said. "I will come back."

Her voice caught on the endearment, covering her mouth with a few fingers, we saw her swallow. A tear formed in her eyes when she again looked at us. She waved goodbye instead of speaking. We turned away and walked back the way we had come. After we exited the greenhouse, I turned to Rick and hugged him myself.

"You made your mom very happy today," I told him.

"But I thought immortals' bodies all healed themselves perfectly. Why didn't her legs regrow?" I asked.

"I don't know," said Rick. "It's too personal a question to ask this soon. Perhaps one day she'll tell me."

The next morning, as we packed, there wasn't a lot for us to do. So we were dressed and ready to leave by the time Ureth and Esperanza came to our guest dome with breakfast.

"We bring you food. May we join you? Perhaps you can give us more news about the world?" said Ureth. "Oh, by the way, we have been keeping an eye on your watercraft. So far there have been no intruders. But there is another craft approaching quickly. They may be pirates."

"Oh, thanks," said Mark. "I'm sure Duffy is on top of it. Yes, we shall tell you more of the world."

"Good, I will send our guards to retrieve your craft and bring it inside our veil before it is spotted." Ureth spoke low to one of the people who had carried a platter and they put it on the table then ran off.

"So, what more would you like to know?" asked Mark.

"I'd like some more details about where you live," said Ureth.

Mark and Gwen picked up the previous story and related what their family was doing. Andrews filled in world details and Rick gave them a summary of the US, while Falon and I spoke of Canada. They peppered us with lots of questions, some of which we couldn't answer, but for the most part we could give them something. By the time the aide returned to let

Ureth know where the yacht was, we had finished eating and the questions had slowed down.

"All of you are welcome here at any time. Now that you know us a little and we have become familiar with you, we can enjoy a friendship. Perhaps we will even open communications between us and your location," said Ureth.

"Good luck with your hunt for family, Lora. Rick, I understand you spoke with your mother," said Esperanza.

"Yes, we reunited. It was very emotional," said Rick. "I would love to stay in touch somehow."

"We'll work on that," said Esperanza.

We picked up our gear and left the dome. A small group of immortals walked with us to the beach. We found the yacht moored just offshore.

"Is this where we should dock next time?" asked Mark.

"Yes, you can come right here and moor. The water is almost shallow enough to walk across," said Ureth.

We hugged and shook hands with everyone who accompanied us, gave them our best wishes, then picked up our gear and started walking out into the waves. At that moment, Duffy was paddling out to us in a lifeboat. We tossed our gear into the boat and swam the rest of the way to the yacht while Duffy brought our gear.

Bertram met us on the dive deck, helped us out of the water, and then helped Duffy with the lifeboat and our gear. Once on board, Andrews took a GPS reading so we could pinpoint the location next time. Duffy walked up to the bridge and got the engines going. I was waving toward shore, when I spotted the vessel they had spoken about. It did look like a pirate.

I pointed it out to Mark.

"Yes, I think we should wait until they've left the area. If we just pop out, it will draw eyes and curiosity."

23—Pirate Attack!

We sailed away from the launch site and held close to the shore to stay inside the veiled area. As the other vessel got closer, Duffy was concerned that our engine noise would be heard. So he cut the engines again, and he watched the pirates cruise around the area for a couple of hours. They appeared to be looking for something; hopefully, it wasn't their yacht. The immortals on the beach had disappeared so they were all alone. The eight friends could only watch the pirates paddle around like bloodhounds.

"I think when they have left, we should leave and go around the long way to return. I don't want them finding this cove," said Mark.

"I'll chart a course to the south, then," said Duffy. "I will continue to use LiDAR and sonar as we circumnavigate the island. The more data we have the better."

"Mark! What are they doing now?" Falon asked him. "I could see the pirates had stopped and were moving around on their deck.

"Huh, give me the glasses please," he said. After watching a few moments he said, "It appears they are getting ready to dive."

"What could they be diving on?" Lora asked.

"Who knows," he said. "I'm going to watch them."

Ten minutes later, he said, "It appears, whatever they want to dive on, they'll need scooters. They have four of them. So they are expecting to go a fair distance."

"I'm afraid they're trying to find us," Falon said.

"They may be, but they have no reason to look for us now. To them, we aren't here, and unless they know about the veil, why would they think anything is here?" said Andrews.

"That is logical, but there is something weird about them," said Mark. "Wait, they are going toward the U-Boat. So maybe they're hoping to salvage something."

"Andrews, can we leave without them seeing us?" Falon asked.

"As long as we're inside the veil, we can see the coastline. We can hug the coast until we cannot see them, and then sneak out on the south side," he said.

"Duffy, silent running if you can, and hug the shoreline as much as possible. Head south and we'll go the long way around the island. Hopefully, they won't expect that maneuver."

"Roger that," said Duffy.

The engines started up, but they were quiet. The yacht slowly moved along the shoreline, slipping through the water and barely making any waves. Lora watched the wake to make sure it stayed as small as possible.

"We'll be near the Dominican Republic when we come around the south end of the island," said Mark.

"Yes, that will work," said Andrews. "Get everyone spotting for us."

Rick, Gwen, Falon, and Lora all picked up glasses and found a different place on the yacht to keep watch for other vessels. Lora went up to the crow's nest as it had the best vantage point.

"Andrews, do we know the extent of the veil?" asked Mark.

"I was given its dimensions, so I will mark that on the map for Duffy. That way he'll be able to stay inside until we know it's clear and we don't pop out of thin air in front of another vessel."

"That map of ours is truly unique," said Falon. "We're not going to want to let it fall into anyone else's hands."

"Agreed," said Mark.

As the yacht made its way south along the coast of the immortal's island, the group got a good view of their compound. It actually took up most of the ground level land. The immortals had told the group that they had facilities underground as well. It was hard to imagine why they did that, but they did come from another planet with all kinds of technology so, perhaps mining equipment was part of it.

Eventually, Duffy lost sight of the pirates, so he looked ahead for other yachts. After all, the yacht had been on a tour and was brought around this way. It was getting close to sunset, and Duffy wanted to get out into open water, citing it was dangerous to stay close to shore without being able to see in the dark, regardless of having charts. No one spotted any lights or ships, so Duffy turned the yacht and headed out to sea.

Everything was going well, until Lora picked up the low hum of engine noise that wasn't ours.

"Lora to Mark."

"Mark here," he answered. "What's up?"

"I hear engines on the port stern side, but I cannot see anything."

"Roger that." Mark peered into the darkness and detected wave movement thanks to the moon.

"Duffy, cut the lights."

The lights on the yacht blinked off a moment later. "Shall I cut the engines?"

"Yes. Tell me what's on the radar."

"Nothing. There are no other ships or yachts in the vicinity."

"Which means these pirates are very sophisticated. They've got some sort of anti-radar system, or they have a stealth vessel."

"Do you want to call Duffy's crew?" asked Andrews.

"No, I don't think it's necessary yet. I believe we can handle a few pirates," said Mark.

"It might be fun," said Rick.

"Indeed," said Andrews.

"Be prepared to be boarded, folks," said Mark on the open channel. "Let them take us, then we can fuck with their minds. But we need to know what they know about the island."

"Everyone to the galley. Let's pretend we're partying like crazy."

Duffy put all the lights back on, and cranked up the volume of the sound system, blasting music in all directions. All of them collected on the galley deck and started dancing. There were lots of bottles out on the table and counter. Two were dirty dancing and two were necking on the couch. They made a great tableau of looking like they weren't paying attention.

When the pirates came up alongside their yacht, the friends didn't flinch. As the pirates came on board by the diving deck, the party appeared to intensify their unawareness. It wasn't until the pirates had them surrounded and yelled at them that the eight of them pretended to scream in fear and back into a huddled group.

"Hands up, everyone. We're taking your yacht. We'll leave you with a paddle and some floatation so you can make your way somewhere," said one of the pirates. The rest sniggered and snorted in amusement.

Two pirates approached Duffy and Bertram and tied them up on the bridge away from the rest of us.

"Down on your knees, now!" yelled another. As we sank to our knees, one of the pirates cable tied the guys' hands together behind their backs. Mark had to bow his head as his anger rose up so they didn't see his eyes and give away his plan.

"Oooooeeee," cried another as he caressed Gwen's breast. The pirate handcuffed Gwen with her hands in front. "We have some nice titties here tonight. Imma gonna want to sample this merch, amigo." Gwen growled at him. "Really, mamacita? You gonna growl at me like a cat? Get your claws out, girl, cause you've just met a tiger, rawr."

Gwen pretended to struggle as he lifted her up by the bicep and took her below deck.

"Take all the women below and lock them in the stateroom. We'll have a party once we figure out who we have here on board." Two of the pirates handcuffed Lora and Falon and tugged them by the arms to the stateroom and threw them inside. They had to pull off the first guy from Gwen and drag him out. They locked the door and went back on deck.

"Guys, you're fucking with the wrong people," said Rick, conversationally.

"Oh ya? How do you figure that, chico?" answered the pirate.

"You're calling me chico?" asked Rick. "*¿Yo un cubano? Ven aquí e insultame.*"

"*Por favor.*"

The pirate got right up in his face and was mugging at Rick. Rick heard Mark whisper, "Now!" and Rick's face exploded into the visage of a demonic vampire. His glowing red eyes, huge fangs dripping venom, and the ugly snarl that ripped out of his throat, as he snapped at the pirate's face, caused the thug to stumble back in fear.

"Whoa, what the fuck?" screamed the first pirate who had been getting in Rick's face.

"Oh fuck! What in hell are you?" shrieked another.

"Your worst nightmare," said Rick calmly and quietly. As he effortlessly broke his restraints, he had an evil smile on his face as he lunged at the pirate. Then his jaws opened wide. The pirate startled for a second, then ran right off the yacht, splashing into the sea. Rick stopped and turned on the next pirate holding a weapon on him. The gun fired and hit Rick in the leg.

"Ouch," said Rick calmly. Then he snarled and leaped at the gunman, taking him down to the deck. Rick was biting his neck, and almost ripped it out.

"Stop, don't kill him yet," said Mark quietly.

"What the fuck is going on here?" yelled the lead pirate as he came around from the back of the yacht. Mark counted another six on board. One for each of them.

"Well, you see, you've happened upon a group of vampires having a party," said Mark calmly. "We were getting hungry and were thinking of getting takeout. Lucky for us, you happened by."

"Take-out? What, you think Domino's will deliver out here?" asked the leader. The others broke out into nervous laughter, letting the three of them know where they were.

"Ah no, Domino's doesn't deliver what we like to eat," said a decidedly feminine voice behind the leader.

He spun around to come face to face with Falon. She hadn't yet displayed her immortal self.

"Come here, big boy, let me show you what I like," she purred. The pirate started walking toward her when she opened her mouth to smile. As she did, Falon's fangs slowly elongated, and her eyes glowed demonically in purple.

The terrified pirate hesitated a moment just before she jumped him, aiming for his neck and biting him with everything she had. He dropped to the deck screaming in ecstasy because her venom only delivered a drug, but she had delivered enough of it to incapacitate him.

Gwen grabbed another by the arm. When the pirate turned around to look at her, he found another demon with fangs and glowing eyes. She twisted his head to expose his neck and kill him. Lora got a third and jumped on his back, wrapping her arm around his neck and choking him into unconsciousness. This left only three more pirates for the guys.

Andrews and Mark were still on their knees, and their heads were still down.

"Thank you, ladies, for the rescue," said Mark.

"We didn't want you to have all the fun," said Gwen.

The three remaining pirates weren't sure what was going on. They leveled their guns at the two men on their knees and yelled, "Everybody get back or we kill these two men."

At that moment, Mark and Andrews broke their restraints and jumped up with their battle faces on: glowing red eyes, long fangs dripping of venom, and utter death written on their countenances. Rick stood beside them and the three slow-walked their way across the deck to the last pirates. One of them thought better of facing off against a vampire and ran for the railing, jumping off the ship. The other two were more than stupid and attacked two of the three immortals. It was an extremely short fight, ending with them in a heap. None were dead, just unconscious.

"Girls, bite them into oblivion. Andrews and Rick, go after the two that jumped off. I'm sure they went back to their boat. I'm going to interrogate this leader."

The pirate leader gave up whatever he knew. He was too afraid he was on his way to hell, so he wanted to unload his guilt. Mark was able to find out that they regularly patrolled these waters looking for pleasure craft to raid. Usually they could scare the occupants into giving them the keys and jumping overboard. Sometimes they were lucky enough to find a rich dude that they held for ransom. He had never heard of or seen any ships disappear in the area, or any invisible islands. In fact, he laughed at the mention of an invisible island or one that would reappear.

Mark finished off the interrogation with an especially frightful face and a *rawr* and made sure the pirate had been double-dosed on venom. The guys then pulled the seacocks in the pirates' yacht so it would sink to the bottom, and set them afloat in one of the tiny dinghies. Their yacht would disappear in a short while, and they'd have to rely on the goodness of whoever passed by to be saved. The pirates drifted away in their boat, babbling about vampires and devils and such.

In contrast, the rest of the cruise back to civilization was calm and quiet once Andrews found and released Duffy and Bertram. Their ship made excellent time sailing, and docked at the harbor exactly a week later. The dock operator was happy to see the yacht again in one piece. He had been worried because he heard there was recent pirate activity in the area.

"Oh don't worry about them, we took care of them," said Mark. "They won't be bothering anyone anymore."

"Gracias, señor," said the dock operator. "The authorities have trouble laying charges because they can't catch them."

"The next time you see them, they'll be spouting insane stories and floating in a dinghy. Very easy for the coast guard to get them."

Duffy gave the dock operator the pirates' last known coordinates. He laughed and translated the story to his employees. They all laughed along with him.

Mark paid the operator for the damage to the yacht and walked out of the office.

Duffy's crew was standing on the dock waiting for Mark.

"That was a great adventure! Will you be going out again?" he asked.

"No, not right now, or the foreseeable future," said Mark. "But I do want to talk to you about bringing you into the fold, and paying you and your crew a salary so that we have your skills at our disposal."

"I'd be open to that discussion," said Duffy. "In my line of work, we use some very sophisticated equipment for detecting and hiding. Navy contracts have equipped my small ship with very fast engines and very sneaky ways of sailing."

"You're definitely the kind of people I need in my organization," said Mark.

"Well, let's talk contracts when you have the time, then. I'm always open to new endeavors," said Duffy. "In the meantime, let my crew unload your yacht and get everything stowed. We will finish processing all the data we collected from the scans we did on the trip."

"That would be wonderful," said Mark. "Full service! You can contact Andrews when you have that done?"

"Of course."

All of the luggage was loaded into the waiting SUVs that drove the group back to the resort. It was lovely to discover the hotel had held the rooms from before. Piling out of the SUVs, they all crashed to their beds.

"Oh, Andrews," said Mark as he was unlocking their room.

"Yeah?

"I think I'd like to hire Duffy for our group, permanently."

"He'd appreciate that. He's a good man and his crew is top notch. Their contracts are sporadic, even if they are lucrative. He'd really like a steady income."

"Well, he offered to crunch the data for us that we collected. He'll be in touch with you when that is done. Then we can get together and discuss next steps."

"Will do. Goodnight."

"Night."

24—Moving On Up

—Lora

You know what they say: one week off followed by one off week.

The trip back to Montreal was uneventful, albeit long. We had so much gear that had to be put in crates and shipped back, because we couldn't take it with us. Mark had to arrange for ship transport. He was surprised that he nearly filled a container. It didn't help that it was December and home was cold, snowy, and not much fun after so many weeks in the sunshine.

Falon and Mark went back to their life, Rick and I went back into ours. At least the holidays were around the corner. Since Rick had moved in, we were cramped for space, so my plan was to do some organizing and try to clear out stuff we didn't need or wasn't being used anymore. I was standing in the middle of the mess that was the dining room. The table was covered with several piles of games and toys the kids never put away, laundry, and various miscellaneous things. I thought to myself, *Some of this has got to go!*

"Lora, hun, I have a surprise for you," said Rick, as he walked in.

"Hmm, sometimes I like surprises," I said without really thinking.

"I have found the perfect house for us!" he screamed in delight. Now there is a good reason he would think this was a positive surprise. As I said, we were really cramped in my small place. But I wasn't prepared for this. I don't know why.

"What? A house? Like to move into?" I blurted.

"I know we haven't talked about this yet. But since I moved in, it has been really cramped here. I know you don't want to live in Georgia full-time, so I thought we could get a bigger place here in Montreal. I went looking, and I found the perfect house. It's even close to Falon and Mark's home."

"Okay, back up, let's start with the basics: how big is it?" I asked.

"Six bedrooms."

"Six bedrooms? That's enormous!"

"Well, your children deserve their own rooms. Anita will have a room, we have a room, and, well, our child will have a room, no?" Rick had such an adorable smile on his face saying that, I just couldn't get angry at him—not that I would get angry. But my resolve crumbled quickly.

Thinking about what he said, it made perfect sense. *Our child?* Was I interested in having another baby? Sort of. I love babies. I had half expected to be pregnant after the turning ceremony and was a little disappointed I wasn't. So yeah, I wanted a baby with him.

"Why Anita?"

"She wants to come up here and do all the cooking and cleaning for us. She's bored in Georgia. When I'm not there, she has nothing to do. Besides, she loves looking after children."

"Okay, what else does it have?" I sighed.

"A huge modern kitchen, six bathrooms, a big family room, dining, living room for entertaining, a theater, three-car garage, large pool, cabana and outdoor kitchen, and a guest house."

"Wow, that is a lot of house. I am afraid to ask about the cost."

"It's only $1.2M—Canadian, that's like $750,000 USD. It's a bargain! It would cost me eight mil easy in Georgia. Please say you'll come and see it with me. Please? We can bring the kids with us."

"Oh great, you'll get them all excited and on your side and I won't stand a chance against that wall of cuteness!" I said, swiping my hand from side to side pointing at all their faces. But I was smiling too.

The kids had come downstairs and were in the hall listening to Rick. They were all jumping up and down saying, "Please, Mom, please, can we?"

How do I say no to that, eh?

"All right, let's go. I'll call Falon on the way and tell her to meet us too."

The drive to the house wasn't long. Rick was right, it was very close to Falon's new place. He turned down this private driveway and pulled up in front of this enormous but beautiful gray stone house, with a gabled front porch and very large double wood doors in the front. The garage was discreetly placed on the side of the house, so you didn't see it from the street. Point in favor.

Walking inside was like walking into a palace in the 1970s. I couldn't see myself living in a place like this. I glanced over at Rick and realized this was like his house down south except with outdated decor. So I looked at it again, from his eyes.

I saw a beautiful entryway with a sweeping circular staircase in the middle. There was an enormous Christmas tree nestled into the curve that was beautifully decorated. And there were already gifts under it. Clearly the former family had not left yet.

"What a beautiful tree. Okay, kiddos, listen up. No running around and no touching. The family still lives here, so mind your manners," I warned them all.

"Oh, that's not necessary," said Rick. "The former family left five months ago."

"Why is there a Christmas tree still here, then? And whose gifts are those?" I asked him.

He looked at me and grinned. "They're for us of course," he said quietly. The kids didn't hear, thank God. They were already off walking around the house. "Since we were away and I didn't know if we'd be back in time for the holidays, I had it set up here just in case we missed it. We could have Christmas if we moved in."

I looked at my mate sideways and squinted at him, thinking. "Rick, have you already purchased this house?" I asked him suspiciously. "We haven't missed the holidays, it's in a few days."

Wow, his reaction to my question was priceless. I swear he looked chagrined, and looked down at his feet like a little boy caught stealing a cookie! It was adorable, but I wasn't going to tell him that.

"Merry Christmas!" he said. "Yes, I've put an offer on it. I know, I know, I didn't talk to you first, but frankly I didn't want to lose the opportunity at the perfect house for us," he blurted out. "Besides, I can afford it, and I want to take care of you and the kids." He hesitated a moment, then added, "I know you're independent and you like to take care of yourself. But we're going to get married, and that means I want to take care of you now."

"Oh, Rick, I do love you, so much. Come on, show me the house you've bought, okay?"

He took my hand and led me everywhere. He was so excited, like a little kid, it was impossible to not catch his fever. He was asking me what I thought of the decor and what I would change. The house was spectacular, albeit sort of stuck in the 1970s. So we could make it ours by remodeling the house to our tastes. That sounded like fun. I'd never had the money to do something like that.

He was right, the kitchen was enormous; dark, but it had lots of windows and space. The bedrooms were a good size, and the master was a bowling alley. But it all needed upgrading—well, it didn't need upgrading, but it sure as heck could use it. It needed to come into the twenty-first century quickly. The 1970s wanted their wallpaper back.

"When can we move in?" I asked.

"As soon as my offer is accepted, I will make the arrangements. We could be in before the end of the next month." Just then, the doorbell rang. I walked to the front and looked outside. It was Falon and Mark.

"Oh My God!" cried Falon. "This place is huge!"

"Nice place," said Mark. "Are you buying the property? It would be a good investment."

"Rick wants to—and to move in soon. Can you imagine this place for parties?" I gushed. "Oh! We could have the wedding here!"

Just then I heard the kids running around upstairs squealing in delight.

"How many bathrooms?" asked Mark.

"Six in total. Master ensuite, a second ensuite, two upstairs to service the bedrooms, guest toilet down here, and one in the guest house."

"You'll need an extra bath upstairs with six bedrooms," said Mark.

"That could be done," said Rick, walking up behind me. "The master is really oversized, so we could take some space from there and put in another bathroom. That makes a lot of sense actually."

"So, what do you say, love of my life?" asked Rick. "You still want to marry me?"

"Yes, I do! Let's take the house," I said. "It'll make a beautiful venue for the wedding."

"Yippee!" Rick grabbed me by the waist and spun me around over his head in delight.

Turned out, Rick was right, we were able to start moving in by the end of the month. But there was a lot of preparation to do. That organizing? Yeah—it happened in earnest. I had the kids go through all their toys and make three piles: keep, give away, and garbage. I learned a thing or two from those home reno programs. I did the same thing to my stuff. Turns out most of my stuff was so shabby and worn, it wasn't worth moving.

"Rick, I don't have furniture worthy of that house," I said one day a few weeks later. I was discouraged and embarrassed.

"Don't worry about that. Let's go shopping for new furniture. We can get what we need to start, and then have a decorator help us with the rest."

"Oh my God, that is so generous. I'm not used to having anyone that could help me with that sort of thing. Thank you."

Our shopping trips to get furniture were a blast. Not only did we combine both our styles, but we got to choose a cohesive look for the house. It would look professionally decorated instead of hand-me-down city. We got new beds and dressers for everyone, including Anita. We also outfitted the family room with chairs, sofas, tables, and lamps. That would get us started. We had all the new stuff shipped directly to the new house, so that saved us a bundle. That was important to me but not so much to Rick. Still, I don't want to waste his money.

When moving day arrived, the movers only had boxes to carry, which made them very grateful. As a result, it went really quickly. I waited in the front hall and directed traffic like a cop, sending the movers to the correct room to deposit the boxes. It took them only three hours to completely move us into the new place.

The Christmas tree was still there, and the gifts were still under it. When the dust settled, Rick brought us all into the front hall, which was a room in itself, and had the kids and I sit on the stairs.

"My family," he started, and choked a little with emotion. "It is my honor to have you in my life. I give you this home as a token of my love and devotion to you. I hope we will be happy here, and have many happy years together. To start us off, I have a late Christmas gift for each of you."

The kids got up and each found a small box with their name on it and took it back to the stairs to open. Minni was the first to get hers open. Inside was a delicate and beautifully hand-crafted ornament with her name and this year's date on it. It was made in her favorite colors and was blown glass. It was really beautiful, especially when held to the light. It sparkled with inner light. Also in the box was a certificate for salsa dance lessons. Dancing in Cuban culture was very important. Minni squealed with delight. She jumped up and ran to Rick to hug him.

"Gracias, Rick, I love the ornament and the dance lessons. I've always wanted to learn," she said. Then she hung the ornament on the tree.

My youngest, Trent, opened his gift next, and it too was a hand-made glass ornament. It had a hockey player somehow suspended in the middle of a double layer of glass bubbles. The player was him, wearing a Montreal Canadiens NHL team jersey. Trent squealed in delight as he recognized his own face. In the bottom of his box was a certificate for dance lessons too, but in his case they were for hip hop.

"Rick, this is amazing, thank you so much," said Trent, shaking Rick's hand instead of a hug. He too hung his ornament.

Pascal, my non-binary child, opened theirs last, and found an ornament with a rainbow ribbon inside with the words "Free to be Me" in script along the rainbow. It was a really beautiful ornament, and it meant a lot to Pascal to be recognized. Pascal also had a certificate for dance lessons, but it would be their choice because Rick wasn't sure what they would prefer.

"Rick, wow. I have no words. Thank you—and I want to see what styles of dance they have at the school please," said Pascal. They hung their ornament too.

"Kids, you can go and start unpacking your boxes please. Put as much away as you can. That means don't leave it on the floor," I said. They all ran upstairs to start unpacking their lives, leaving me with my husband-to-be.

"The last gift is for you, mamacita," he said. Handing me a similarly sized box, I was expecting an ornament and dance lessons too.

However, when I opened it, I nearly fainted. Yes, there was a beautiful ornament inside, but there was also a little blue box. When I took it out and opened it, my hands were shaking. As soon as I opened it, I started crying. It was the most gorgeous diamond ring I had ever seen. It was so big, I knew it would take a serious adjustment to wear it—and goddess help me for wearing gloves! Oh my, it took my breath away. I had a river of tears rolling down my face just looking at it.

"Lora? Mamacita? Are you okay?" asked Rick, suddenly concerned he'd done something wrong.

"Oh my, yes, I'm fine. My breath was stolen for a moment, that's all. Oh Rick, yes!"

"Well, I knew the answer to the question already, I just wanted to seal the deal with the proper ring. Please try it on. I want to make sure it fits well."

"My hands are shaking, you come and do it please." So he stepped over to me and took the ring from the box, knelt down, and slipped the ring on my finger. It fit perfectly. I felt like Cinderella, except you know it was a ring, not a shoe. My three kids cheered and screamed in delight as they witnessed his proposal from the balcony upstairs. I hadn't realized they were watching, so I looked up at them, smiling, and they were all beaming.

"Congratulations, Mom!" they yelled together. "Rick, welcome to the family, Dad," said Minni. Rick's breath hitched in his throat at the sentiment, and stood and hugged me a long time.

"What else do you have, Mom?" asked Pascal.

I looked inside the box again, and there was a hand-blown glass ornament that had a scene from Atlanta and a date. *What a romantic he is!* It was the day we met.

"It's the time and place we met, and I fell in love with you," he said. I heard a quiet "Awww" from Minni upstairs.

"I will treasure that memory always," I said, and went and hung it on the tree too.

"Mom, do you get dance lessons?" asked Minni.

Looking inside the box, yes, there was a piece of paper. It was for dance lesson for two—my choice.

"It looks like we're all going to be a dancing family!" I said.

"In Cuba, in my culture, dance is very important. We all learn how to dance, the salsa if nothing else. But the traditional dance of Cuba is called *danzón*. It's sort of like Argentine Tango, but it has African beats, and lyrical music. We also love to dance the mambo to big band music."

"Oh, all of that sounds like fun! I'm in," I said to him. Turning to my kids, I added, "Okay, you guys go unpack and I'll call you for food. We'll order in tonight, then we can have a movie."

There was a chorus of "Yeahs" as they went to their rooms to unpack. Rick took my hand and twirled me around in a few dance moves that I easily followed. But that was because he was a good lead.

"You're going to learn fast. You can follow well," he said.

"All those years of dancing I did," I said with a smirk.

After dinner, we invited Falon and Mark over for a movie. Down in the home theater, the kids sat on the floor while the adults got large reclining seats. We were lucky, the former owners didn't dismantle the home theater and take it with them. According to Rick, they were retiring to a much smaller place, and didn't want to move all the heavy chairs and equipment. So it was a gift for us.

"What movie do we want to see?" I asked everyone.

"How about a Christmas movie?" asked Minni.

"*Elf*!" cried one kid.

"*Polar Express*!" cried another.

"How about the Dickens story?" asked Mark.

"*A Christmas Carol*?" I asked.

"Yeah, that's the one, then we can do one for the kids," said Rick. "It's easy, because the library of movies is accessible from the console on your chairs."

We looked down at the chairs' arms and indeed found a console with a menu on it that listed the movies available.

"Wow! That's handy," I said. "Can it be added to?"

"Yes. We've got access to Netflix here as well," said Rick. "Of course, we have hardware for Blu-ray discs too."

"4k or 8K?" asked Mark.

"4K but it will take all Blu-ray formats. This is the most modern room in the whole house. I believe they built it about ten years ago when 4K came out."

Rick and I sat in the back watching all our friends and family having a good time. He leaned over to me and said, "Now all we have to do is plan our wedding."

I looked at him and had the perfect idea. "I wasn't kidding about the venue. What do you think about getting married here, at the house?"

"I love that idea! Justin will cater of course, and we have the space. When?"

"What about waiting until we can use the pool?"

"I like that idea, very much. So June. Date?"

"I've always been partial to thirteen," I said.

"June 13th it is. Let's tell everyone!"

We stood up and clanged on our cups for everyone's attention. When all eyes were on us, I spoke.

"Everyone, friends, family, we have picked a date for the wedding! We're getting married next summer on June 13th, right here at the house. So mark your calendars!"

A loud cheer came up as everyone was congratulating us. Now all I had to do was get it planned!

25—Training

—Lora

ow that we had picked a date, I had a wedding to plan and a new house to redecorate—and I still had research to do! Luckily, Anita moved to Montreal two weeks later, and she was a major help in getting the house set up. The woman had a way of making work disappear.

When Anita arrived and we showed her the new bedroom, she clapped her hands in delight. I think she unpacked herself in a day. She was so happy to be taking care of people again, she cried.

My first priority was still to find my ancestors. It was April, so I decided to get Anita working on some of the wedding details while I did the research.

I needed to go back to the occult store and track down more information. I planned to bring Rick with me again, because two sets of eyes were better than one and he knew what I was looking for.

We returned to the exact same room we had been in before. I pulled out the books we had found last time and set them on the table while we looked for others. In the back of my mind, I thought about visiting my great-great-grandmother again to see what she could add to the search. I'm sure she had a trick or two.

We went looking for more books written by Group 32 or Group 35 members. We found more than a few. So both of us sat down with a stack and started reading.

"Oh! Look, look, look at what I just found!" cried Rick excitedly.

I rushed over and looked over his shoulder.

"This month, a baby girl we called Esperanza was born. Immediately, we noticed a difference with her than with other babies. Ezzie was able to move things when she looked at them. This telekinetic ability was new, and we suspected it was a result of blending human DNA with our DNA. Her mom was of mixed race and her dad was immortal."

"Could this be a coincidence?" asked Rick.

"The name?"

"Yeah, isn't the entity here called Esperanza?" asked Rick.

"Yes, but that doesn't mean it's the same individual," I answered.

"Can we ask? That would be cool!"

"Esperanza, do you hear me?" I asked the voice in the room.

"Yes, Lora O'Reilly, I can. What can I do for you?" asked the disembodied voice.

"Esperanza, where did you come from? What are you?"

"I am the echo of a soul who lived long ago."

"Can you tell us which soul?"

"I was considered a wise-woman, and my name was Esperanza."

"Ask her where she lived," suggested Rick.

"Esperanza, do you remember where you came from?" asked Lora.

"I was born on a tropical island with hot breezes and waving palm trees. The island's heart was unquiet, spitting red fire and causing my people to seek refuge on another island. I perished in the flames."

"How did you come to be here?" asked Lora.

"My soul was trapped by a magic-wielder and pressed into service as this entity's host."

"Oh, that's not good," I murmured.

"Esperanza, your people may be the ones we are looking for. A group of immortals who referred to themselves as Group 32. They came to the Caribbean archipelago about three thousand years ago. They settled on the island today known as Cuba, but they left that island about around the time of the conquistadors. Was the magic-wielder one of your descendants?"

"Yes, quite possibly. I had twelve children, both boys and girls. They all had gifts that manifested when they became adults. Their gifts were magical to the humans, but normal to us. Only a descendant would have been able to call my soul."

"Lora, so this Esperanza may be the one who is in my family tree, which sounds like the one who is written about in the journal. This may be a connection."

"I think we need to go back to 3G and get some information and training," I said. "You can come with me this time and meet her."

"Mirror, take me to my great-great-grandmother."

The mirror started swirling as the image in the mirror shifted and it became a portal. Rick behind me gasped as he watched blue skies and forest appear.

"That looks about right," I said. "Okay, love, I'll be back very soon. Just doing a test hop."

I turned away from Rick and stepped through the mirror. Unfortunately, it was not on the ground, but suspended about six feet up, so I had a bit of a fall. Landing on the ground hurt like the dickens, but I didn't think I broke a limb. But it posed a problem for getting back to the portal.

Will it work from down here? I'll look around without moving from this spot.

Turning in a full circle, I scanned the area I had landed in. There was no doubt this was where 3G was. But no one came to greet me this time.

"Mirror, return me to my time."

I watched as a spot about six feet above me opened up as a portal. Rick poked his head out and threw a rope down. I grabbed on quickly, and he pulled me up as fast as he could go. He got me through the portal just as it snapped shut, nearly taking off my foot.

"Oh, that was too close!" I said.

"What did you see?"

"Well, the place looked familiar, but there was no way to tell for sure. I didn't move from my spot because the portal was six feet off the ground. So I need to add that instruction to the request. I was warned the mirror had a nasty sense of humor."

"I saw the portal open but didn't see you. That's why I looked through," said Rick.

"Good thing. Your action to use a rope was a godsend. Thank you. I had no idea how I was going to manage that jump," I said. "I wasn't specific enough."

Reforming my request to be as specific as possible, I again cast the spell that would open a portal to my great-great-grandmother. As soon as the mirror cleared, there she was standing just beyond with a huge smile on her face. She beckoned us to come through.

We both walked through the mirror, and I dropped a scarf I had and put a rock on top of it to mark our return location. I turned and looked around and then at him.

"Innogen, wonderful to see you again!" I gushed as I ran up and hugged her.

"I see you brought me your beau," said Innogen. "My, what a handsome man. Come, children. I have a meal ready for us before we begin."

26—Finding Group 12

—Lora

Rick and I spent what felt like days with Innogen. She put me through all kinds of exercises to open my magic, to get me to feel the energy around me. It was difficult and exhausting. Yet every time I said I was too tired she pushed energy into me and we kept going. She wanted me to have magic like her. I hadn't known it took so much work and practice.

Rick helped by getting me to breathe, centering me, and keeping me relaxed. When I felt my temper rising, he could help me bring it down.

"You two work well together," said Innogen at the end of a particularly difficult session.

"Thank you," said Rick.

At the end of our time together I had mastered—well, maybe not quite mastered—casting and moving, and had learned how to use the energy between Rick and I like a battery for my magic.

"That was some trip!" said Rick, after the meals were placed in front of us. When we got home, we were starved, in spite of being fed by Innogen while we were there.

"It was," I said. "We learned so much from 3G."

"Mmm, this steak is done to perfection!"

"Mine is too, and I love the mashed potatoes. I hadn't realized how hungry I was."

We sat in silence for a few minutes, just enjoying our meals. We had gone to our favorite steakhouse, which was around the corner from the occult store.

"I think 3G's story about Group 12 will help me find them," I said. "I think I remember seeing a volume on it at the back of the store."

"Shall we do that tomorrow? I have to check in on the restaurant, and Justin."

"Of course. After dinner, I want to get home and decompress before the kids come back."

Two days later was the soonest I could get back to the occult store. So I decided to make the trip myself.

Before I took the trip, I wanted to find that volume about Group 12 and do some reading.

"Esperanza, do you know of a book about Group 12?" I asked once I was back at the occult store.

"Ye, Lora O'Reilly, Group 12 was instrumental in creating this place. They were the ones who stored all this information."

"Wait, I thought the occult store was in Montreal?"

"Your entrance to it is. But it lies outside the boundary of space and time, in a magical dimension where all magical beings can access it."

"Can I enter the store in Montreal and exit in Ireland?" I asked.

"Yes."

"Oh! That is very handy," I said. "Okay, show me where the volumes on Group 12 are please."

"Group 12 is this way," said the disembodied voice. "Please follow the light."

I took off after the floating orb as it wound its way around walls, up and down stairs, and through doorways. The orb eventually stopped at a large open room lined with shelves.

"The original Group 12 split into two," explained Esperanza. "One group became significantly diluted by human DNA. They embraced the magical offspring of immortals, letting the others go their own way. Today, that group is a hybrid group of humans and immortals of over fifty people. The others remain isolated like the other immortals."

"So the group I need to make contact with is in the coven. Where are they located?"

"I believe they live in a castle, south of Dublin."

I walked around the library and picked up one text after another on *The Collected Magical Knowledge of the Goddess*. The group believed in the combined power of thirteen individuals, through ritual and physical expression.

"What does that mean?" I asked out loud.

"What do you mean, Lora O'Reilly?" asked the voice.

"The combined power of thirteen individuals through ritual and physical expression," I said.

"They believe that having coitus as a group increases their power."

"So they believed that getting thirteen people having sex together would raise their magical ability?" I asked.

"Yes."

Huh. Well, we certainly did feel a sense of power when we were all together. I'll have to test that theory. Perhaps just the two of us will make a difference.

Reading some more, I discovered that they had settled near a town called Marlowe. They had built a castle there and surrounded it with lots of heavily forested land so that it was difficult to find. The castle had its own food sources and water.

"Okay, Esperanza, I'm leaving for a while." Once outside, I went to an internet café and looked up Marlowe Castle. There was nothing. Looking up Marlowe just as a town also got nothing.

How am I going to find them? I looked for ancient maps of Ireland that might still have old names on it.

I'm going to have to go to a regular library.

Leaving the internet café, I took a trip out to Park and visited the Mordecai-Richler Library to see if I could see some ancient maps of Ireland. After searching several hours through their very extensive collection, I had to give up.

"I'll have to take a different direction," I said out loud. "Perhaps 3G can help me pinpoint where they went." Returning to the occult store, I went back to the time bridge mirror and stepped through for my 3G.

"Lora, you have returned," said Innogen. "It's nice to see you, granddaughter."

"3G, were you expecting me?"

"Yes," said Innogen. "I knew you would need some information from me. Are you going to try to save the witches?"

"Yes, I want to try. I've learned some interesting things."

"Like what?"

"Well, for example, the witches, the ones who performed the ritual that backfired and sucked us all into the other dimension, were offspring of immortal/human couplings. They currently form a coven in Ireland somewhere."

"Good. What else have you learned?" asked Innogen.

"Because they are immortal, they use sexual rituals to gather their power."

"Yes, that is correct. The immortals have an innate ability to create life and other things when tapping into that most sacred of powers—the expression of true love. It's the deepest connection humans or immortals alike have at our disposal. Our problem is that they do not have true love in their circle, so they can only tap into sexual energy. And that's not strong enough."

"How did they create enough power the first time?" I asked.

"They didn't. That's why it failed and backfired on them."

"Can you help me find them in Ireland?" I asked.

"I believe I can. Watch this scrying spell. You can perform it in your time."

I paid close attention to the patterns Innogen drew and the materials she used to prepare herself for the spell. I listened very carefully to the incantation to memorize it—repeating the words in my head over and over again until I felt I would remember.

"Now, when you do this, you need a grade-four hickory wand. Do you have one?" asked Innogen.

"No, I don't."

"Here, then, take mine. Stow it inside your clothes. It should make it back."

"Thank you, 3G. I will be back."

"Oh, I know. You will need my help to cast the spell to bring them back."

I looked at my 3G and wondered at that statement as I asked the mirror to bring me back.

As soon as the occult store materialized in front of me, I went looking for the materials I would need and a piece of paper to inscribe the spell on so I could put it in my grimoire. I also purchased an additional wand. You can't have too many of those.

"Esperanza, is there a room where I can cast a scrying spell?" I asked, after my purchases were finished.

"Yes, Lora, follow me." Again, a glowing orb of light appeared and floated away from me. I had to walk quickly to keep up this time as it led me into a quiet area of the store away from the items to purchase. There, I found a small room with a table and candleholders ready.

Thanking the disembodied voice, I closed the door and set up the scrying spell as my 3G had done. Pulling out the sheet of paper, I carefully cast the incantation over the bowl and placed the herbs and wood in the bowl. Pouring a few drops of paraffin in the bowl over the herbs, I took the candles and lit them. They created a dancing flame of orange and blue as the materials were incinerated.

In the smoke, an image appeared. It was a ruined castle with wild bushes growing inside the structure.

I directed the image so I could look around. Off to the left of the old castle was a low, wide building, similar to a barn, built into the side of a hill. There was a well-worn path that went from the doors of the building up to the castle.

"Where is this?" I asked out loud.

"The castle of Carlow," said the disembodied voice.

"Are you sure?"

"Yes. I grew up close to there."

I dissipated the spell and packed up the materials I had purchased and put them in my backpack.

"Esperanza, thank you for your help. I can leave now. I've got what I need."

"Good-bye, Lora O'Reilly," said the disembodied voice.

And I was outside.

Pulling out my phone, I called Rick.

"Rick, I've found them!" I said excitedly as soon as he picked up the phone.

"Wonderful, what's next?"

"I'm coming home, then we can discuss this with the group."

When I got home, it was close to dinner. The kids were fed and they were helping Anita with cleaning up the kitchen.

"Wow," I said. "What did you say to get them to help?"

"I told them that if they wanted tacos tomorrow, they had to clean the kitchen tonight," smiled Anita.

"You're a natural parent," I said. "Good work. And thank you for feeding them."

"No problem. I made dinner for everyone."

I spoke to each of my kids, hugged them and thanked them for helping out. I then returned to the kitchen, where Anita had a bottle of wine open for us, and a meal on the table.

"So what did you find?" asked Rick once we were sitting.

"I found the current coven's location—they're living at a place called Carlow Castle. It's a ruin though, and there's a large flat structure nearby that seems to be part of the picture too. I also learned from 3G that the coven has been trying for a while to free the witches, and the reason they fail is because there is not enough power in the coven."

"How is that possible?" asked Rick. "Don't they have a lot of members?"

"Yes, in fact they have fifty. But that is not the reason they don't have enough power. They cannot tap into the same power we can."

"What power is that?" he asked.

"True love. Our true love connection allows us to touch a greater power and summon it. When we were on the yacht, that power that happened was because of all of our connections to each other. We can tap into a deep well of magic through our connection."

"Our sex drives the power?"

"Yes, but not just sex: sex between mated souls," I said. "It's why the immortals are so promiscuous. They are generating and using the power to create life and things."

"Wow. Okay, what's next, then?"

"I want to experiment with you and me first, to see if I can accomplish something that normally I wouldn't be able to do. I need to see if we can perform a ritual in under one hour."

"You mean one hour to have mind-blowing sex, perform a ritual, and get out?" he asked.

"Yes, that."

"No pressure."

"None at all," I grinned.

After the kids were well asleep, we set up the living room for a ritual. We moved the furniture, brought in pillows, and lit candles and incense.

I was sitting in a lotus position, chanting as the smoke from the incense was twirling in vertical columns, practicing what Innogen had taught me. The air was charged with magic, and it felt electric in the room. Rick joined me on the floor in a lotus position, hands, palms up on his knees. I opened my eyes when I felt his presence.

"Lora, your eyes are now glowing green!" cried Rick. He watched as green swirls of power wove around my body, and when I lifted my hand the tendrils of green wove through my fingers.

"That is the color of my magical energy."

"What do you need me to do?" asked Rick.

"Make love to me. I will channel it."

He reached out, taking hold of me gently as if I was a treasure. Opening up my flower and gently stroking me, he took my nipple in his mouth. Bringing my arousal up, I took hold of him with my hands. We melted into each other, and as our arousal grew our pheromones were released, increasing each other's libido. Like swirling smoke, our heartbeats slowed and synchronized as our bodies got deeper into each other's arousal.

Rick looked around and saw bands of gold swirls weaving around us, intertwining with my green magic, which had become amplified. It now suffused the gold and included both of us. He reached for me again, to continue our journey to climax.

As we got closer to release, the level of hormones transported us to a different plane, where there was only the deepest of connections. The bands of our power had grown and mixed purple, gold, and green.

When I felt the release was imminent, I broke from my partner and whispered my incantation, pulling all the energy into my body. The power swirled closer and closer to me, wrapping itself on my skin. I felt our climax begin, released my incantation, and an explosion of power reverberated through the room and the house, making everything shake and rattle. As we gasped out our releases and the final shudders took our bodies, we sprawled on the floor in a heap.

"Oh my God, there's a unicorn in the room!" cried Rick.

My eyes sprung open to behold the most magnificent creature standing calmly in the center of the room, looking a little displeased with how messy it was.

"Benevolent unicorn, I welcome you," I said, bowing from my spot on the floor.

"Why have you summoned me?" spoke the unicorn.

"To see if I could bring one of the most treasured and powerful beings here," I said. "It was a test of sorts before we try to rescue the witches from the far dimension."

"Ah, I see. Well, you have succeeded. Well done. You have the right power," said the unicorn, looking at us. Then he/she touched both of us on the forehead with his/her horn. We felt the zing of magic he/she bestowed on us.

"I have given each of you a kernel that you may use in case you get into a tight space. Immortals rarely need our help, but just in case, you have it. I shall leave now. Good luck, Lora O'Reilly, in your endeavor." Then the unicorn blinked out of sight.

"That just happened?" asked Rick. "Did we just see and speak to a unicorn?"

"Yup, that was so cool!" I said.

I looked at the clock. It said 2:35 a.m. Not fast enough! "Well, we've proven that our lovemaking enhances the magic. But we need to do it in less than an hour. Did you feel our heartbeats synchronize?" I asked.

"Yes."

"When that happens, we need to go through the time portal. Do you think we can do that?"

"Let's try," said Rick.

"Okay, this time, when our hearts synchronize, I want to get up and walk into the kitchen and back and see if we can continue."

"Let's try." I looked at the clock: 2:45 a.m. I started meditating again to bring my magic up. This time, because we were already flooded with adrenaline and pheromones, our arousal was faster. As our hearts synchronized, I peeked at the magic, and it was just as big as the first time. When I felt the time was right, I stood with Rick, and held hands to maintain contact while we shadow-walked the short distance to the kitchen and back.

We fell back into our climax, building higher than before. I pulled in the power until it was wrapped around me, and released my spell as we experienced orgasm together, biting each other.

Neither of us blacked out, so our eyes were open fully as the incantation happened and a brilliant white bird appeared in the middle of the room. I looked at the clock: 3:15 a.m. Much better!

"We did it!" I cried in happiness. "We did that in thirty minutes."

"What was that bird that appeared?"

"That was a fire-bird. Mythical to humans, but real to us."

"So am I to believe we need a pre-magic fuck first, then do magic?" asked Rick.

"So it would seem," I said. "Want another rehearsal?"

"Not tonight!"

"Just as well, I'm tired with all the casting." I stood up and took Rick's hand and led him upstairs to our room.

"That was fascinating tonight," said Rick. He was holding me up against his body as we lay on the bed, my head was resting on his bicep.

"It was," I said, as I drifted off to sleep.

27—Off to Ireland

—Lora

Before we made travel plans to leave for Ireland, I wanted to go back in time once more to Esperanza, to confirm the data we were going to provide.

I set off for the occult store once more with my grimoire that had the family tree in the back. Once I crossed time, I quickly walked to the village and asked for Esperanza.

"Lora, you're back," she said. "Excellent! We have that information for you. We found Aedanmar in our records as a child of an immortal named Esperanza and a human. She moved to Group 12 after some sort of split with Group 32. Twelve settled in the British Isles. That group recorded a split as well and some left. We do not know if Aedanmar went or stayed, though Esperanza stayed with my group. She shows up in Ireland in 1207 your time."

I flipped open my grimoire to the family tree page. I was now able to put a date next to my ancestor's name. She had a birth date. And she had a location.

"Thank you, Esperanza, for all your help." I was escorted out of the village to the spot where I returned. The villagers were wide-eyed when they witnessed me pop out of thin air, but they were likely more disturbed when I disappeared into thin air. Oh well! Rick had booked flights for us that evening to Dublin. Mama was in town now, so she was going to take care of the children. There was only one week before we were moving into the new house, so everything was chaotic. Rick wasn't sure this was the best time to go on a trip, but I was very keen. At least, we would be returning to the new house.

Anita had been left in charge with money and cheques to pay the movers, and to hire whoever she needed to help with setting up the house. Rick knew that he could trust me to get everything done.

All we had to do was go to Ireland, locate a coven, and find my mother. It was exciting to think that we might come into contact with my ancestors soon.

The flight was uneventful, which was good, seeing as it went over water the whole way. Landing in Dublin, we saw how flat and green Ireland is. Once we picked up our car and got on the highway, everything was so green!

I felt like I had come home. I was just a young girl when I moved away, but Ireland was in my blood. It was difficult getting used to driving on the left side of the road. I was not used to seeing traffic coming toward us on the other side, and traffic roundabouts were nuts.

Coming into the area of the castle, we were surprised to see a small city around it. In fact, houses and businesses were built right up against the castle walls.

This didn't match my scrying image. But at least the castle matched the image I was given.

We located an inn called the Seven Oaks Inn just a little north of the castle. It was a nice, small place with clean rooms and a good price. Most importantly, the hotel was in the middle of the city and it was easy to explore. It's not as if we would have posted an advertisement for locating a coven. We would need to ask around discreetly.

Checked into our hotel room, we unpacked.

"Hon, how are we going to find this group?" asked Rick.

"I'm not sure," I said. "What about hanging out in some pubs and asking the people who live around here?"

"Asking about what? Witches, Covens?"

"Perhaps just about my roots. If I pose as a Canadian who's looking for my ancestors, maybe that will let us ask lots of questions."

"Let's try. Are you hungry?"

"Yes, let's go for a walk and find a pub," I said.

Stopping at the concierge desk, we asked about local pubs that served dinner and were given several names. They were all within walking distance, so we could leave the car at the hotel.

The first pub was The Irishman. We went in and sat at the bar. Rick ordered a couple of pints and some food for the two of us. We sat and ate companionably chatting about what we had seen so far.

"So, where are ye from?" asked the barkeep.

"Canada," I said. "I'm here looking for my familial roots."

"So ye're from Carlow?" he said. "T'is ah close-knit village. So we should be able t' help you."

"That would be great!" I said. "I have a little bit of information. My family name is O'Reilly, and I have the name of an ancestor Aedanmar. She was a maternal ancestor."

"Aedanmar, t'is an unusual name, and should be good t' find. We Irish like t' use historical names and repeat them every other generation. If ye can find a current one, chances are they could be related."

"A good tip, thanks," I said.

"Excuse me, I overheard you were looking for your family?" asked a woman behind us.

Turning around, I saw a woman dressed in a long robe.

"Yes, I am."

"Maybe I can help," said the old woman.

"Oh, go on with you, Nelly. She don' be wantin' yur magic notions. The girl just landed and she'll be wantin' information," said the barkeep, shooing the woman away.

"Oh, that's alright," I said. "I'll take any help I can get. I have no idea where to start."

"Come with me, then, missy," said the woman, walking toward the door.

"Barkeep, please keep our seats, we'll be right back," said Rick.

"No problem," he answered. "Just don' promise anyt'ing or give over any money."

Rick nodded and followed me out the door. Once outside, the old woman walked across the street to a shuttered storefront and went inside.

It was dark when we walked in, and our eyes automatically adapted. Being immortal, that meant they started to glow.

When the old woman turned back toward us, she gasped as she noticed our eyes.

"I knew it!" she cried. "Yer immortals, aren't ya?"

I decided to play dumb first. "What do you mean … immortals?"

"Well, look at yer eyes, they're all aglow," said the old woman. "I knows the immortals have glowy eyes."

"What do you want, really?" asked Rick.

"You were looking for yer family. I sensed you were immortal, so I can help you," said the woman.

"How?" asked Rick.

"'Cause my mam knew yous, God rest her soul," said the woman. "They hid us from the others."

"What others?" I asked.

"The others, the ones who practice witchcraft, the ones who follow the old religion."

"Who are they?" I asked, getting a little excited at our quick good luck.

"They are the…" the old woman started, then looking around furtively, dropped her voice to a whisper: "…the coven."

"Like a coven of witches?" asked Rick.

"Shhhh! Be quiet, else you'll bring them down on you!" screeched the woman.

"Are they bad people?" I asked.

"They're dangerous people."

"Dangerous how?" *This is like pulling teeth!*

"They can curse you, do'cha know?" said the old woman, her accent getting thicker.

"Where can we find these groups of people?" asked Rick, wanting to cut to the chase.

"I can take ye t'em immortals for ah quid," said the woman.

"Ah, no. I'll give yu no money. If you don't want to tell us, we can find it ourselves, thank you," said Rick.

"Wait, don't you take Euros here?" I asked.

"Yes, ta's what I mean'."

"Okay, Lora, I think we should go back to our supper." Rick looked at me meaningfully.

"Come on, I'm still hungry." We moved to leave. I had the door open already and one foot out of the door.

"Wait! Okay, I'll take you there without a payment. If you are pleased with what I show you, perhaps you'll give an old woman a donation?" Her accent suddenly cleared up.

I stopped mid-stride. "Deal," I said. "Let's go now."

"Let me go pay the barkeep, first," said Rick. "Don't go anywhere until I'm back."

I watched as Rick ran across the street to pay the barkeep. But once he was gone, the crone locked the door and took my hand, and we escaped through a hatch in the back of the room.

I was returned by the crone the next morning to see Rick lying on the ground in the back of the building. Clearly, he had planned on waiting until we returned. Kneeling down beside him, I gently shook his shoulder.

"Rick, wake up!" I said. "Rick, wake up!"

Rick opened his eyes and squinted because of the sunshine. He looked up into my face and gasped in relief. He jumped up and grabbed me in a huge hug.

"Where did you go last night? I looked everywhere!"

"I know, I'm sorry about that. As soon as you left, she pulled my hand and we walked through some sort of portal and ended up in a different place entirely. I now believe she was a witch too."

"Did you meet the immortals? Did you get to see anyone?" he asked. "Here, let's walk back to the hotel and you can tell me everything over breakfast. I am starving."

"So am I." We walked arm in arm back to our hotel, and dropped the food bag in the room and went to breakfast in the restaurant. We ordered two large Irish breakfasts, and a pot of coffee.

"So what happened on this end?" I asked him.

"I left you to go across to the pub to pay. He gave me a bag of food as take out. But when I came back across the street, the door was locked and I could not see you anywhere. I banged on the door and peered through the glass.

"I screamed your name but nothing happened, I heard no one. It was unnerving. I walked back and forth across the front of the store and discovered a narrow alley, not much wider than my shoulders. I squeezed down the alley and came around the back of the building. I saw a light on the second floor, it was flickering like candlelight. So I cupped my hands around my mouth and screamed your name again.

"I saw the candle go out, and a window opened. "Shush yur noise out there!" said a craggy old man. When I told him I was looking for my wife and that you had gone into your store and disappeared, he said, "Nonsense, no one has come into our store. Now away wit' ya."

"I peered into the back property and didn't find anything that would give a clue to your whereabouts. So I squeezed through the alley again and sat on the walk by the front door, determined to wait for you."

When the food arrived, we dug in and sat and ate for most of the meal. It wasn't until I had finished my plate and on my third cup of coffee that I started to tell my side of the tale.

"As I said, she just grabbed my hand and pulled me. I sensed the portal we went through because it was like the time bridge we use at home. Perhaps the store she took us to was an occult store," I said. "Once the haziness cleared, we were in a clearing in open countryside, there was a stream close by. I could hear the water running.

"There were several large buildings that were flat and one large house—more like a manor really—in the center. I heard a dog barking in the distance. When I spun around, the old woman was gone. So she must have returned immediately. I marked the ground with a piece of tissue I found in my pocket wrapped it around a stone. I figured I would have to get back there to return just like the mirror.

"I started walking toward the manor house, not making a secret that I was there—I spoke out loud to make sure people would hear me. Before I got to the door, it opened and someone was standing in the doorway. They challenged me by asking me how I got there. I told them I was brought here through a portal by an old woman who had since disappeared. The person laughed at that, saying she really was a scared rabbit. They then asked me who I was and where I came from. So I told them. They listened for a moment, then closed the door.

"I stood there waiting in case they would come back, but they didn't. When I started to see light in the sky, I knew I had been there too long, so I started back to my tissue, which took a while to find, and then to return here. I materialized inside the shop again, startling the owner, I imagine. He let me out, and that's when I found you."

"Wow, that's quite a story," said Rick. "So who do you think it was? People like us or the other group?"

"I think it was the other group. Seeing as I want to talk to both groups, I don't care who I find first," I said. "One interesting thing: where I ended up matched the image I was given by the scrying."

"That's good. The connection between the castle and the building is now made. We get back and forth with a portal. That's why the castle can be in the middle of the city," said Rick. "We should go walk the grounds of the castle."

We finished up our breakfast and set off for the castle, which was only a few blocks away. When we got close, we could see the tips of the towers that remained above the buildings that lined the street. It was spooky, because the ruins were really just that: a ruined building. A plaque outside the castle told the story:

In the 1800s, a mad doctor wanted to turn the castle into an insane asylum. He decided he wanted to 'redecorate' the interior of the castle, so he placed explosives under the foundation of some of the walls. The explosion undermined the foundations so much that all the walls collapsed except the one between the two remaining towers.

The jagged scars on the walls left from the walls being destroyed were visible today.

When we walked up to the building, we discovered the outline of the castle's walls still in the ground. There were at least two more turrets outlined, and there was what looked like the bottom of a grand circular staircase in the middle. It went down into the ground like black, open jaws. We also found doorways in the remaining wall, and turrets that were padlocked with gates, probably to keep people from destroying what was left of the poor castle. The outer walls surrounding the keep were still intact, and they outlined a garden that someone had planted on the grounds. We found all kinds of nooks and crannies that went into the keep's basement that were barred from exploration. Again, probably for safety reasons. But it left one wondering what was there.

We took lots and lots of photos of everything we found, from as many angles as we could. When we got back to our room, we displayed the photos on the laptop screen so we could blow them up.

"Look at this. The top of this tower is intact, and I remember seeing a gate at the bottom of it."

"Look at this one, the gate was open. I didn't notice that while we were there."

"There are lots of places to explore here. It's just a matter of getting access without people noticing," I said. "I suggest we go back tonight."

"I want to see where that doorway goes, and what is down those stairs in the middle of the castle. We may need some equipment though. Did you notice parking around the castle?"

"I saw cars parked along the street in front of it."

"Good! Then we can load our car and use it to carry everything," said Rick.

"What do you think we should take?"

"Ropes, lights, lock picks, helmets, walkies, cameras—off the top of my head."

"Well, we better find a hardware store, then!" I said. "I'll look for that."

It took us a couple of hours to collect all the things we would need. Some of the salespeople looked strangely at our purchases, and we used "spelunking" as the reason. We didn't find lock picks, of course, so we purchased some fine tools that would do the same thing.

We returned to the same pub for supper. The barkeep recognized us and came right over.

"Good evening, folks. What can I get you?"

"We'll have the same thing. It was so good yesterday," answered Rick.

The barkeep poured off two pints and slid them down the bar for us to catch, and put in the order for food to the kitchen. He then came back with some pretzels to munch on in the meantime.

"You never returned last night. I hope that old woman didn't cause you trouble," said the barkeep.

"Nah, no trouble, but she did have a lead for us to follow tomorrow," said Rick.

"Any little bit of information helps," I said.

"Well, I was asking some of my patrons for ya, and one of us heard of a woman named Aedanmar that used to live around these parts. But he hadn't seen or heard of her for a decade or more."

"Oh, that's interesting. Will that gentleman be in tonight?" I asked.

"I expect so, he's a regular here. Oh look, there he is now. Come here, Robert."

"Was someone calling me a gentleman? I'll have you know I won't be insulted that way!" he said with a twinkle in his eye. "Hi there, I'm Robert O'Shaunnesy. Pleased to make yur acquaintance."

"Hullo, I'm Lora O'Reilly, and this is my husband, Rick Benal," I said. "Very pleased to meet you too."

"A Robertson, aye? There were lots of us in these parts, but they've disappeared now," said Robert. "The name you had was Aedanmar, no?"

"Wait a minute, why did you say Robertson?" I asked.

"Well, 'cause you look like one," said Robert. "You said yur name is O'Reilly? I'll bet anyt'ing yur granmam was a Robertson."

"Yes, she was—but it was my 3G."

"3G you say? As in great-great-grandmother?"

"Aye."

"Well, then, Aedanmar was a Robertson you see."

"She was the first name of the first ancestor I had in my family tree. We knew our ancestral female, just not who she was," I said.

"Do you have any dates?" Asked Robert.

"Not precise ones yet," I said. "It's why it's been so difficult to find anything."

"Well, I don't know if my information is going to help you much. But there was an old wise woman around these here parts. She died a few years back in an old folks home. T' nursing staff may remember her and know who her family was. Her name was Aedanmar you see. She was very old, perhaps 120 years when she finally succumbed to death. She spit in its eye, I tell ya. My mam and granmam often went to her for advice and treatments. She was trusted with many things that we didn't trust doctors for. We Irish are a picky bunch."

"Do you remember where your mam went to see her?" I asked.

"Oh yes. T'was a very old manor outside o' town. My family had held t' property for hundreds o' years, perhaps more, and t' place was a huge sprawling place with lots o' buildings. She saw my customers in a small building closer to t' road."

"You don't happen to remember the street or address, would you?" asked Rick.

"Hmm, let me think a minute. I was small back then, but hmm … it was on Ballincarrig. That was it. Ballincarrig. Outside of town. No, I don'remember t' number."

"What was the name of the seniors' home?" I asked.

"Hillview House," said Robert. "It's down t'ward t' south side of the town."

"Many thanks, Robert. You have been very helpful," I said. "Can we buy you a pint to show our appreciation?"

"That would be grand, thank ye."

Rick and I spent the rest of the evening laughing with the locals at the pub and getting to know the history of the area, which was quite storied. We talked at length about the mad doctor who destroyed the castle and why. Many of the locals had side stories which added even more color to the main story.

28—Tunnel Spelunking

—Lora

It was about 10:30 when I decided we should get going and scope out the castle. So, saying our goodbyes, we left the pub and walked to the car.

The short drive to the castle only took a few minutes and we were rewarded with an open parking spot close by. But the castle was lit up at night with spotlights: That was unfortunate. However, there were no visitors on the property.

"Why don't I walk up the road, casually, while you stay here and see if I'm visible from the street?" I said. "We may get away with being up there."

"That's a good idea. I'll stay in the car so I'm not obvious," said Rick. "After all, that's what would most likely happen—someone spotting us from their car."

I got out of the car and casually walked to the castle side, where I reached the staircase. I stopped to "retie" my shoelaces, while looking around for people. With the coast clear, I ran up the steps and walked into the center of the clearing. Rick watched as my head bobbed past the vegetation of the garden and then disappeared.

"Lora, are you in? Over," said Rick through his handheld radio.

"Yes?"

"Wherever you are I cannot see your head," said Rick.

"Good, I'm walking around the garden. It is sunken down a couple of steps from the top of the stairs."

"There is still no one on the street," said Rick.

"Good, I'll come back and we can get our packs."

I reappeared a few minutes later, jogging down the stairs. I made a point of continuing along the same sidewalk down to the corner, crossing the street to return to the car. If someone had been watching, it would have looked like I was just jogging. Except for the shoes.

I reached the car, stopped, and got in.

"Well done," said Rick.

"I kind of like this espionage business," I said. "It's fun!"

"Don't say that until we have finished! You'll jinx us," said Rick.

"Oh, don't tell me you're superstitious!"

"No, not really," he said with a grin. "It just seemed like the thing to say."

Grabbing our packs, we got out of the car and retraced my steps to the castle. Once we were on the garden level, Rick crouched because he was so much taller than me.

"Where shall we go first?" asked Rick.

"I vote for the center staircase here at the circular opening," I suggested.

I walked over toward the circular opening and looked over the barrier in front of the steps. There wasn't much light because the gardens were not lit.

Shining my flashlight down the stairs, I couldn't see any obstruction on the stairs, and they looked pretty stable. So I stepped over the barrier and started down the circular stairway.

As soon as Rick determined we were sufficiently below ground level, he straightened up. He too had pulled out his flashlight and was scanning around us as we descended.

The stairway went a long distance into the ground, much more than a single story would go. The room we found ourselves in at the bottom was vast. It clearly reached beyond the castle walls that were visible above ground, perhaps even under the roads. There were huge stone columns evenly spaced, holding up the ceiling. There was a musty, earthen smell in the air, telling you clearly you were underground. Some of the stone walls had moisture dripping down, likely from openings in the ground. There was no light whatsoever. So Rick and I donned our hard hats with headlamps in order to explore hands free.

As we walked around, we found rock falls and small piles of debris. Clearly, this huge room had been cleaned up after the explosion. We discovered several side rooms that were blocked off with thick wooden doors. The doors had huge steel or iron hinges, perhaps made in the 1800s. We also found what looked like a hallway on this level—but we couldn't reach it, due to a large fissure in the floor.

Returning to the staircase, we continued down to another level. From the top, we couldn't see how far down it was, but if it was the same distance as the other space, it was another twelve or so feet.

"Which way, boss?" asked Rick when we reached the bottom.

I looked around. "This level isn't as big as the previous one," I said.

"No, it seems much smaller. It's just as tall, but there isn't as much floor space down here."

"Let's go that way," I said. "I think that is toward the back of the castle, and it looks like there is some sort of hallway there."

"Lead on, Macduff!" he answered.

Carefully picking our way around debris, we walked around the staircase and toward the dark opening in the back. Our lights barely illuminated twenty feet in front of us, the darkness was so complete. However, it did bounce off the walls of stone, showing us that the darkness was indeed a hall of some kind.

"Ha! There is a corridor here. It's very narrow. What do you think?" I asked.

"Let's follow it and see where it goes," said Rick.

"I'll follow you."

"Aren't you going to go first to protect me?" he asked.

"Yeah, right," I laughed.

I started down the corridor. There were alcoves along the side—for candles or torches, perhaps? Apparently so: About a hundred meters in, we found one with a torch in it still.

Rick pulled out some matches and tried to light the torch. Amazingly, it worked. A strong flame erupted, spilling more light into the corridor. Now we could see it was curved as well as downward sloping. The stone was beautifully laid, with an arched roof with hardly any cracks, and all the pieces were perfectly cut. It was masterful work.

"Wow, look at the stonework!" said Rick. "This is a mason's wet dream."

"It's always interesting to find work done by so-called unskilled primitives that rivals or is better than the work done by modern man," I said.

"Indeed. There were many people whose skills were much more advanced centuries ago than today. Those skills have been lost."

"Let's keep going," I said, moving forward.

The corridor continued on a downward slope, albeit gentle. But it changed direction a few times, curving the opposite way first, then back on itself. The slope was so slight that you barely noticed you were going down. Yet, while the sound of our footsteps didn't change, the sense of us changed subtly. The sound of our walking seemed more muffled and deeper in tenor. I had the feeling we were quite deep in the ground.

We came to an arched end of the corridor. There was another torch in an alcove on the wall, and that too worked when we lit it. Light from its flame illuminated the end wall and revealed a great door carved into it.

There were all kinds of runes and words in an unknown language carved into the door. But the door wouldn't budge at all, ending our exploration to this point. I got out my camera and started taking closeup pictures of the door with its runes and writing in detail.

"This is as far as we can go here. Shall we go back and find another passageway?" asked Rick.

"Yup. Should we leave the torch lit?"

"If we do, and people are actually using this corridor for something, then they'll know someone else was down here. That may or may not be a problem."

"Well, let's extinguish it, then. We have flashlights, and if they go out, I can create light."

Backtracking our steps, we found another arched doorway. This time the door had been left open. There was another torch on the wall too. We lit that one and brought it with us through the doorway. Again the corridor slanted down, but steeper this time. We had walked about five meters when we came to a set of stairs.

"Do we continue?" I asked.

"I can't see the bottom. Let me go down and call back up."

I waited for Rick. I turned off my flashlight to conserve batteries, and my eyes naturally adjusted.

Oh, I'd forgotten about that!"

Suddenly, I could see detail in the darkness. There were runes and writing all over the tunnel. The runes were glowing with some substance. Clearly, these were made by supernatural beings, maybe even immortals. I hadn't seen them in the torch light.

"Rick!" I stage-whispered into the dark. "Can you hear me?"

"Yes, clearly," came the answer. "What's up?"

"Turn off the flashlight and look at the stones!"

I heard the click as he turned off the light, then a gasp as he saw the rune covered walls of the tunnel.

"Wow, that is a lot of writing," he said. "Can you read any of it?"

"No, not really," I said. "But I'm going to see if I can take some photos and we can look it up in my grimoire."

"Did you bring it with you?"

"Yes, it's on my phone."

"Clever woman," said Rick. "I'm at the bottom now. I seem to have descended about fifty steps. It's very damp down here. Water is dripping from the ceiling and down the walls. If I were to guess, I think this tunnel goes under water."

"How far do you think we have walked from the castle?" I asked as I heard his footsteps echoing back up the stairs.

"I'd say close to a hundred meters. It's very difficult to judge distance underground. You kind of have to tell from the time you've walked," said Rick. He had arrived back where I was waiting. "Do you want to continue?"

"Did we bring GPS devices with us?" I asked as I was feeling around the walls at the top of the stairs. "Oh! I found something."

Rick came over and looked at what I found. "It looks like a handle cut into the rock. Let's pull on it and see if it opens."

As he pulled, I watched to see what would happen. Slowly, a crack appeared in the rock wall in the shape of a rounded door. When Rick had opened it wide enough to go through, we discovered another flight of stairs, going up this time.

"Let's follow them, shall we?" I asked. So we did. The flight went up at least fifteen feet to a grate. We could tell we were at the surface, and we heard running water nearby.

"We can use the GPS now," said Rick. He took off his pack and pulled out the map of Carlow and the GPS, then proceeded to get a reading on our location.

"We're at 52.835755, -6.935401, says the device," I said, reading it off the screen.

"Well, then that puts us around here, give or take a few feet," said Rick pointing to a spot on the map next to a small river.

"So maybe the tunnel goes under that river?" I asked.

"Let's find out," said Rick. Picking up his pack again, he rolled up the map but kept it handy. He would now track our progress on the map. I kept the GPS handy as well, in case there were other stairs going to the surface. Down we went back to the stairs in the tunnel.

The tunnel was indeed wet, but not flooded. There were puddles on the floor and water running down the sides in places, but it didn't look like it was in any danger of collapsing. So we kept exploring, and ten minutes later we came to another dead end with a doorway.

"Another of these doors again, with runes. I don't think we'll get past it," I said.

"Wait, I think I can read these runes, sort of. They resemble something from a memory."

"Interesting. You want to take a crack at it?" I asked.

"I think it's the immortal language," said Rick. "Not that I know it or anything, but it's vaguely familiar."

"Look, there is a hand impression here on the door," I said. "I wonder if that is a scanner, like we have to scan fingerprints?"

I placed my hand on the handprint of the door. The door's runes started to warm, then glow yellow. The glow spread from rune to rune until the door was completely glowing, then it sprung open, swinging away from me.

"Oh my! I didn't expect that," I exclaimed. I looked at my hand and saw an imprint of the handprint design on my palm. "Huh, look at this, Rick."

I showed him my hand and he looked at the door. "It has marked you," he said. "Shhh, I hear voices."

The two of us turned off our lights quickly and moved off to the side to wait for whoever was coming. There was nowhere for us to hide.

29—Finding a Coven

—Lora

"Who goes there?" came a muffled voice from the other side of the door. "Name yourself or suffer the wrath of this coven!"

"Hello! My name is Lora, Lora O'Reilly," I said. "I come with my mate, and we come in peace. I'm looking for my family."

From the gloom, six women appeared, wearing dark green cloaks with the hoods up. Their eyes were glowing green like emeralds, and their hands were extended with green lightning flicking between their fingers. We stood and stared at each other. Were these women members of the coven I was looking for?

We all stood there for what felt like an eternity. The women were staring at me and Rick, and we stared back. Neither Rick nor I showed any fear, which intrigued them immensely.

"How did you get here?" asked one of the women.

"We followed clues that led us to Carlow Castle," said Rick. "We started to explore the castle this evening and found the tunnels. We followed them here."

"How did you open our perimeter door? It is warded against intruders," asked another of the women.

"I don't know," I answered. "First, I have to ask: are you women members of the Carlow Coven?"

"Yes, we are. Why do you seek us?"

"First, the answer to your previous question is, I noticed a handprint depression on the door, and for some reason I was compelled to put my own hand on it. The hand started to get warm, then the door's runes filled with light and the door opened. A few seconds later, we heard you coming."

"The door opened for you?" asked yet another woman, now confirmed as a witch. "That is highly unusual."

"I believe I may be related to you or someone in your coven. My ancestor's name was Aedanmar. It was written in my grimoire by my great-great-grandmother."

"Grimoire? You're a witch?" asked the first witch.

"Yes. Born so."

"And your mate, is he a witch too?"

"No, my mate is immortal, as am I."

"Immortal?" said the first witch. "There are no immortals left in this world."

"Yes, there are," said Rick. At that point, Rick must have generated aggression in himself by thinking of someone he wanted to kill, because his fangs elongated quickly and his eyes glowed red. "We exist, we are just in hiding."

All the witches took a step back from Rick, except for the first one who spoke. She remained fixed in my place in front of us.

"I do not scare easily, mate of Lora O'Reilly. You can pull all your power around you, but my sisters and I can overpower you easily."

"Whoa, whoa, whoa! Everyone take a beat!" I cried, holding my arms out to everyone. "This is not a competition to see who has more power. My mate was simply providing proof of his claim."

The tension dropped noticeably as everyone's energy lessened.

"That's better. Is there somewhere we can go to speak?" I asked. "Or should we return tomorrow?"

The first witch glanced at her sisters. "You can return tomorrow, we will have a proper welcome for you," she said. "My name is Amarlyis. I am related to Aedanmar."

"Oh! Wonderful to meet you, Amarlyis," I said.

"What time would you like us here?" asked Rick.

"Come for noon," said Amarlyis. The witches retreated back into the gloom and the door closed behind them.

"Well, that was abrupt," said Rick. "I guess there's nothing left to do here. Funny, they don't look like witches. Let's go back to our room. We now know where this leads, and that it won't take very long with immortal abilities to navigate. We can chart it on the map."

"And what do witches look like?" I asked.

"You know, gnarly and bent with craggy hands and long noses that have warts," he said jokingly.

"Oh really?" I asked. "Is that what you think I am? Craggy?"

"Not at all," Rick said quickly, realizing his danger at that moment. "You're gorgeous, and don't look like a witch at all! Oh my, I stepped in it, didn't I?"

"Yup."

"You know what I mean, they were all remarkably attractive women. More than average. They could all be models."

"That's probably the influence of the immortal blood mixed into their line," I said. "Why don't we go back to our room."

"Good idea."

Picking up our packs and turning off the flashlights, we jogged back all the way using our immortal sight and speed. Once we got back, we were able to approximate the location of the tunnel using the one GPS reading we got. We found the river it went under, and we guessed the location of the entrance. It wasn't a particularly long tunnel, only about a mile.

We went to bed but stayed awake most of the night talking about our adventure. The sun was just about to burst over the horizon when Rick started to lightly play with my breasts. I became aroused and my scent became intoxicating to him as he rolled on top of me and kissed me deeply. I responded in kind, with my tongue exploring his mouth. Our heat flared and our limbs entwined and our hearts synchronized. As our lovemaking grew more impassioned, our power built and drew into us. When we brought each other to climax, our power burst from us in a small wave, emanating in all directions.

The next day, the coven prepared a luncheon dinner for us. As soon as we heard the ward on the door open, we knew someone was sent to retrieve us and bring us to the main house.

When Rick and I arrived, we were escorted to a circle of stones behind a large stone manor. The circle had perfectly balanced lintels across all the stones, connecting them into a ring. There were twelve stones, a witch standing in front of each stone, with one standing in the very center of the circle.

We were brought inside the circle. My skin sizzled as the power of the coven danced across it as I passed through the barrier. Rick must have had the same sensation, but it affected him by stimulating his libido. His eyes started glowing gold and his cock became quite hard in his pants. He gasped as his body reacted. I looked at him and noticed the gold, swirling eyes. I chuckled lightly at his expense.

"Not funny," he whispered.

"Yes, it is," I replied.

"What caused it?"

"Their power."

A coven member bid us to stop, and left the circle.

"Honored guests, welcome to our coven. Within its walls and wards, we are protected from the prying eyes of humans," announced Amarlyis.

"Thank you," said Rick and I together.

"We are honored to be here," I continued. "Why the circle?"

"We welcome you within the stones to see your power. I felt it last night, and wished to see if you would help us."

"You felt it last night?" I asked. And then I remembered our lovemaking. *Could it be that we generate power every time?*

"Surely, you are not creating magical power without a reason?" asked Amarlyis. "That would be such a waste. We need to preserve our magical power. Tell me, how is it so easy for you?"

Thinking, I realized what Esperanza had told me about true love and that the coven didn't have that going for them.

"We are mated," I said. "We share a bond far deeper than sisters, brothers, or coven members. We share a true love bond."

There were a number of gasps from the circle and outside.

"I am not an immortal," said Amarlyis. "Like some of my ancestors, I have a long life, but I will die of old age. But I understood the nature of that power. The depth of that power. I once held such power when I had a true love mate. But she is gone."

It was silent at that admission. We all glanced sideways, some uncomfortable in the silence.

"Would you be willing to share?" asked Amarlyis, suddenly snapping out of her reverie.

"I don't know you that well, it would be awkward," I explained. I was stalling, because we had no such difficulties with the immortals.

"Then please, let us get to know one another! Come participate with us in a midday ritual we do to thank God and goddess for our bounty and our lives."

At that point, all the coven members inside the stone circle dropped their robes, displaying fully nude bodies. Their chanting and dance were provocative to say the least, and as they finished their ritual, Rick and I were flush with arousal. It was the immortal in us—remember, lusty people!

After redonning their robes, the coven members all came and sat in concentric circles on the ground around the center altar stone, where Amarlyis and us were seated. Food and wine started being passed around and we all shared the meal. The three of us in the center had private service as novices brought us all manner of food and wine. The novices were dressed sort of like nuns, except the fabric was quite transparent. They weren't wearing any head coverings, but the robes covered them head to toe, sort of.

There was jovial conversation all around Rick and me. My hearing picked up parts of conversations here and there. People were wondering who we were, where we came from, and most importantly why we were here.

I turned toward Amarlyis to speak to her.

"So tell me, if you would, how long has there been a coven here?"

"A formal coven has occupied this space for about 1200 years. Originally, a monastery was built on what is called Castle Hill. Only a graveyard remains today. We predate them, and watched as Carlow Castle was built in 1207. It was then destroyed in 1814 by a madman. There have been people in this area for ten thousand years actually."

"Really? That is very interesting. Do you know where we came from?" I asked.

"The people who originally settled in this area came from very far away, and were quite different. Our history shows that when we first came here, there were no humans. In fact, humans only started walking across the land bridge from Europe around 10,500 years ago.

"We met our ancestors back then, who had already established a community. Eventually, there was interbreeding, and witches were born. We are the cross between those beings and humans. We inherited our power from them, but it manifested differently in every child. Some didn't have any power at all. As human history was laid down, our community became feared and hated so we withdrew from humans completely. Our ancestors did the same, but much earlier than us."

"Who are they? Your ancestors?" I asked.

"We called them immortals, because we never saw them age or die. But they weren't human, and we don't know where they came from. Some humans worshiped them as gods, but not us."

"Do you know where they are today?" asked Rick.

"We know where they were. But we have not seen each other for hundreds of years. When you said you were an immortal, we thought maybe you were one of them. But you're not, are you?"

"No, I am from a different group of those people. We settled in the Caribbean," said Rick.

"So there was more than one group?" asked Amarlyis.

"Yes. According to my research, there were originally thirty-five groups that spread out across our planet," I said.

"Fascinating," remarked Amarlyis. "Why do you come to us now?"

"I'm glad you asked," I said. "I wasn't sure how to open up this topic. I have two reasons for being here. The first is to find my family. I believe I am descended from people of your group."

"You mentioned that," said Amarlyis. "What's the second reason?"

"The second is to learn something specific from you. Through my research I learned that a very powerful witch, in the Caribbean area, tried a spell to bring the immortals back from their hiding. Her name was Esperanza and her spell backfired, and instead some of the witches were sucked into another dimension to be lost forever. When she died, a ritual was done to capture her soul and force it into an object to prevent her from moving on. Today, that soul is the disembodied voice that helps supernatural people find things in the occult store. I want to free her and the witches."

"I see." Amarlyis was silent for several minutes, apparently processing this information.

"Why do you want to free the witches?" asked Amarlyis.

"Because my great-great-grandmother told me I needed to," I said.

"Who is your great-great-grandmother?"

"Her name is Innogen."

Amarlyis gasped audibly. "I haven't heard that name in centuries. If she is your great-great-grandmother, then you definitely come from this coven. Innogen was my sister. I miss her terribly."

"You're my aunt?" I asked.

"It's more complex than that. Let me explain. My grandmother was the Esperanza in your story, and she had a daughter and a son. The son married a mixed-race woman and the daughter married a human. My mother, Esperanza, was the daughter of the son. My father, Padaro, was the son of the daughter.

"Esperanza tried to bring the immortals back. She failed. On her death, I trapped her soul.My parents had many children. One was Innogen. We were siblings, but many decades apart in years. Innogen and I had a falling out over the burial of my mother's body. She left the coven."

"I understand that Innogen had a difficult time," I said. "My grandmother gave up on magic completely. My mother didn't know that we were witches. She had magic, but my grandmother, mother, and I were never trained. I discovered my magic on my own, and did what I could to learn, but without a teacher, it has been very slow. When I found Innogen, suddenly my whole world opened up."

"Who will train you now?" asked Amarlyis.

"Innogen said she would train me," I said.

"How is that possible? My sister is dead!"

"No, she's not. She is in a pocket dimension," I said. "I can go to her through the time portal in the occult store. Esperanza showed me how."

"Occult store? Time portal?" asked Amarlyis. "What nonsense are you speaking about? Are you referring to the Vault?"

"I don't know. In Montreal, I happened upon a door that goes into an occult store. I was directed there by a colleague of mine years ago. It's a repository of all things magical, and a store for us to purchase supplies. It's hidden from the human world, so you have to be taken there by someone else the first time in order to find it.

"Ever since, I've been using the occult store as a library of sorts. I access it through Montreal, but Esperanza says it's everywhere and anywhere. She gave me a spell to create a local door wherever I am."

"Show me," demanded Amarlyis.

"Okay." I then stood with Rick. We faced each other and clasped hands while I chanted some strange words. Amarlyis gasped again, as the power started to swirl around the two of us in wisps of green light. When I finished the incantation, we clapped our hands together and a doorway appeared out of thin air beside us.

The whole group gasped collectively.

"This is the occult store. Would you like to see it?" I asked Amarlyis.

The witch scrambled to her feet and joined Rick and I as I opened the door and walked through. All three of us disappeared inside and then the door closed and disappeared too.

Amarlyis gazed around in wonder at the spectacle of the occult store. She walked slowly around it and lovingly touched some of the objects. She was quietly crying as she saw what was there.

"Amarlyis, what is wrong?" I asked.

"Nothing, nothing at all. This is the Vault. It was created so long ago, and then we lost our way here. This is where I trapped my mother's soul so that I would have her."

"Amarlyis, you're here," said the disembodied voice.

"Mother!" cried Amarlyis.

"Now you know how to reach me again," said Esperanza.

"I will share this with everyone in our coven, Mother."

We popped out of another doorway I created from the occult store to an immediate din of voices.

"Amarlyis, where did you go?" cried several of the witches.

"My sisters and brothers, oh my, the Vault is restored to us!" cried Amarlyis. "It truly is a storehouse for all the occult and the supernatural. My mother is there!

"Is there knowledge there to help us in our pledge to return our sisters and brothers?" asked one of the witches.

"There is more knowledge there than you can imagine," said Amarlyis. "My mother is there as the guiding voice." Amarlyis choked up a little at the mention of her mother. "We can finally fulfill our pledge."

"Your pledge?" I asked. "What's that?"

"We too have been trying to bring back our sisters, so your personal account confirms you are one of us, truly. We have not succeeded because we do not have enough knowledge or power or both."

"What have you done so far?" I asked.

"We were taught the spell by Innogen before she left. It requires the power of thirteen, and the cast must be done at the peak of sexual intercourse when the power is at its greatest. But it never worked for us."

"I know why," I said. "It's because none of you are true love mates. Your coven is men and women you love, respect, and abide by, but there are no true love mates, are there?"

"No, none of us have that sort of love. I did once, a long time ago. But she denied us and left. My broken heart has never quite healed. When I do my magic, I try to tap into that love I felt, and I can feel the power it would give me, but the power never comes."

"That's why you don't waste it, and you asked us how we could," I said.

"Yes."

"We have three true love couples in our group. We are all immortal, and I am an immortal witch. I can generate the power. Innogen told me she can cast the spell for us, I just have to get everyone in the same place. Where will the witches materialize when we do this spell?"

"They will come to us, wherever we are," said Amarlyis.

"Do we need to perform this within a stone circle?" I said. "I cannot bring Innogen here. I must go to her to learn the spell first. To do that, I have to return to the occult store. I will return in a day or two. Rick?"

As Amarlyis gathered the coven around her and told them more about what she saw at the occult store, we got up purposefully and strode outside the stone circle. "We will be back!" I cried as we called the occult store again and disappeared. Rick and I got to the occult store, then passed through the time portal to see my 3G. As we approached the convent, Innogen appeared from between the hedges.

"Lora, good to see you again. What brings you here?"

"I've found my ancestors and their coven. I've met Amarlyis. She is leading the coven."

"Oh good! Amarlyis is leading, you say? She's my sister. She's also tricky, so watch your back. Did you discover any further information about your mother or grandmother?"

"Only that you had a 'falling out' with Amarlyis and left with my grandmother and never spoke to them again," I said.

"It wasn't a 'falling out.' My sister was angry that the coven was considering rescuing the witches. I was the loudest voice in favor of that, so I was put here by Amarlyis. I challenged her authority, and her response was to trick me into walking into this dimension."

"I see," I said. "So I shouldn't trust her at all. Do we want to learn the spell that we have been trying to perform to release the witches or not?"

"Yes, if you can, learn that spell. I will compare it to mine."

"Amarlyis said that their spell will draw the witches to them rather than just releasing them," said Rick.

"Yeah, that sounds like her. It would be an attempt to strengthen her coven and gain more power. My spell simply releases them. They would return to our own place and time. Of course, that will change history. So maybe that's not a good idea. I should rethink that. Hmm."

"What if we brought them to my place and time?" I asked. "We could find a place to perform the ritual that is far from other people."

"That's a tall task in this century," said Rick.

"But if we brought them here, then they could walk out on their own and then Esperanza can let them exit wherever they want, one at a time," I said.

"That's a possibility, but I don't know if that will work," said Innogen. "I cannot leave this place. I have to be brought out. However, we could do it in the occult store. You could bring me out of here, and then we can do the ritual there."

"Sounds like a plan," I said. "So, first, get the spell from Amarlyis. Then get you out, then release the witches, then release Esperanza."

"Releasing Esperanza by force will destroy the occult store," warned Innogen. "No one will have access again. Ask them when you get back. It would be a shame to lose that repository of knowledge. It needs a soul to keep it tethered to your dimension."

"Oh, that's a shame. Maybe I can find another soul to replace her," I thought out loud.

"It has to be a magical soul, dear. Not just anyone will do," said Innogen. "I could do it. That would guarantee that I would be available to train you and watch over you. Yeah, I like that idea."

"But, Innogen, then I won't be able to see you anymore or hug you!" I cried.

"Dear Lora, you speak to Esperanza every time you're there," said Innogen. "That is all we need. Besides, I'm quite familiar with the spell to bind a soul to that place. So it's settled, no arguments! Go now, go learn that spell that Amarlyis is using and then come back here. Bring this beautiful man with you. We will need his power to get me out of here."

"Okay. Wait! How do we release Esperanza and then capture your soul without losing the occult store?"

"Oh, yes. Well, you see, there has always been a magical soul in the occult store. The spell actually replaces one with another. Over the thousands of years of its existence, magical beings have volunteered their souls to keep it going. It's always been a temporary thing, until Amarlyis trapped Esperanza there with no intention of releasing her."

"Yes, she mentioned she was Esperanza's daughter," I said.

"Correct."

"How does it all fit together?"

"Ureth had a wife with the same name, Esperanza, and they led group 32 in the Caribbean. They had many children. One of their sons, Mitar, married a mixed-race woman, Llyuthea. They had a daughter called Esperanza after her grandmother.

"One of Ureth's daughters, Aedanmar, mated Mak, an immortal, and they had a son named Padaro. Esperanza II mated Padaro and had me, then Amarlyis many decades later."

"After the failed spell that trapped twelve individuals, I wanted to try rescuing them. Aedanmar and Amarlyis disagreed and trapped me here. When our mother was dying, Amarlyis feared losing her forever, so she trapped our mother's soul to protect her.Shortly after that, she and Aedanmar left group 32 and went to Ireland."

"Yes. If we are both related to Esperanza, does that mean I'm related to Rick?"

"No, dear. Shonia comes from the first Esperanza's line, but through a different child."

"Oh, that's good!" I said in relief.

Rick and I prepared to leave. At the last moment Innogen yelled, "Watch your back, dear!" and we stepped through the mirror and returned to the occult store.

"Esperanza, Innogen just told me that we need to replace you so that you can be released. Is that correct?" I asked.

"Yes, Lora O'Reilly, that is correct. Another magical being must voluntarily offer her soul to replace mine so that I may leave and move on. It has always been thus, until I was trapped here. By forcing my soul here, the previous soul was lost."

"Oh, that's sad," I said. Then I outlined the plan for releasing her, the lost witches, and Innogen. When I was finished, I was a little out of breath.

"I have the perfect space for the rituals," said the disembodied voice. "There is a cave that is part of the occult store, reserved for special rituals that need secrecy. It is large and well lit and also shaped to concentrate power in the middle. Very few know of its existence, because it is only asked for maybe once a millennium."

"Can you show us?" asked Rick.

"Of course. Follow the light please."

We walked a long way it seemed and far down into the "ground," or down many stairs at least, until we arrived at an immense cavern with a large platform in the middle.

"Oh my God, it can't be!" I cried. I ran forward and looked up and around the enormous place. "Rick, is this the same cave we were looking at in Cuba?"

"It certainly looks like it," he said. "Look at the details on the walls."

"Esperanza, where is this cave?"

"Lora, it is located on a very cold island. I can sense the cold myself. We are deep underground here, and far from human civilization. I am aware of several other such locations around the globe. I believe the one you speak of was built by group 32."

"Is this the original location?" I asked. "I feel like I'm standing on holy ground."

"Yes, it is."

"This will be perfect, Esperanza. Absolutely perfect. Innogen will be very pleased," I said. "Okay, step two: I need to learn the spell from Amarlyis. Esperanza, please take us out to their coven."

Rick and I appeared out of thin air in the middle of the stone circle. Coven members who were walking around were startled by our sudden appearance, and initially threw fireballs at us in self defense. Once I identified us, and asked for Amarlyis, their attacks stopped and we were taken inside the manor.

"You're back," said Amarlyis. "Did you find what you were looking for?"

"Yes, but there's a change of plans. Instead of doing the ritual here, we have a better place to bring all the witches. It helps concentrate the magic. My friends will meet us there, so between our power and your coven's, we should be able to accomplish the impossible! But I need to learn your ritual properly. Can you run me through it?"

"Whoa, I haven't agreed to go anywhere else. I want the witches here, in our coven."

"Don't you think offering them a place is better than forcing them? I asked.

"They will be out of time!" cried Amarlyis.

"That's exactly the reason they shouldn't be trapped yet again," I said patiently. "Rick, could you go and make that phone call for me?"

"Yup, be right back!"

30—Gathering Players

—Rick

While Lora disappeared to speak with Innogen, I walked out of the manor and down the road a short ways to make a call.

"Falon speaking, how can I help you?"

"Falon, it's Rick."

"Rick, what's up?'

"You remember the occult store Lora took you to?"

"Yes, it was a cool place."

"Do you think you can find your way there again?"

"Yes, no problem. Why?"

"Lora and her great-great-grandmother are working on a plan to rescue the witches that were trapped in another dimension. She needs all six of us, and our libidos, to power a magical ritual to open a portal to let them come here."

"All right, then, that's a simple explanation. Weird, but simple. When?"

"What time is it there?"

"Almost 4:00 p.m."

"We're five hours ahead of you. So let's say 6:00 p.m. your time, two days from now. That will be 11:00 p.m. our time."

"Got it. And when we get there, are there any instructions we need to follow?" asked Falon.

"Yes, ask Esperanza to take you to the ritual site."

"Got it. Two days from now, at 6:00 p.m., the four of us will be at the occult store, and once there, be taken to the ritual site. Do we bring anything?"

"Blankets, lots of blankets, pillows, lube—you know, the usual." He was grinning and Falon laughed.

"Sex rituals it is! Bye."

Chuckling to myself, I hung up the phone and walked back to the manor and found the two women sitting close together with Lora, mimicking Amarylis' moves and words. She was studying Amarlyis' moves carefully.

So she had prevailed, no surprise there, and is learning the ritual, I thought as I sat down in a chair to wait patiently and watch.

I loved watching her anyway. It always got me going. I reflected on what we were planning on doing in two days, and my body started responding to the thoughts. *Enough of that, you!* I told myself. The last thing I wanted was to get excited and interrupt the women. Well, perhaps it wasn't the last thing.

A short while later, Lora seemed confident enough with the ritual and thanked Amarlyis for the lesson.

"Are we going to have the opportunity to participate?" asked Amarlyis.

"I believe we need you, yes," Lora said. "Do you remember the incantation for the occult store?"

"Yes."

"Rick—what are the arrangements?"

"Two days from now, at 11:00 p.m. this time, return to the occult store and ask Esperanza to take you to the ritual site. Bring lots of blankets and pillows. It's cold there."

"So, two days from now. We'll be there," said Amarlyis.

"Come on, love, let's go get something to eat before we get some sleep," said Lora.

"Sleep, yeah, that's what we'll do," I said, looking at her beautiful face.

31—Releasing the Witches

—Lora

Rick and I made our way back to the hotel in Carlow. By the time we got there it was very late. All the pubs were closed and so were the stores.

We asked the concierge if we could get a meal and he told us to not worry, he'd have something brought up for us. We zombie-walked to our room and flopped on the bed. We were so tired. Today had been very long and stressful.

Soon, there was a knock on the door, and a chipper young man pushed a trolley into the room with the scent of steaming food.

"Here you go, two large bowls of Irish stew, a loaf of bread and cream, and several pints of beer to wash it down," said the steward.

"Oh, that smells wonderful! Thank you so much." Rick left him a tip on the bar because he didn't know if tips were included, then we pulled up some chairs and dug into the fragrant stew. There were large chunks of meat, carrots, potatoes, and turnips with a thick, savory broth. It was heavenly. The bread was really fresh, like it had just come out of the oven, while the clotted cream was a nice touch.

We ate every bite, and did indeed wash it down with a pint or two each. Stomachs full, we lay on the bed and held each other. We had a couple of days to prepare for the event of a lifetime.

"You were adorable," said Rick.

"When?" I asked.

"When you were learning the ritual from Amarlyis. I was watching you and couldn't help getting turned on by you. I had to have a stern talk with you-know-who so he wouldn't embarrass us in public."

"We're not in public now."

"That's true." He pulled me closer and leaned in to kiss me. It felt like days since we had made love, and my body responded instantly to his heat with a fire of my own. I watched his nostrils flare as he picked up the scent of my arousal. He pulled me on top against his hips. I could feel the very prominent bulge developing.

A quiet groan escaped my lips, and shivers lifted the hairs on my body in excitement, as he slipped his hands under my shirt and undid my bra. That felt wonderful, to get out of the wires. My breasts sprang free and hung down. He slid my shirt off my body and finished removing my bra. Then he just stared for a minute.

"Ah, your breasts are so beautiful, mamacita. I want to bury my face in them."

I leaned over and he pressed his face into my cleavage, holding my breasts and rubbing his face. I listened as he inhaled the scent of me and pulled back and kissed each nipple. Then he buried his face again while his fingers tweaked my nipples until they were hard.

I pressed myself on his cock until he started groaning himself. Letting go of my boobs, he let me sit up so I could undo his pants. Rick never wore underwear, so as soon as I opened the zipper, his cock came out to play. He was beautifully formed, long, very long, thick and strong, with a slight curve which touched me deep inside in just the right place. I took his cock in my hands and started to rub him up and down. He danced in my fingers.

Rick's hands went to my jeans and undid the zipper. I was wearing a thong, so he played with the lace, teasing me a little until his fingers slipped underneath and found my folds. I was already substantially wet, and as his fingers touched the moisture, he sighed and moaned in pleasure.

"Let's take off these clothes, mamacita, and enjoy each other's bodies."

I rolled off him and we both shucked our remaining clothes quickly. Rick pulled back the sheets and we both jumped back into bed. I landed on my back diagonally across the bed. Rick came up between my legs and planted his nose at my mound and inhaled my scent again, deeply.

"I love your smell, mamacita. It drives me wild," he said as he showed me the swirling in his eyes, and how his fangs had elongated. He licked me slowly, drawing my moisture up and sipping it. Then he buried his tongue in my folds and started to make my body go crazy with sensations as he brought my arousal to a heightened place.

Leaving me, he stood up. I whimpered like a puppy, hungry and wanting him so much I touched myself. He watched me for a moment, then took his cock and rubbed his head in my slit, covering himself in my juice. Each time he slightly dipped inside, my motor revved. He teased me and teased me, until I was panting and couldn't wait anymore.

"Take me, I need you so much!"

He plunged into me with vigor. The invasion into my flesh crossed the line and my body had its first orgasm. He kept still as my shudders subsided. I could feel him deep inside, filling me completely, and it felt like we were one. He slowly started to move, and I met every thrust with one of my own. He grew longer and harder with each thrust until he tipped me, pushing against that hard-to-reach place at the end of my channel. It always hurt a little, but it was a good hurt that sent me over the edge again.

As my second orgasm happened, he was coming too. I could feel that point at which he stopped controlling things and let go. His animal took over as he hammered himself into me, hitting the end each time. That in turn caused my orgasm to crescendo and multiply until he climaxed with me. His seed poured out, and he took my offered neck and bit down, delivering the venom that would send me over the top, but as he bit me I took my own bite on his neck, which was suitably exposed.

Together, as he finished pouring his seed and pumping into me, we soared on a wind of euphoria, entwined by love.

I was so used to the venom now, I didn't black out any longer. So I remembered and felt every moment. That added to the climax and left us feeling completely fulfilled.

"Oh God, I love you so much," said Rick. "Will you marry me?"

"Hey, I already asked!"

"So you did. What did I answer?" he teased.

"You said yes. Are you changing your answer?"

"Never. I want to be married to you forever. I want to be inside you forever."

"Well, that could get awkward," I said, teasing him.

"Only occasionally.

I pulled up the blankets to cover us without detaching, and Rick snuggled beside me. We both loved that he could stay connected long after our lovemaking. We fell asleep that way.

The sun woke us up the next morning. We were still entangled in the sheets. I opened my eyes and his beautiful brown eyes were watching me.

"Have you been awake long?" I asked.

"No, only a few minutes. You wiggle your nose in your sleep. It's adorable."

"You make me sound like a rabbit," I said.

"You know what rabbits do, don't you?" he asked.

"Ah yes, fuck like bunnies. Great, frequent, fast, and unsatisfying sex with a dozen kids afterward. No thanks!" I said, laughing. Rick laughed with me.

"Seriously, what shall we do today?" he asked.

"I want to touch base with Falon and Innogen. I will also need to buy supplies for the rituals and have that all in place."

"Well, we can split the tasks if you want."

"No, I like to go together. Most of the supplies we will get through the occult store anyway. The first ritual will be for Innogen, to release her from that pocket dimension."

After breakfast, I called Falon. "Falon, it's me."

"Hi, Me, how's it going?"

"Lots of news. But I would rather tell you in person. I need to amend the plan a little."

"What's the change?"

"Can you get everyone to the occult store in a few hours?"

"I think so. It's very early here, so I should be able to grab everyone before they start their day."

"I'll see you there in an hour, then."

"Bye."

"Rick, let's get to the occult store too. I can start shopping while we wait for everyone to come."

An hour later, I was collecting my materials and putting them on the counter, when Falon and the rest of the gang walked in the store.

"Hi, everyone! welcome to the occult store," I said.

"This place is very cool," said Gwen.

"Uh huh," said the rest.

"First thing we need to do is travel through time to get Innogen back here," I said. "When we get there, we will only have one hour to return, because time moves differently there."

"Got it," said everyone.

"Esperanza, please take us to the time mirror."

A glowing orb of light appeared in the middle of the group. Andrews and Gwen gasped in surprise. The orb started moving and our group of six immortals followed through the gloomy interior of the store. I went last because I was carrying the things I would need for the ritual.

When we got to the mirror, I reviewed the rules with everyone and made sure they all were clear on what they could and could not do. Grasping hands, I took us through to my 3G. She was waiting at the portal's exit point.

"Welcome, everyone, to my very own pocket dimension," said Innogen. "I need your help to escape this place back to the occult store."

"What do you need us to do?" asked Mark.

"All I need you to do is to lock hands with everyone in a circle," said Innogen. "I will do the rest."

Our six immortals stood in a circle around Innogen and locked hands. Following her directions, we focused on the hands we were linked to and thought about the love we had for each other, and in particular the love we each had for our mate.

Innogen was counting on the libidos of the males to spike everyone, and that is exactly what they did. As soon as they started thinking about their love for their mates, the guys' bodies reacted—subtly at first, but then the reactions grew. As their arousal increased, we females picked up the scent. This started a circuit of sorts, where everyone started reacting to each other, building up the arousal in the group like a battery.

As the power built among the six of us, wisps of gold energy started twirling around us, individually at first, then each couple. I watched through my lashes as Innogen was speaking something under her breath and the energy intensified swirling around us faster.

Her own energy, green in color, twined around her hands. I saw her lips move faster as she sped up her incantation. Power flowed all around her, creating a cocoon of green bands. Innogen raised her hands, and like a lightning rod drew our gold energy toward her. The seven of us were like batteries connected in sequence, charging up. The energy took on the form of a mist flowing around us and through us, not unlike a magnetic field. As our energy merged with Innogen's green energy, I knew the moment had come.

Innogen spoke aloud this time and cast her spell. Her body absorbed all the power and then exploded out of her like a great ring of gold, spreading across the dimension. Quickly, the aspects of the dimension started to dissolve, and winked out of existence.

"Now, everyone, go back through the mirror—quickly—holding hands," yelled Innogen.

One by one, we popped back through the mirror and moved out of the way for the next person. Lastly, Innogen came through, and I sighed in relief.

"Innogen, you made it!" I ran and hugged her. She hugged me back tightly.

"The six of you have so much power, it's incredible," she cried. "There was no doubt in my mind it would work."

"What's next?" asked Falon.

"Esperanza, how long were we gone?" asked Innogen.

"You were gone for over twelve hours."

"How is that possible?" I asked. "I thought the limit was one hour."

"Because we were wielding magic, the time changed," said Innogen. "Also, because I was casting a spell to destroy that dimension, it didn't matter."

"So how long do we have before the big ritual?" asked Rick.

"About fifteen hours."

"Some of that should be spent sleeping, people. Why don't we all go back to the hotel to eat and rest?" suggested Rick.

"Good idea," said Gwen.

Leaving the occult store, everyone ended up in our room, so we went down to the front desk and rented three more. Mark enquired about food, and we were directed to the hotel's dining hall. I ordered the Irish stew again, and a few others followed my lead.

Once we all had food and pints, we were happily munching and talking. Innogen told us many stories about her life, and we filled her in on the past few centuries.

Innogen was particularly interested in stories about how the immortals turned humans. Being a supernatural herself, she didn't really need that, especially since she was volunteering to take over the occult store from Esperanza.

"Okay, kids," started Innogen, to Gwen and Mark, chuckling. "This is what we'll need from you for the next ritual."

She outlined the plan to bring back the witches and what the ritual would need.

"You mean we'll need to have sex this time?" asked Andrews.

"Yes, copulation will increase your power a hundred-fold. I saw how much you have, it's incredible, but you will need to bring about all your creation energy to perform this feat."

"The coven will be there too, Innogen. So perhaps they can contribute the same way," I suggested.

"The more the merrier," she answered. "Now, this is what is going to happen: the ritual will get really wild. We need to open up a vortex to the dimension. This requires an immense amount of power. No single witch can do this. However, with your help, I believe I can.

"Once the vortex is opened, we have to pull the stranded witches through to this side," Innogen continued. "So you have to maintain the open vortex—which means sustained power. We don't know what condition they will be in. When they arrive here, the witches will be confused, very confused. We cannot tell them where or when they are immediately. That will require a soft touch.

"Once we have dealt with all the freed witches, I will volunteer myself to replace Esperanza so that she can go free. That means my body will die and my soul will be absorbed by the occult store."

Innogen paused in her explanation, looking at each of us. "Do you understand?" she asked us.

"Uh huh," we all nodded and agreed.

"Are we going to need to get into sex, or do what we did to get you here?" asked Andrews.

"I'm not sure," said Innogen. "I expect that it will be somewhere in the middle, and perhaps toward a group climax. The challenge for you six will be to get romantic in front of everyone."

"I don't think that will be as much of a problem as you think," said Mark. "Our internal animal takes over, and arousal becomes inevitable as the charge of the energy hits us. With so many becoming sexually aroused, it may be easier than we thought."

"Well, let's go back to the occult store and get things set up," said Innogen.

"We can do that from our room," I said.

"I'll meet you there, let me go pay the bill," said Mark. The rest of us went up to mine and Rick's room. I opened the doorway to the occult store as soon as Mark arrived, and we all went through.

"Let's go to the ritual site. Esperanza? Can you take us there?"

"Of course."

Within half an hour we were entering the huge space for the ritual. I heard gasps coming out of Falon and the rest, as they saw the room we had been brought to.

"Oh my God! This is another launch room from the immortals!" yelled Falon.

"So it would seem," I said. "According to Esperanza, this is the original, and it may be the one under the Antarctic ice."

"It is a little cold here," noticed Gwen. "And dark."

"Let us work on that," said Rick and Andrews. Rick set about looking for means to get heat, checking the exterior walls for some kind of control box.

Andrews stood on the platform and just stared. "I think the floor was designed to hold torches of some kind." He went down the stairs and started scanning the walls of the platform. There were glyphs on most things, but it was anyone's guess what they did.

Pressing things and levers randomly, Andrews discovered a control that brought torches up out of the floor. There were hundreds of them arranged in concentric circles around the perimeter of the platform. Once lit, they put out a considerable amount of heat. Of course, we had no way of knowing how long the torches would last or what fuel they burned. That would be a surprise.

Within minutes, the huge open space began to feel warmer. The seven of us got up on top of the platform and went toward the middle. We then arranged ourselves in a circle with Innogen in the middle again. This time, the circle was large enough for us to stretch out on the floor.

"Guys, let's treat this like the ritual we did for turning. We had an audience then of strangers, and it doesn't matter once we're focused on each other," suggested Falon.

We spread the blankets and pillows down on the hard surface of the platform, then started to remove our clothes.

A bright orb of light burst into the room, followed by forty people. This was the coven.

"Welcome, Éadrom agus Dorcha Coven," said Innogen.

"Innogen! My sister. How is it possible that you're here?" cried Amarlyis.

"These six have restored me," she answered, pointing to the six immortals around her. All of our eyes were glowing in the darkness as they stood there. We were unashamed of our nakedness.

"Six immortals, I see," said Amarlyis.

"Shall we get started?" asked Innogen. "Sister, I will need your help in the chant. Please join me in the center of this circle."

"Of course, sister." Amarlyis motioned to her coven to spread out on the platform around the circle evenly, giving us a wide margin. The forty witches formed a second circle, clasping hands around us as Amarlyis walked into the center.

"Together, sister," said Innogen, "we shall perform the ritual and say the incantation to open the vortex and pull our sisters home. It shall be difficult and dangerous. I will need you to keep the focus on maintaining the open vortex as I pull them home. You will need all the power your coven can generate. Let us begin."

The two women also stripped naked, and the coven followed suit. The two women held hands in the middle, focusing on our ritual.

"Ah, before we begin, may I ask a question?" asked Falon.

"Of course, dear," said Innogen. "Go ahead."

"Why is magic done naked? I'm not complaining or anything, just wondering."

With a chuckle, Innogen smiled and turned toward the group. "We disrobe so that there is nothing between us and the magic. Sometimes the magic becomes incendiary, and that can be dangerous. So we remove easily burned materials."

"Oh, thank you. That makes sense," said Falon.

The six of us started with thinking of our mates, like before feeling the love we had for each other. And just like before our thoughts had power, and that power created reactions, which led to scents, which engaged our libidos.

I could feel the arousal starting without even trying. The zing that was traveling back and forth between me and Rick on one side and Andrews on the other excited every cell in my body.

It took no time at all for my nether regions to react to the scent of my mate becoming aroused. My mind imagined his fingers in my folds, caressing me, and I became quite wet as my body felt us.

I let go of Andrews' hand and pulled Rick toward me. He took me in his arms and ravaged my mouth as his fingers sought my wet folds—thrusting his fingers deep inside me in his excitement, and making my own libido ramp up even more. I took hold of his member that was trapped between us and worked the length of him, causing him to lengthen and get harder. He was secreting beads of cum that I rubbed all over his head. His hands left their work and grabbed my ass, lifting me off the floor so he could get under me and bring me down on his cock. I wrapped my legs around his hips to hang on while I wrapped my arms around his neck. Rick was kissing me deeply, ravaging my lips as his cock pushed its way inside me. He held still for a moment as the swell of the wave passed over us unbroken. The energy was building as each wave got higher and higher.

Rick's knees buckled with the effort, so he brought us down to the floor and laid me out on the blankets. He had to separate us to do this, but it was only for a moment. We took time to explore each other's bodies, rippling the energy higher and higher, but pausing to hold it inside. It was difficult, because all I wanted to do was release myself and climax with my guy.

Mark and Falon were doing the same thing, she sitting in his lap and doing a very slow grind so that they were creating lots of tension but not releasing it.

Gwen and Andrews were doing a slow burn too, touching, kissing, and nipping each other into a froth.

All of us had to still ourselves for moments at a time to swallow the need to climax, and to keep building the energy. Soon, I saw the energy swirling around each of us. Mine was green like my 3G's, and Rick's was gold. Our energies mingled, threaded, and danced around us in rhythm to our motions.

Rick paused again. He was as on the very edge of climax as was I, and we were both squirming with need. Our heartbeats synchronized in that moment, and a surge of power exited our bodies. Our energy had joined with the others now, and it was circling and meandering around all six of us.

Innogen and her sister were still in the middle of our circle, and their green energy could be seen stretching from them up into the air above us. They were chanting quietly, focusing everything they had on creating a vortex.

Rick slowly started thrusting again, withdrawing until his head was out, holding it at the opening, teasing me, making me beg, and then plummeting inside, punching the end of my channel, sending shivers of pain and pleasure through me. Again and again this wrapped the coil even tighter inside, tightened the spring. Great gold and green bands of power were writhing in waves circling higher and faster in this ancient room.

As the six of us paused again at the same time, we heard our six hearts synchronize. The explosion of energy from us sent a wave spiraling upward to join Innogen's energy. It was forming a vortex.

As the swirling power was drawn into a tighter circle, Innogen drew it down to her, molded it into the shape and size she needed, and then cast a spell into it, opening it up into a vast vortex above us. Innogen worked hard to control the vortex; sweat was dripping down her neck and the strain on her body was taking a toll. Amarlyis worked on maintaining it—the two witches were working at a level that was very nearly beyond them. Without the aid of the immortals, they would have failed again.

Our energy was still being held tightly, but we were becoming exhausted.

"You can start your climax now," called out Innogen. "Just don't do it quickly. The coven will pick up your energy and help."

"We need new stimulation," cried Mark.

"Use your venom," said Innogen.

"But that will push us into orgasm," said Mark.

"Small amounts."

So that's what we did. Administering tiny amounts to each other juiced us without bursting the bubble we had created. With all six of us re-engaged, the power rekindled.

We climbed the energy rail together, spreading the venom around to keep it going. I heard gasps and moans around us—the coven was participating in their own sex. Opening my eyes, I glanced at Innogen and saw that she was bathed in gold energy. It was all wrapped tightly around her as she wielded it.

Out of the corner of my eye, I saw robed figures materialize. As soon as they were solid, they collapsed on the floor. A coven member ran to them with a blanket and a pillow to take care of them. Another had water and was getting them to drink.

Innogen suddenly collapsed to the floor. She looked at me and whispered, "Release."

All of us then released all of our energy and climaxed together. The amount of energy that exploded from us was incredible. As it rolled outward in a wave, it hit the curved walls of the room. All of a sudden, we saw glyphs illuminating and glowing on the walls. The energy traveled up the walls, lighting them up as it escaped through the top hole. The entire room lit with golden energy.

Amarlyis had let the vortex go and fallen to the floor, exhausted too. She crawled over to her sister and was quietly speaking with her. The six of us were in a heap of gelatinous flesh. I don't know how long we all lay there, surrounded by the coven, the torches, and the new witches, but it was quite a while. I woke up starving.

I recognized Rick's arms wrapped around me, keeping me warm. I glanced around. All the couples were reunited. Rolling over, I kissed Rick on the nose, and waited to see his eyes open.

"Hello, beautiful," he said in his usual greeting after lovemaking.

"Hi, handsome," I answered him. "How do you feel?"

"Drained," he said. "But good. You?"

"Strangely, I feel wonderful. Must be all the venom I got."

I heard the rustle of clothing being put on and the low murmur of voices of people trying to be quiet. The torches were still burning, but their flames were quite low now, so they didn't offer much light in such a cavernous place.

Innogen was awake and dressed, and sitting on the floor with her sister. They were speaking quietly. When Innogen saw us wake up, she stood.

"Everyone, may I have your attention for a moment, please?" she spoke loudly. "I want to thank you all for your effort in this endeavor. I could not have done this without all of you." She looked at her sister too. "We have rescued all twelve witches and they seem to be in fair health."

There was a cheer from everyone at that. One of those rescued stood up to speak.

"I thank you, my brethren, for your sacrifice and effort to bring us back. We understand this is not our time, and that we will have a lot to learn and get used to. After speaking to my sisters, we have decided to stay here in this space until we can reintegrate into this century. We will have the help of Innogen, because she will become the voice of the occult."

"That is the last ritual we need to do," said Amarlyis. "It would be my honor to do this for you, sister."

"In a minute. First, I must speak to my great-great-granddaughter, alone."

"Esperanza, as your last task, could you please take our coven home?" asked Amarlyis.

"Of course." All of the Irish coven members winked out of the room, leaving only the six of us, the recovered coven, Innogen, and Amarlyis.

"Amarlyis, I don't need you to do this spell. You may leave."

"Mmphfmm," was the noise coming out of her throat. "Fine, I'll leave." And she was gone.

"Esperanza, I, Innogen of the Coven of Light and Dark, volunteer to take your place as the Voice of the Occult, releasing your soul to become reborn."

I watched as Esperanza appeared almost in solid form in front of me. I saw her lovely curly hair and green eyes as she reached out with a hand to touch Innogen with love reflected on her face. Then her image dissolved and she was gone. Innogen started to glow, and got brighter and brighter until I could not look at her, her body transparent like a ray of light. Then she disappeared.

"Innogen, are you still here?" I asked the darkness.

"Yes, dear child. I will forever be here until the next supernatural volunteers to take my place," answered the disembodied voice. But it was different this time; I recognized it as my 3G.

"Take us home, Grandmother, please."

"Of course, my dear."

The six of us popped out of the space and back into our hotel room in Carlow a moment later.

"Did that just happen?" asked Falon.

"Yes, it did," answered Mark.

"Is anyone else hungry?" I asked.

"You're always hungry! Are you pregnant?" asked Gwen.

"Oh!" I said. "I might be. I don't know."

Excerpt from Book 6

IMMORTAL NEXUS

1—Carlow, Ireland

It was an epic night, bringing all those souls back from the pocket dimension where they had been trapped. The power of the magic still vibrated through us, sparking off and sizzling.

We six immortals had succeeded in reviving the ancient magic their ancestors had relied on. Through the energy of sexual connectivity, we had opened a vast portal to another world and brought thirteen men and women back home.

It was an epic night indeed. My great-great grandmother, Innogen, also released Esperanza from her prison and took her place in the occult store. Now I would forever be able to communicate and learn from her. I couldn't wait. There was a large part of me that was more interested in returning to the vast room where we did the magic, just to be there where it happened. But I had to take care of the physical right now. I was starving after all that work and jumping through dimensions.

"Are you pregnant?" asked Gwen.

"Oh!" I said, snapping back from my reverie. "I don't know."

"I think I am," murmured Gwen.

"Oh, that's wonderful!" cried Falon. "Congratulations, Gwen and Andrews!"

"What!" said Andrews. "Did you say pregnant?"

"Gwen was ripe for a child," said Mark. "She just needed a potent male."

"Yes, my love," said Gwen. "You put a baby in me."

"Now what?" asked Falon.

"Oh my God," said Andrews, feeling a little stunned.

"I vote for sleep," said Mark. He took hold of Falon's hand and led her back to their room.

"Bye, all!" called Falon over her shoulder.

"Come here, lover," said Gwen, pulling Andrews into her arms. "Let's go get something to eat in our room, eh?" Gwen and Andrews left as well, leaving me and Rick alone in our room.

"You did it, love," he said, nuzzling me.

"We did it," I said. "But what do we do now?"

"Are you pregnant?" he asked shyly.

"I don't know. It's very possible with all the intense sex we've been having. It's nice, not having to wear protection anymore. I used to hate having to ask those questions: Are you clean? When were you last tested? Do you have condoms?"

"Yes, it's certainly one of the more enjoyable perks of being intimate with an immortal. We don't catch or pass on human diseases. In fact, even having sex with you as a human I wasn't at risk, nor were you. Pregnancy is another situation though. Why don't we go get some food and a test?"

"Sounds like a plan."

The streets of Carlow were quiet with most shops closed, but "our" pub was open so we went in to get some food.

"Welcome back, you two," said the barkeep. "It's rather late, isn't it?"

"Yes, but we were hungry after a very long hard day. Would you have anything to munch on?" I asked.

"Well, I believe there is some bread just out of the oven, and some stew leftovers and a wee bit of lamb as well. Let me put some plates together for you."

"Thank you!"

In no time at all, two heaping plates were placed in front of us filled with the savory smell of roasted lamb and the heavenly scent of a fresh loaf of bread with a pot of cream butter, plus two cold pints to go with it.

Rick and I spent no time talking but dug into the wonderful food, groaning with pleasure while we were chewing. Eventually, I pushed back from the bar with my plate empty, smiling like a fool and moaning about an over-full stomach.

"Oh my God, that was so good!" I said at last.

"I agree," said Rick.

"I'm going to miss this place."

"Why?" asked the barkeep.

"Well, we'll be going home to Canada tomorrow."

"Then you'll have to come back for a visit, now don' ye know," said the barkeep.

"Oh, we will, you can count on that!" said Rick. "I want your recipe for the stew."

"Ah well, that there's a family secret, I'm afraid."

"I couldn't bribe you, eh?" asked Rick.

"We may be able to come to some sort of a deal," said the barkeep, with a finger sly to his nose.

Rick and I then returned the long way to our hotel room.

"Hun, I think I need to go check on the witches and see how they are doing," I said. "It's going to be a shock for them to suddenly be in the twenty-first century."

"Okay, can we do this tomorrow morning? I'm kind of more interested in getting you between the sheets, *mamacita*," Rick replied.

"Hmmm, I like the sound of that," I answered. "Let's stop on the way and get that test."

There was one drugstore in the area and it was unfortunately closed. So the two of us went back to the hotel. I stood in the hallway a moment as Rick unlocked the door to our room. We could hear murmurs coming from all the other rooms where our friends were staying. It didn't sound like anyone was engaged in anything more than pillow talk.

As Rick pushed open the door, our room was welcoming, cool and quiet. He took my hand and led me to the bed, where he slowly stripped away my clothes and then got down on his knees and put his ear to my belly.

"Hello in there," said Rick. "If anyone is listening, I want to introduce myself. I'm your papa."

Tears came to my eyes at the tenderness with which he touched me and kissed me. I'd never had a partner who was so caring about their child, let alone their unborn child.

"Little one, I will protect you with my own life. I love you and I cannot wait to meet you."

"Ah, Rick, that's so sweet," I said.

"To have a child with you would be the *pièce de résistance* of life."

"For me too," I said. "I would love to raise a child with you. I just need to tell my mortal children that their siblings won't get older the same way that they will."

"We will cross that bridge when we get to it," Rick said. Standing up, he took his own clothes off and uncharacteristically dropped them on the floor. Picking me up in his arms, he walked to the bedside, placed me down on the sheets and laid on top of me.

"All I want to do right now is hold you and love you," he said.

What he did was worship me. It brought tears to my eyes again as he kissed me tenderly and held me gently.

"Is something wrong?" Rick asked.

"No, my love, nothing is wrong. It's just all so right now."

"Not yet, we are not married."

"Well, that will have to be planned now that we are finished with this latest adventure."

"And it will. But for now, let me love you."

I felt the whisper of his lips cover my skin in kisses and the flutter of his breath as he passed over all of me. The small delicate sounds vibrated in me, stirring the resting tiger that was inside, awakening and stretching as if to be ready.

The more Rick did, the more that tiger revved up, until I was alternating between small growls of pleasure and purring in happiness. Rick was gentle with me, maybe because I might be pregnant, or perhaps just because that was his mood. But our lovemaking was not urgent, or fast, or hard, or any other over-the-top, excited ways. It was smooth, and sexy, and held a great deal of reverence.

When we came back down from our shared climax, he spooned me and held me like a treasure until we both fell asleep.

What's Next ?

Book 6 - Immortal Nexus

- Andrews and Gwen talk about family

- We meet a new immortal, and a new couple

- Andrews tells the story of how he was hired by aliens

- Someone gets pregnant

- Gwen reminisces about her time living with the First Nations

- Escalata II is finished and launches with a bang

- Lots of good lovin' happens too!

About The Author

Linda Ashton Trott

Ms Trott, a native of Montreal, Canada, currently lives in the nation's capital with her husband of twenty-four years, their four cats, and eight Japanese Koi.

When not writing, Ms Trott can be found in their backyard relaxing by the pond or editing her husband's stories.

Ms Trott has always had an interest in all things supernatural, the occult, UFOs, aliens, and the paranormal. It seemed natural to combine one or more of these elements into a unique universe in which to tell interesting stories.

These are not children's stories. "It's funny, I never sat down with the intention of writing Adult books," Linda once said. "But here they are. I wanted to express physical love honestly without cutesy acronyms and vague names."

These stories contain explicit language and hot, steamy sex scenes that will leave you panting.

Books In This Series

The Immortal Stories Series

The Immortals are a race of beings that came to Earth many tens of thousands of years ago. Their stories stretch across time and have become woven into the history of humans. Their society is hidden from humans even though they live among them. Forbidden from developing romantic liaisons with humans, some break the rules and form close bonds and get married. But this always comes with consequences.

1 - Immortal Desire

One immortal and one human.

As Zisis's world collides with Falon's, she is left to cope and deal with the blowback. Their love affair is erotic, passionate, and stirs the soul, but it is ill-fated. This is a story of romance, heartbreak, hardship, and survival. The sex is hot and steamy, the highs euphoric, and the lows devastating.

2 - Immortal Fulfillment

What a twist! What has Mark done?

After a nasty life twist has her rethinking a relationship with her Texan, Falon needs to decide which direction to go. Is she back to square one? Certainly not! Between hurricanes, hot tub invites, and road trips with hot, sexy guys, there is plenty of action and adventure.

3 - Immortal Peril

The Family is NOT happy!

Lora meets Rick, a talented dessert chef in an up-and-coming restaurant in Atlanta, Georgia, while visiting her best friend, Falon, who is on contract work there. Lora and Rick hit it off in ways she can't believe—one hot weekend in Miami and she can't get him out of her mind. So, when invited to Atlanta again, this time by Rick, she doesn't hesitate!

When Mark disappears without a trace, Falon is left to find out what happened.

4 - Immortal Victory

Out of the fire and into the frying pan!

Falon gets out of one problem only to find herself in danger again. An ancient enemy is targeting the immortals and will stop at nothing to eliminate them. Dodging assassins and traps, Falon decides to end homelessness, one person at a time.

Her BFF Lora discovers that true love sex generates magical energy while she looks for her ancestors.

Gwen finds a partner in Andrews.

5 - Immortal Hunt

Having just survived a coordinated attack from an ancient enemy, the immortals rejoice and celebrate their success. Attention turns toward locating their ancestors when a news item catches Lora's attention and gives her a very important clue to finding them. The immortals are off on a great adventure to distant places. Pirates, witches, time travel, spooky castles, and volcanic caves are some of the encounters happening this time. Don't miss out on the adventure!

6 - Immortal Nexus

New is old, and old is new

Surely, saving a coven of witches from a pocket dimension would be a highlight in life. But it's not. The immortals return home to everyday life; family, moving, school, raising teens, and of course, spicy lovemaking.

 We meet a new character with a deep past. And when a new couple moves in across the street, Falon notices some familiar characteristics. She makes it her mission to meet the new neighbors.

Family matters are front and center in this story. The close-knit group of immortals is becoming a family, and some stories need sharing like Andrews' tale of being hired by aliens.

Justin and Rick finally open the new restaurant. It was a New Year's Eve celebration with a bang!

7 - Immortal Generation — Coming 2023

Short Stories

First Contact: An Immortal Origin Story

The Immortal's Origin Story started 33,000 years ago, when they arrived on Earth. *First Contact* follows the story of how the immortals meet the first humans and what happens when they interact and live together.

Praise for the Series

What are readers saying about this new series?

"Yet again I've got an ARC for this author and I've got to say that these books just get better and better. I loved this one [Book 6] and it is my favourite so far out of the series. There is now so many new people with there own stories that I don't think it will get boring any time soon. My favourite couple were Falon and Mark but I have quickly fallen in love with Margaret and Abeo and I didn't see the twist and turns right at the end. Brilliant book by a brilliant author."

... Sam ***** Amazon

"Linda Ashton Trott has a real gift for crafting intricate sex scenes that are highly charged and also entirely believable. She really brings you into the bedroom in a joyful way. The will-they-or-won't-they story keeps you wondering, right up to the plot twist at the end, which sets readers up for Book 2."

... Amy **** Amazon

"Ohhhhh! This book was good! Hot hot scenes with enough of a story in between to keep you hooked. We all need to

become Leopard Ladies! Nice quick read. Can't wait to read book 2 of the series!"

... Josée **** Goodreads

"Brilliant book loved the storyline and I couldn't put it down once I started. I loved the characters and got really absorbed in to their lives and feelings.

all I can say is Wow I loved every part of it (#3). I'm really sad that the book ended the way it did as I wanted to carry on reading and finding out what was going to happen. I love this series and all the characters. Hopefully there should be another one."

... Sam ***** Amazon

"Picking up where the first book ended, this installment of the series was the heroine's journey of self-discovery in order to make the right decisions for her, something I really enjoyed!

This book was sexy, fun and the character development was great! Ioved how the heroine slowly took back control of her life and found empowerment in her spontaneity."

...Nikita **** Goodreads

"wow! amazing, fast paced and enthralling new world! Wonderful characters that charmed me from the beginning. Honestly this was a wonderfully perfect read to help me escape from the world for a bit.

Amazing (#3). I love this world and it's characters. Great storyline and well written. This series has been amazing to read. Definitely need to pick them up."

... Naomi ***** Amazon

"Yet again I'm absolutely totally blown away by this book (#4). I love the characters and the story line. Linda has written a fantastic book with steamy scenes that I didn't think were possible but brilliant. I loved the fact that we're now starting to see smaller named characters have a bigger role. It's very well written and can't wait to read more of the series."

*...Sam ***** Amazon*

Being an Indie Author

I've chosen to publish independently. This means I don't have the big machine of a traditional publishing company behind me. Reviews are very important on Amazon because they determine how visible you are in the marketplace. That makes your review, and every other review I receive, the most important tool in my marketing toolbox. If you've enjoyed reading this book, please consider spending a few minutes leaving me a review on Amazon. It doesn't have to be long.

Thank you!

See my website at www.lindaashtontrott.com to join the mailing list. You will not be inundated with mail, I promise! It will let you know when the latest book is released and if there are freebies.

Visit my Amazon author's page at https://www.amazon.com/~/e/B09TG29J19

www.ingramcontent.com/pod-product-compliance
Lightning Source LLC
Chambersburg PA
CBHW070631260626
47161CB00007B/2658